JUMPIN' THE RAILS!

To: Nancy
With the first
field trip 2007 —
nine years later
came this adventure!
Thank you for bringing
your class and inspiring
a novel!
Love, Sheila
xxoo

JUMPIN' THE RAILS!

Sheila W. Slavich

Cover art is a painting by artist Connie Wilkerson-Arp
Back cover photo of West Point Train Car Shed:
Courtesy of Doug and Katie Roberts

Library of Congress Control Number:		2016901357
ISBN:	Hardcover	978-1-5144-5396-4
	Softcover	978-1-5144-5395-7
	eBook	978-1-5144-5394-0

Print information available on the last page.

Rev. date: 03/09/2016

To order additional copies of this book, contact:
Xlibris
1-888-795-4274
www.Xlibris.com
Orders@Xlibris.com
716079

CONTENTS

Prologue ix

Chapter One: A Modern-Day Southern Belle 1
Chapter Two: Aleks's Secret Notebook 13
Chapter Three: Adam Meets His Family at the Griggs Plantation.... 23
Chapter Four: Fiction or Nonfiction: That is the Question! 29
Chapter Five: Boston and the Notebook 39
Chapter Six: Gettysburg 49
Chapter Seven: Second Day of Gettysburg 55
Chapter Eight: Under the Cover of Night 69
Chapter Nine: Gettysburg, July 3, 1863 75
Chapter Ten: The Bayly Family 83
Chapter Eleven: The Long Journey Home 89
Chapter Twelve: Eureka! 101
Chapter Thirteen: International Threat 109
Chapter Fourteen: Sweet Home Alabama 115
Chapter Fifteen: The Proof is in the Pudding 119
Chapter Sixteen: The Mystery's Missing Pieces 131
Chapter Seventeen: Down Yonder in the Chattahoochee 137
Chapter Eighteen: Preparing for the Battle 143
Chapter Nineteen: Time Piece Turns, Tick-Tock, Tick-Tock 147
Chapter Twenty: The Griggs Plantation 1865 151
Chapter Twenty-One: General Is Shot 157
Chapter Twenty-Two: Morning of the Battle of West Point 1865.... 161
Chapter Twenty-Three: General Tyler Captured by Men in Blue.... 169
Chapter Twenty-Four: Operation Fort Tyler 181
Chapter Twenty-Five: Jumpin' the Rails to 2015 187
Chapter Twenty-Six: The Griggs Home 2015 193
Chapter Twenty-Seven: Modern-day Changes 201
Chapter Twenty-Eight: The Judge and the General 207
Chapter Twenty-Nine: Fighting Breaks Out at the Fort 211
Chapter Thirty: After the Cannon Fire 217

Chapter Thirty-One: Hostages 223
Chapter Thirty-Two: Missing Persons 231
Chapter Thirty-Three: Time Travelers & the Investigation 235

About Jumpin' the Rails! II 255
Author's Note...259
Acknowledgments 261

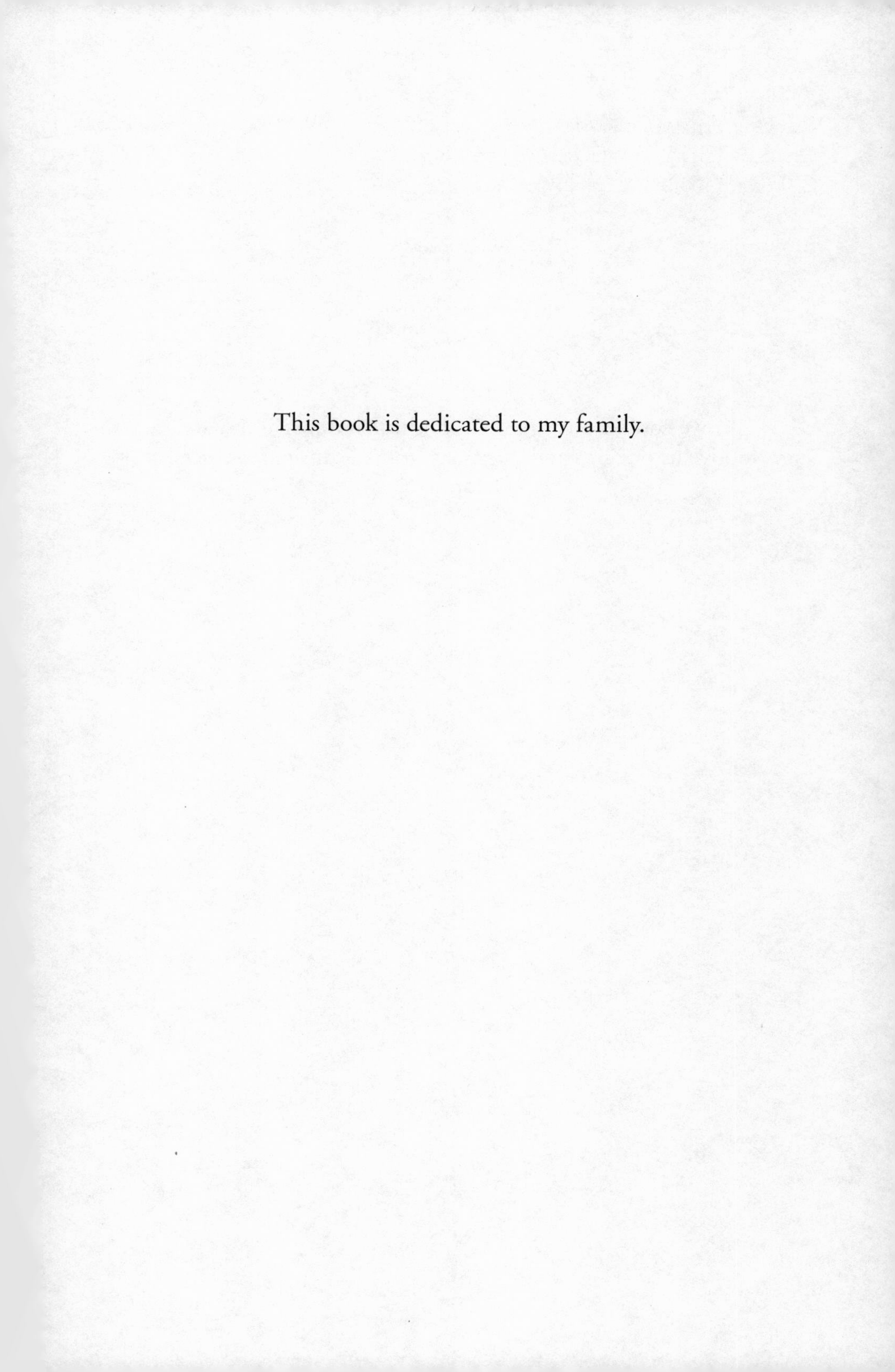

This book is dedicated to my family.

If we confess our sins, he is faithful and just and will
forgive us our sins and purify us from all unrighteousness.
—1 John 1:9

PROLOGUE

The disadvantage of men not knowing the past is that they do not know the present. History is a hill or high point of vantage, from which alone men see the town in which they live or the age in which they are living.

—G. K. Chesterton
(English author and inspiration to C. S. Lewis)

Spring 1860

THE NOON SUN beat down on the two men walking past the house on the hill; they were making their way to the fields and stopped to rest.

"This is the highest point in the area. Look over there. That's downtown West Point, and to the left of those buildings is the river," said Asa as he scooped up soil from the edge of his field. The dirt sifted through his fingers like sand–leaving a red-colored clump in his palm–he slung it across the field like an outfielder—when the bases are loaded.

He continued, "Seems like plants would wither up and die in this rocky soil. I tried my hand at tilling it, and it's more stubborn than a mule. I grew up on a farm in England and always said this was the one thing I wouldn't do. I've swept more barns, fed more chickens, corralled more cows, and harvested more crops than most field hands. I thought I was brilliant when I talked my father into giving my brother the farm and sending me to America.

"I was brilliant until I met Mrs. Griggs. Someone should have warned me about the charms of Southern women. All she had to do was smile at me, and I became unfit to hold a candle. Shortly thereafter, I bought the farm. My father-in-law said that a cotton crop here is the same as a crop of gold coins.

"Well, I reckon we better get started then."

The man standing next to Asa uttered short responses—"Yesa, Masser" accompanied by head nods.

Asa and the man standing next to him were strangers. Earlier in the morning, Asa had won the bid for the man at a slave auction in downtown West Point, Georgia. The prize slave was worth nearly $1,500, but Asa had paid more because this slave had a reputation of trustworthiness, intelligence, and strength. Other bidders were skeptical, but not Asa; he'd spoken to the owner and discovered the sale was due to financial reasons.

From the looks of it, the entire plantation had turned out at the auction to say their good-byes to Asa's new slave. The large black man shared the auction block with a young boy who held tightly to him. Asa wished he could afford to buy the young boy too.

"We'll purchase him as soon as we can," Asa assured the slave. "I have a son about his years."

Tears streamed down the slave boy's cheeks, he looked back helplessly as his new owner drove the carriage in the opposite direction of the Griggs Plantation.

The slave boy was his son.

"You may visit him anytime," Dr. Griggs had said.

Mrs. Lois Ann Griggs didn't attend slave auctions but had caught glimpses when she shopped at the mercantile downtown. She heard children scream as they were sold and pried from their mothers' arms. Mrs. Griggs knew the loss of children, not by force but by disease and miscarriage. "To forcibly take children from their mothers is a crime against humanity, Dr. Griggs. God, have mercy on us."

Lois Ann argued daily with Asa about slavery. It was an issue that headlined every newspaper and was the topic of discussion at every dinner table in America; arguments ranged from religious to economic.

"As long as we treat them right and teach them how to be civilized, these creatures are much better off here than under the oppression of Africa," Asa argued. "They were owned by brutalizing black men who would rather kill them than have them work an honest day and teach them about God and family."

"But, Asa, where does it say in our Constitution that all men are not created equal? Isn't this the reason our ancestors left Europe? Didn't they leave to have the same opportunities everyone else had? Birth does not separate us from opportunity. Why should it separate them? Aren't we acting as the kings and queens of these people?"

"No, Lois Ann, we are not their kings and queens; we are their masters. And besides, this is not our conflict; it is our nation's."

Their conversation on the topic of slavery would circle around and around like a spinning top that never came to rest.

Now that Asa had taken on the plantation, he saw slavery as a necessity for the farm's survival. He didn't like slave auctions either; this morning had been his first.

* * *

From the window of the house, the men's shadows could be seen traveling down the hill to the back entrance.

"Oh, it's you, Dr. Griggs!"

"Why? Who did you expect, my dear?"

"I saw your shadows, but the sun blinded me so that I couldn't see your faces. I knew there were two of you, but I was uncertain as to whom the shadows belonged. You see, Dr. Griggs, the shadows looked the same."

"I know what you mean to imply, Mrs. Griggs, but now is not the time for this discussion."

"Adam, this is Mrs. Griggs."

The man turned his broad face toward hers but was careful not to look her in the eye. "It's a pleasure ta meet ya, Ms. Griggs."

"It's nice to meet you too, Adam. You will be Adam Griggs from now on. You need not be afraid here. We will treat you like family. Mammy, please go fetch Adam some provisions and show him to his quarters."

* * *

The war came to the South and four years later left it devastated. The Civil War killed more Americans than all American-fought wars combined; by some accounts, more than seven hundred thousand perished. Most of its battles were fought on Southern soil, tearing up rails, burning buildings and homes, and leaving land unplanted and families impoverished.

The end of the war meant the end of slavery, and with the end of slavery came four million newly freed men and women in need of employment and shelter. Typically, they worked as sharecroppers for their former masters while others set up shantytowns not far from the plantations where they'd lived in shacks. Their new conditions were less than desirable. The makeshift homes were unsanitary, food was scarce, and disease was rampant.

Adam chose to stay on the Griggs Plantation and work as a sharecropper, but he died a year later from a wound he received at the Battle of West Point.

Secondary education in the United States included little history of the Civil War; much was forgotten, and with ignorance came fear of the past. Young black people seldom spoke of the advancements made by their ancestors because their ancestors had not passed on the stories. Freed slaves desired a better future for their children and grandchildren and chose to stay quiet about their slavery because for some their stories were too painful to share.

The Griggs Plantation, however, served as a permanent reminder of the South's fall, slavery, and a nation divided. Its scars from the cannonballs were still visible in the home's limestone wall. What had changed for the plantation was its size; farming income fell with the stock market crash of 1929, and the family sold off acres one by one until only two remained.

CHAPTER ONE

A Modern-Day Southern Belle

CATHERINE GRIGGS NESS was a modern-day Southern belle with a linen fan on her dresser and a hoopskirt in her closet—well, not quite *in* her closet; it protruded from the closet and held it ajar. She wore the hoop with her 1860s-period ball gown, lace gloves, and lavender hair ribbons.

"Uhh!" She pushed and bent her hoop inside the closet. "There!" The petite miss proclaimed victory over it once again. With hands on her hips, she stopped and glanced admiringly into the mirror. She favored her grandmother thrice removed. She had auburn hair and blue eyes that won her whatever she wanted—or at least it seemed that way to her big brother. The hoopskirt, however, was unaffected by her charms and had the final say. *Bam* went the door, and out popped the skirt. She threw up her hands in surrender. The antiquated undergarment would remain there, peeking out, until she retrieved it for the next reenactment event.

Catherine lived in the home that had been built by her Griggs ancestors more than 150 years earlier. The 1858 Greek Revival on the hill stood with its more contemporary neighbors and remained one of the most beautiful homes on one of the most beautiful streets in this small Alabama town, which sat right on the edge of Georgia.

Living in this home and raising her family here was something that Colleen, Catherine's mother, knew she would do from the time she was a young girl. She was the oldest of her two siblings, and according to birthright, the house was hers to care for and pass on.

Colleen looked younger than her stated age of forty-five—at least ten years younger. Her layered blonde hair fell at her shoulders. It highlighted her porcelain skin, which she religiously protected from the sun with her wide-brimmed hats and generous applications of sunscreen. Some said she hadn't changed since high school but only she knew she could still fit into her majorette uniform. She was always busy with her family, her hobbies, or volunteer jobs at school or in the community.

She was allergic to dust and left the housekeeping to the maid. That is why, to Catherine's surprise she found her mother cleaning out the top of the closet in her brother's room across the hallway. Aleks was away at college. He'd left to start his first year at the Massachusetts Institute of Technology (MIT) in August. He wasn't an average nerd; Catherine would be the first to admit that. Her brother was smart and athletic. To make things even better for him, he was model good-looking with his swishy blond hair, blue eyes, and, if he was without his shirt on, abs. All Catherine's friends had crushes on her brother.

Colleen was throwing things down from the top shelf. Playing cards and pieces of Aleks's past were in a pile on the floor beneath the chair she was using as a ladder.

"What are you doing?" Catherine asked her mother.

"Your brother has asked us to bring a few of his things to Boston. He wanted his binoculars. I thought they were up on his closet shelf. I'm not finding them," she said. "How's your packing coming along?"

"I'm about to start. I have my clothes out on my bed. Just need to get my suitcase down from the attic," Catherine said. "Would you come with me? I hate going up there alone."

"Yes, of course, and I need to get Aleks's notebook from the attic," Colleen said.

"You know, Mama, I've been thinking; a visitor from the 1850s would feel right at home in our house!"

"Why's that?" Colleen said with a laugh.

"First of all, it's not normal to have hoops and corsets in 2014. I used to think everyone dressed up for Civil War reenactments. People from the North think we are odd. My friend who recently moved here from Vermont said that when I spoke of 'the war,' she thought I meant the Revolutionary War. I said, 'No, everybody around here knows that *the war* means the Civil War.' Someone else in my social studies class said they did reenactments too. I asked them if they were Confederate or Union. I even invited them to join us this spring on the anniversary of the battle. Well, turns out they are neither Confederate nor Union because they are from Montana, and in Montana, it's all about Custer's Last Stand. My teacher told us that everyone's war is different. 'The war in your own backyard or your region is the one that lives on forever.'

What does that mean? How can history live on if it's history? Sounds like a big contradiction to me. What do you think, Mama?"

"Catherine, I think your teacher is correct. If the British had fought the Revolutionary War in Alabama, then the men would dress in blue and red coats and the ladies like Molly Pitcher, and if Little Bighorn had occurred on the hill behind our home, I suspect we would have Native American reenactors—"

"I know," Cat interrupted. "Daddy would dress up like Custer?" she said with a chuckle.

"Oh, here they are," she said. Colleen had found the binoculars toward the back of the shelf. "They're dirty; looks like they've been through the war," she said jokingly.

"Time to head to the attic!" Colleen said.

* * *

The attic was not a traditional attic. It was a storage area on the third floor of the house and sat just off Catherine's parents' room.

She bounded up the stairs, two at a time, to the third story.

"Georgia, Georgia, the whole day through, just an old sweet song keeps Georgia on my mind." Catherine's voice streamed through the rafters. She was singing away spiders and stowaway mice.

"Eww!" she shrieked. "I have cobwebs all over my face." She whined and spit. "I can't see back here. Aaahh! A m-m-mouse!" Cat let out a bloodcurdling scream, bumped her head on a rafter, and ran out from the dark space.

"You okay, Cat?" Colleen asked.

"I will never ever go back there again," she said, rubbing her head. "Daddy needs to put some lights back there!"

"Is your head okay, honey?"

"Yes, ma'am, I'm fine," Catherine said. By her scream, it had sounded like she'd been mortally wounded.

"Is the notebook in a box?" she asked.

"Yes, Aleks said it's in a cardboard box with his name on it," Colleen said.

"Seems silly to me that he wants a box of childhood memorabilia!" Cat proclaimed.

"It's not an entire box. He said it's one notebook. Do you remember the notebook with Einstein on the cover? Adam gave it to him," Colleen said.

Adam was Aleks's oldest and closest childhood friend. They'd grown up together like brothers. They were also opposites in the sense that Aleks was growing up in a white home of privilege and his friend was from a middle-class black family. Their friendship was the product of the working relationship that their parents and some of their ancestors had shared since the 1850s.

"I remember it because he'd never let me look at it," Catherine said. "You know, Mama, we should have thrown out his things when he chose MIT over Auburn."

"Aleks loves Auburn. He needed a fresh start after the investigation, and he's always wanted to attend MIT. It's been a dream of his since he was a young boy. Remember the afghan Gram made him when he was in middle school? It was MIT colors."

"War Eagle fly down the field, ever to conquer, never to yield …"

"Cat, is that your stuffed Aubie playing Auburn's fight song?"

"Yes, ma'am, it's so old I can't believe that tiger still plays!" Catherine said.

"I found something over here in the corner, behind the scuba gear," Colleen said.

She brushed off layers of dust from the top. It had Aleks's name on it. She carried it toward the attic door and opened it, and there it was lying on the top. "This is it. Here's his notebook," Colleen said.

Colleen's phone rang. A patient with an emergency was calling for Dr. Ness. She covered the phone and whispered to Catherine that she was heading downstairs where there was better reception.

Catherine still needed her suitcase. She glanced around, looking for pink in the midst of green plastic and brown cardboard boxes filled with photos and Christmas decorations.

"Here it is, and I didn't even have to go back into the dark area," she said to herself. She picked up the suitcase and noticed Aleks's notebook had been left on the box next to the door. "I guess Mama forgot this when she got the phone call," she said.

"Hmmm," she said, sitting down with her back to the door. *He won't know if I take a peek,* she thought.

She carefully opened the notebook in the middle and started reading. It held her attention for only a moment, and then she flipped through the notebook front to back. His handwriting changed—in the front it was small print and in the last entry it was in cursive and severely slanted to the left. It was barely legible. *Aleks doesn't use cursive,* she thought. His school notes were always printed, and the letters were so small no one knew how even he was able to read what he'd written. She had only seen him write his signature in cursive, and this didn't even look like a messy version of his signature. *Maybe someone else wrote the other entries*, she wondered.

Toward the back, there was a sketch of a house. *He always drew homes with large floor plans.* This one looked familiar at first. She turned the notebook on its side to see the front view of the house. It was their house. The sketch was labeled "Griggs House 1861." It didn't look exactly like it looked now, more like the photos and paintings of the original house that their mother had shown her. He had labeled the rooms. The parlor and the dining room were in the front of the house, off the second-floor balcony entrance. These rooms were now their bedrooms. And the modern-day dining room had been a bedroom for Dr. and Mrs. Griggs and the downstairs rooms were labeled as the kitchen and slaves quarters.

"How did Aleks know this?" she asked herself. There was yet another drawing of the house—a modern drawing. "He made our den into an H. G. Wells room," she said with a laugh. He had labeled it in parentheses, "Interactive Theater Room." She was sure Aleks meant it had time-travel capabilities. He had always told her that time travel would be the entertainment of the future.

In that room, he had drawn a cabinet, and on the cabinet, he had labeled one section "Artifacts" and another section "Time Travel."

What was in the cabinets, she wasn't sure.

She put down the notebook and then looked in the box to see what else was in there—old wrestling medals, a few treasured photos from a summer in England, and notes from his favorite teachers. Aleks was selective about what he saved, so Catherine knew the items in the box must be special to him.

At the bottom was the hollow book that Gram had given him. She slid it open and found folded pieces of parchment paper and an antique ink pen. "Notes from girls?" She smiled. She carefully opened one folded square to find that, no, it was not a love note but a sketch of a battlefield. She unfolded another and then another only to find more of the same. One location was labeled "Gettysburg." It was detailed with names of officers: Meade, Pickett, and Longstreet. *Hmmm,* she thought, *this still doesn't add up to anything that makes a lick of sense.* The writing on the maps was definitely Aleks's. It was small and neat and looked more like his normal writing. *This must have been from his history class,* she thought. *It was taught by one of his favorite teachers.*

She placed the hollow book by her feet and picked up the notebook again. She had always wanted to look in her brother's Einstein notebook. He would sit at the drafting table in his room and write in it, his arm and shoulder covering his paper.

She had thought it strange the way he'd jump when she'd come in and speak to him while he was writing, and she noticed it had gotten worse after Adam's disappearance. The only time she'd see the notebook would be when he was writing in it; otherwise, it remained hidden. Last year, on a day when she had the day off from school because of parent-teacher conferences and he was at school, she had spent the entire day searching for the notebook and never found it. When he had come home, he had accused her of being in his room. How he could tell she'd been snooping, she had no idea. She thought he must have a hidden camera because she was careful to put everything back in its place.

But here she was in the attic, alone with his Einstein notebook. *Now's my chance,* she thought, and with a grin the size of the Chattahoochee River, she dove in.

As she flipped through, it appeared that each page was full. The beginning of the notebook had formulas and Newton's laws. She remembered her brother used to recite them over and over again. Then she opened to the center of the notebook; there she found some answers to her questions. The journal entry was dated, and at the top of the page was a quote.

* * *

Imagination is more important than knowledge.
—Albert Einstein

Journal Entry
April 16, 2014
(Aleks's senior year of high school)

"I made a discovery this morning that proves my Wellsian travels and possibly the existence of an alternate history. The proof is on the tree house table."

* * *

Catherine closed the book and examined its cover. It was Aleks's notebook all right. Questions raced through her mind. *What is Wellsian travel? The proof is on the tree house table?*

Almost six years earlier, Catherine had watched her brother drag the table up the hill. It was a simple structure: a wood block for a top set on four spindles.

"Where are you going with that old thing?" Catherine hollered.

"To my tree house."

"It doesn't look nice, Aleks."

"It happens to be an antique, Cat! Dad said it's likely as old as the house. He gave it to me."

The truth was that Aleks's dad had put the table in the trash pile and Aleks had saved it from the dump.

Aleks situated the table on his front porch. The cedar-lined tree house was in the backyard, elevated six feet high on wooden stilts with a staircase from the ground to the porch. The structure, sheltered by a canopy of trees, sat on the unattended outer edge of the family's property. This area was thick with fresh evergreens, two-hundred-year-old oaks, dogwoods, and kudzu. Their parents had the tree house built for Aleks's ninth birthday.

* * *

Catherine reopened the journal, flipped back to the April entry, and continued to read.

> Adam carved today's date in the table. There is no other explanation for the dates on the underside of the table. He made the mark right next to his initials that he'd carved on our first time-travel trip. He showed me the initials and the date he carved after we returned from 1861. He did it to have proof of our travels. These new dates appeared right next to that date. When I looked at the table a month ago, those dates were not there.
>
> Now it reads, "AG (Adam Griggs) 1861, 4-16-1864—AN (Aleks Ness) 4-16-14." It's today's date with my initials! He's communicating with me.
>
> I made the discovery when I returned to lock up the tree house this afternoon. Thanks to General, the table was lying on its side. He pulled it over with his leash when the reenactors fired the cannons at the fort.
>
> Adam's here! Now I can get back to him.
>
> When he didn't make it through the portal with me from Gettysburg in 1863, I didn't know where to look for him! But I know where he is now! He's here! He's right here!
>
> I know I can get back to the Griggs House 1864. We time-traveled to the house in 1861. Why not now?
>
> Point the compass on the rock; timepiece turns, tick-tock, tick-tock! This went through my mind all night last night. Adam made this up, and we must have said it over and over again during the last three years. This has to be a sign.
>
> I haven't traveled since Adam's disappearance because I was afraid I wouldn't be able to return.
>
> Now I'm going back to the Griggs House to rescue Adam. If I don't make it back, then that's the chance I have to take to save my friend.

* * *

"This is crazy. Has Aleks gone crazy? Poor buddy, he must be making up a story so that he can deal with this awful situation." She always referred to him as buddy when she was mothering him.

Catherine sat in the attic and read for at least an hour more. A hand tap on her shoulder brought her to her feet. She turned to see her 220-pound, five-foot-eleven-inch father standing behind her. Ivan, now fifty-five years old, was a former college running back. He'd injured his knee in his second year, and his future plans had changed from pro football to medical school. The cardiologist still carried the looks of an athlete, just a little heavier and with less hair.

"You scared me!" Cat hollered.

"Did you think it was the ghost of General Tyler?"

"You're not funny, Daddy. You know there's no such thing as ghosts."

"Maybe not but you jumped awfully high! Either that or you feel guilty about reading your brother's private notebook. You know he doesn't allow you to look in it."

"How do you know that?" she asked.

"Let's see, because I heard you ask him over and over again and then it would turn into a shouting match of him telling you to leave his room. Then you'd come ask your mother why he wouldn't let you look at it. It never changed. You wanted it, and he always told you no. Now come on downstairs and give me the notebook."

"It's okay, Daddy. There's nothing in here anyway. I'll give it to Mama."

* * *

Catherine knew Aleks's friend who was mentioned in the journal had been gone for more than two years and was classified as a missing person. Aleks had told the police he and Adam had gone downtown that day and jumped on the train, and then when he jumped off at their usual spot near LaGrange, Adam had not gotten off. Authorities from three counties searched the railroad line and the tracks, questioned townspeople, and investigated the railroad company. The worst of it was when the national media sensationalized it and all but convicted Aleks of a racial crime, but without evidence it began to fade and more sensational stories took the spotlight off of Adam's disappearance. As the year came to a close, the police department announced that Aleks was no longer a suspect.

The weeks following Adam's disappearance were stressful. Catherine would hear Aleks up during the night. Her bedroom was directly across from his in the front of the house. First, she'd hear the train whistle, and shortly thereafter, the front door to the balcony would squeak, followed by the sound of Aleks's feet hitting the patio below as he'd jump from the second-floor balcony.

She assumed he was looking for him on the train, but that didn't make sense to her, and her brother wouldn't talk to her about it.

Could this be true? Could Adam be in another time? she wondered.

The door to Catherine's bedroom creaked open.

"Hey, honey, are you packed?" Colleen asked.

Catherine jumped when the door opened.

"I'm sorry. I didn't mean to startle you. We have an 8:00 a.m. flight. I wanted to make sure you were packed."

"Yes, ma'am." Catherine slid the journal beneath her pillow, jumped up, and started placing her clothes in her suitcase.

Colleen replaced an outfit that Catherine had pulled from her closet with one of her daughter's favorites. "Are you okay?" Colleen asked. "I've never seen you wear your school uniform on the weekend."

Her thoughts were not on her trip but instead on the journal and maps she'd discovered. "I'm fine," she said. "You can go pack. I can do this by myself," Catherine said closing the door behind her mother.

Catherine commenced talking to herself. "What table? Wait a minute! The table! The table on his porch!" She threw the rest of the clothes in her suitcase and ran to the tree house. When she turned the table over, her eyes hit the mark like a bull's-eye. The initials were exactly as her brother had described in the journal, as were the dates.

A cold chill swept over her. All her life, she'd listened as her brother and father discussed science fiction. Terms like *black hole*, *wormhole*, *speed of light*, and *Einstein's theory of relativity* were discussed as often as most folks talked college football.

She sat on the tree house porch paralyzed by her discovery. She thought back to her brother's conversations with their dad. *If it wasn't science they talked or read about, then it was science fiction.* The bookshelves in Aleks's room were filled with books written by H. G. Wells, Jules Verne, Stephen Hawking, and Charles Darwin.

The sound of "War Eagle" startled Catherine from her daydream. Auburn's fight song was her cell phone ringtone. Her brother was calling.

"Hey, Cat! Mom said she found the notebook I need?"

"Yes, it was in the attic."

"Listen, Cat, whatever you do, don't open it. I need you to put it in a manila envelope and seal it with duct tape," he said cautiously. "And one more thing, you're the best! I have lab now. Gotta go! Thanks Cat! Love you."

Before she could confess that she'd read his journal or could ask him a bazillion questions, he was gone. Catherine felt unsettled but mostly eager to find out what her brother was up to. She took a picture of the initials and dates on the table. *When I get back in the house, I'll take photos of the journal as well—in case the airport loses the notebook or he tries to deny anything. It happens,* she thought.

The fourteen-year-old Nancy Drew secured her evidence and then jumped into bed, pulled back the ruffles on her comforter, and slid between her high-thread-count cotton sheets, not to sleep but to read. The journal entries covered several years. Some events she remembered, while others seemed straight from an H. G. Wells novel.

CHAPTER TWO

Aleks's Secret Notebook

CATHERINE SETTLED INTO her bed and opened to the front of the notebook and began a new entry.

* * *

It is a miracle that curiosity survives formal education.
—Albert Einstein

Journal Entry
April 17, 2011
Griggs Plantation (1861)

Yesterday, Adam and I traveled to 1861 West Point and met our ancestors. Sounds absolutely crazy! I know it does and I wouldn't believe it if Adam hadn't been there with me. We didn't look much different from the people who lived 150 years ago, thanks to our Fort Tyler reenactment clothing, but there were lots of other differences. They called Adam a "darkie" and said they'd never seen such a smart "darkie." I felt so bad for him! Who speaks to other people this way? I've heard inappropriate things said—but never to someone's face.

This is how it happened. We were hiding from my little sister in the shed—the old green shed that's covered in vines behind my tree house. I had my dad's railroad watch. I'd snuck it from my dad's dresser cache earlier in the day. He said it would be mine one day—passed down from his ancestor who'd worked as a railroad engineer during the 1800s. I'd convinced myself that maybe today was "one day" and slid it in my pocket.

Adam and I sat in the shed and looked it over. The watch is a Waltham with low serial numbers, which makes it more valuable. We decided I'd better return it sooner than later or our parents would switch us both if we lost it. Even though at 15-years-old, we were getting a little too old to switch or at least we thought so. Once when we'd taken a Civil War sword from the safe, our mothers switched us and then made us pull weeds in the flowerbeds. We laughed; remembering how we'd moaned and groaned like the switches hurt but the truth was neither one of them could give a decent spanking. After we dried our pretend tears—compliments of the sink, we were sent out to weed the flowerbeds. The weeding punishment didn't hurt too much either because we suddenly came down with a virus. We ran the thermometers under hot water to show them we were both running high temperatures. Adam's mom was at my house working that day—so we were both sent to my room and spent the rest of the day watching movies, being served meals in bed—all the luxuries that come with a sudden virus.

In spite of our fear of a good switching, we kept the watch all afternoon and returned it the next day. We studied the watch carefully. The inscription on the back read, "Counting the minutes until your return. Devotedly Yours, Carrie Leah."

"Who was she?" Adam asked.

"She was married to the railroad engineer, my great-great-great grandmother. This old compass is also from the same family," Aleks said taking it from his other pocket. It was cracked and not as carefully kept as the railroad watch.

We spent an hour playing some stupid game where we'd guess our location with the compass. The problem was that the compass wasn't working and with boredom setting in we gave up hiding from my sister and ventured outside to sit on a flat boulder near the back side of the shed. Adam and I sat there in the shady spot and drank from our canteens. We laid our artifacts on the rock next to us. The rock is part of an outcropping that runs near the tree house but goes unnoticed because of vines and underbrush. It is dark gray with quartz throughout, making it look like stars in a night sky.

When I glanced at the compass, it was spinning. We'd move it, and it would stop. We'd point it at the rock again, and it would start spinning. I grabbed the railroad watch and discovered its mechanisms were moving; it was keeping time, unlike before.

Shortly after that, Adam stood up and leaned against the shed. I have difficulty explaining what happened next except to compare it to the pull of a vacuum sweeper on your hand when you cover the opening of the hose to feel its suction. It felt like that only 10 times more powerful and the vacuum-like suction pulled our entire bodies into the shed. We fell through the darkness, and then we heard the noise. It was deafening, and there was blinding light. Within seconds, we found ourselves riding on a train platform between two boxcars. We leaned out and looked around to see and hear what we'd only heard about and seen once in an old photo, but there it was as clear as day and right in front of us. It was the old depot in downtown West Point, and we were headed into the train shed—both of these buildings no longer exist.

We jumped off the train and walked to the Chattahoochee House Hotel, which according to my parents ceased to exist sometime in the early 1980s. It stood right next to the station, near the riverbank. We found the hotel to be a large building and extremely crowded.

It was the busiest I'd ever seen our little town with the exception of our annual Christmas parade. There was more traffic from horses and buggies than anyone from the twenty-first century would believe. This was thanks to the 1850s railroad engineer who didn't match the gauge of the tracks, making the transfer at West Point necessary for everyone traveling from Atlanta to Montgomery.

Jeff Davis, president of the Confederacy, himself passed through West Point twice, once on his way to his inauguration in Montgomery and then again twenty years after the war when Dr. J. W. Griggs, Asa's son, welcomed him on behalf of the citizens of West Point.

We walked through the dirt streets and stopped at the slave auction. The sight of it made us feel sick to our stomachs. There were black people chained and dressed in dirty rags. We both figured the sooner we left that area the better and headed to my house.

Adam and I were not used to crossing roads with horses and buggies and were hit by a buggy on our way. We scared the lady in the buggy to death. She screamed, and we laughed our heads off because she sounded just like my mama when we scare her. We ran from the accident and up the hill but stopped suddenly at a familiar sight. It was my house—newly built and it was just as we'd been told–a large plantation.

* * *

From down the street, they spotted two children in the front yard under the shade of a large oak.

"Let's talk to the kids," Aleks said.

"You think that's a good idea?" Adam asked. "I'm nothing but a slave to these people. Nothing about me matters except my skin color."

Aleks knew Adam was right and the revelation was like a punch in the gut. He placed his arm on Adam's shoulder to console him.

Adam pointed over at the fields, "See what they're doing!"

Aleks looked over at the field workers planting crops. There were too many to count.

"I never thought about it until now," Aleks admitted.

"Why would you? It's my heritage, not yours. Your family owned the slaves and you know what, not much has changed. We are still here working your plantation," Adam said.

Adam sounded bitter. His mother worked for Aleks's family as a housekeeper and cook, and his father did yard and masonry work for the Ness family and others around town. The boys attended different schools and churches.

"It all started with my ancestor, Big Adam. He was a slave who was owned by your great-great-great-grandfather."

"Really?" Aleks said, trying to sound naive, but he was unconvincing.

"Of course! My parents don't know a lot of stories about our ancestors but we know they worked for the Griggs Plantation. My family has the same last name as your ancestors, and it's not because we are related," Adam said.

"I never thought about it before," Aleks said.

"Everyone in our town is like that. There are white Smiths and black Smiths."

"Blacksmiths, did you hear what you just said?" Aleks joked.

"This isn't a joking matter," Adam said.

"No, but don't you think you are taking this all too seriously. What our ancestors did shouldn't keep us from being friends and it hasn't–look at us—we are best friends!"

"That sounds good, but our history does affect us, it affects everything from what schools we attend to what neighborhood we live in. My daddy said that most white folks around here don't think it's proper for whites and blacks to live in the same neighborhoods or socialize and that there are black folks who don't like it either," Adam said.

"That was our parents' and grandparents' generations, not ours. We are like brothers," Aleks insisted.

He wanted to convince his friend, and it seemed possible. After all, they'd discovered time travel; surely a biracial friendship was possible.

"We'll be racial trailblazers," Aleks said.

"Yeah, sort of like modern-day abolitionists," Adam said.

"That's right, let's go meet our ancestors," Aleks said.

"I'm not sure this is such a great idea," Adam said.

"I see what you're saying, but we need access to the backyard so we can travel back home," Aleks said. "I don't know how else to get home."

He reached over and punched Adam in the arm.

"Ouch!"

"Did you feel that?" Aleks asked.

"Of course I felt that!" Adam hollered.

"Just making sure this isn't a dream."

"Next time ask me to punch you," Adam said.

"I can't believe we're here. Do you know what this means?" Aleks asked.

"Yes, we need to get back to the future."

"That's one of my favorite movies," Aleks said.

"Would you be serious?" Adam said and ran ahead in frustration.

"McFly! McFly!" Aleks called after him, and Adam waited for him to catch up.

"How do I say that again? Yesa, masser?" Adam asked.

"Yes, that's all you have to say. Don't be nervous. I've got this," Aleks said.

The young men walked up the hill and into the front yard. They approached the children.

"Pardon me. Do you live on this plantation?" Aleks asked the blond-headed boy, who looked about eight, and the dark-haired girl, who looked about fourteen.

"Yes, we do," said the girl.

"Who's that talkin' to you, Miss Persia?"

Aleks and Adam looked toward the house. From under the balcony came a determined-looking black woman. She was barely five feet tall, round as a barrel and walked at a sprinter's pace.

“What you boys needs wit’ Masser J. W. and Miss Persia?”

“I’m sorry,” Aleks said. “I am Aleksandr Ness, and this is my friend Adam.”

The woman looked directly at Aleks and said, “I’s Ms. Griggs’s house servant and nanny to her chil’ren. Yous can speaks wit’ me,” she said with a proud white grin.

The boys were caught off-guard. They had not planned on this encounter with her, but Aleks quickly regrouped.

“We are headed to Montgomery from Atlanta to visit my grandparents, and our train has been delayed until tomorrow. My friend and I were taking a look around before getting a room at the hotel downtown. We saw the children in the yard and were just being friendly and saying hello to them.”

While Aleks was spinning the tale, Adam walked around to the side of the house, trying his best to view and assess the topography of the backyard, and then returned to Aleks’s side. “Excuse me, Masser Aleks,” he said, tugging at Aleks’s shirt. “I don’t see a shed.”

“Masser Aleks. Dis here is Miss Persia Griggs and her younger brother, Masser J. W.”

The boys sat on the front lawn with the Griggs children and Mammy.

“Are you sure you’re not a Yankee?” J. W. asked.

“Why would you think that?” Aleks asked.

“Because you sound like one,” J. W. said.

“I assure you, we are not Yankees,” Aleks said.

“You know we’re gonna lick those Yankees and do it on their own soil too. That’s what my pa says.”

“That’s enough, J. W.,” Persia said. “You are using poor manners. Mama will whip you if she hears you talkin’ like this.”

“Yes, indeed, Masser J. W., Mrs. Griggs gonna gives you a whoopin’ for dat sassy mouth,” Mammy said.

A bell rang out from the house, and a woman’s voice declared, “It’s dinnertime.”

“Who is that?” Aleks asked.

“That’s Dorothy,” Persia said. “Mammy, can they stay and join us? Can they?”

“Let me check wit’ Dorothy,” Mammy said.

They went up the bricked staircase to the balcony. Persia grabbed Aleks's arm and pulled him back. "Your servant has to eat with our servants. My mama will switch us all if you bring your body servant in the front door. He needs to enter underneath the staircase—through the servants' quarters."

"Dat's right. You's best be listen' to Miss Persia. We have rules 'round dis house," Mammy said as she walked proudly through the main entrance.

"It's not a problem, Ms. Persia. I'll go in the servants' entrance," Adam said.

"Your darkie speaks like he is a white boy," said Persia.

"We were raised together," Aleks said.

"J. W., please show Adam where the servants are eating underneath the balcony," Persia instructed him as she and Aleks continued up the front staircase to the main entrance of the house.

"Please don't misunderstand me, Aleks. It's not that my mama is for slavery, but if we treat the darkies like white folks, then we won't be welcome anywhere in this town, ever again. There's a lady who lives down the road … well, she treats her house servants like they are white, and she no longer receives invitations to any of the barbecues or balls. Mother says we'd surely be off every invitation in town, and my dance card would be dreadfully empty."

"You're not old enough to have a dance card!" hollered J. W. as he walked down the steps.

"When I am old enough to have a dance card. Well, you know what I mean. To make it worse for that family, the one I was telling you about, their daughter married a light-skinned boy who tries to pass himself off as white. They are a sweet couple and would do anything to help anyone, but people treat them like they have a terrible disease. That's what my mama told me."

"You're bleeding!" Persia gasped and fell to the floor right in front of Mammy.

"Oh dear, look what you done. You done gone made Miss Persia have da vapors," Mammy said, scolding Aleks.

"I'm sorry," he said.

Persia was laid out in the main hallway right inside the front door. Mammy had Aleks pick up Persia and carry her to a sofa.

"She ain't never liked blood, and da heat's done got her too. Dis child can't be round such t'ings," Mammy explained as she pulled up a french chair and fanned Persia.

"Here I is carryin' on and you's bleedin'," she said, seeing an open wound on Aleks's leg. "Ms. Griggs! Ms. Griggs!" Mammy called out for Mrs. Griggs to help her.

"What is it, Mammy?" Mrs. Griggs asked, entering the parlor from the main hallway.

"Oh my, what happened to Persia?" she asked, touching her daughter's forehead.

"She done come down wit' de vapors at da sight of dis young man's injury," Mammy explained.

"You all right now, darling?" Mrs. Griggs asked Persia.

Persia opened her eyes slightly and gave a reassuring nod.

"Well, Mammy, you can go get a wet towel for her head now that I'm here," Mrs. Griggs said.

"Oh my, look at your knee," she said, giving Aleks a reassuring smile. "If you are here to see Dr. Griggs, I'm afraid he is not in this morning but I am his wife and know enough about doctoring to tend to your knee. Come over here," she said, motioning him to follow her to the chair by the window.

"I'm Aleks Ness," he said.

"It's nice to meet you, Aleks," she said.

"Wow!" Aleks exclaimed. At that moment, he realized that he was in his bedroom, but it looked nothing like his bedroom except for the windows overlooking the balcony were the same.

"What is it?" Mrs. Griggs asked.

"Oh, ah, your home is so beautiful," he said.

He was amazed at how different but yet how similar his family home was 150 years earlier. Where his poster bed stood was a settee, and there were two french chairs in front of a fireplace. He paused for a moment to look at the family portraits of Dr. and Mrs. Griggs and their children. Aleks glanced at the portraits and then back at Mrs. Griggs and couldn't help but smile.

"You sure are in a pleasant mood to be injured," she said.

Traditionally, the parlor was the first room to the left of the entrance and the dining room was the first room on the right of the entrance. He could see the room across the hallway from where he was, and where Catherine's bed should have been sat a dining room table.

The rooms were the same fifteen-by-fifteen-foot squares. He looked down at the flooring and saw that the home's heart-pine floors were a much lighter color; there were not as many scratches either.

"Sit here," insisted Mrs. Griggs.

When Mammy returned with Persia's cool cloth, Mrs. Griggs sent her on another errand for water and fresh linen strips.

Mrs. Griggs was a petite woman with brown hair pulled back in a bun at the nape of her neck. She wore a day dress and looked ready for church. She spoke in a soothing, aristocratic Southern drawl. "I don't believe we've met before," she said as she gently wiped his knee with water and wrapped the wound. She asked him about himself and his family, how he had obtained the injury, and if he would stay for dinner.

"I'm not surprised at all that this is a carriage wound. Our little town is so crowded with the cotton exchange and that horrible slave auction that I'm surprised anyone ever survives crossing the main street.

"I've heard these train delays last a day and sometimes a week now that the trains are being used to transfer Confederate troops and supplies. Where are you and your servant staying while you wait for your train?" she asked.

"We had planned to stay at the hotel downtown."

"Do you have someone traveling with you?" she asked.

"Yes, my friend, Adam—I mean, he is my house servant. He is downstairs with your servants," Aleks said.

"We have plenty of room here. Won't you stay with us?" She didn't hesitant long enough to hear his answer. "Well, then, you will sleep in J. W.'s room and your body servant will stay downstairs with the house servants."

"Thank you for your hospitality!" he said.

"Mammy, tell Jim that our guest and his servant will be staying with us until their train leaves for Montgomery. Please have him show Adam the house servants' quarters."

CHAPTER THREE

Adam Meets His Family at the Griggs Plantation

Journal Entry
April 17, 2011, continued …

WHILE I WAS having dinner in the dining room, Adam had dinner downstairs with his ancestors. He told me about it when we arrived home.

Adam said he followed Jim through the familiar doors of the downstairs entry where he had been many times before. Everything was different; the black-and-white marble entry was a dirt floor, and the mahogany banister and railings that led upstairs were new, no marks or scratches. To the right of the entry was the living area for the house servants. *Wow,* he thought, *no TV.* To his left was the kitchen, and the cooking smells were wafting into the entrance. A tall, thin black woman came out to greet him and let him know he would assist in the kitchen during his stay. She looked so familiar to Adam that she made him feel at home.

* * *

Her name was Dorothy, and he was happy to work with her. He had always wondered about the stove in Dr. Ness's study. He had never seen it used until now.

"I's needin' ya to wuk dis dough till you gets all da lumps out," she said with a smile.

"Yes, ma'am."

"Where ya say you comes from?"

"We are from Atlanta."

"You mus' be the masser's son 'cuz you talk mighty white and be lookin' mighty light," she said under her breath.

As far as Adam knew, his father and mother were both of African descent, but he was much lighter than Dorothy and the other house servants. Adam marveled at how different his life was compared to what it would have been in the 1800s. He worked his knuckles through the biscuit dough.

"You hadn't done much cookin' before, haz ya?" she said and then showed him the proper way to knead.

Dorothy stepped into the room that Adam knew as the laundry room. He heard her busy at work, and it was at that moment he stopped kneading the dough, took his pocketknife, and scratched his initials on the bottom side of the biscuit table. He had just enough time to place his mark before Dorothy was back with her next task.

"How's it comin', boy?"

"I'm finished."

She placed the biscuits on a cooking sheet and onto the fire. When they finished baking, she told him to get one for himself.

"These are the best you've ever made," he said.

"You has my biscuits before, has ya?" she said with a laugh.

"Oh, no, ma'am, I bet these are the best you've ever made. They are awesome."

"Awesome? What's dat? Is dat like sayin' da'z awful?"

"Oh, no, ma'am, awesome means it's the best."

"Dat's mighty nice of ya, boy. Now, load dis on de dumbwaiter in de entry. Mrs. Griggs is waitin' fur de biscuits to feed your young masser. She tol' me he nearly ate de whole first basket all by hisself."

Adam slipped a biscuit in his pocket for later and placed a dozen on the silver tray for the dumbwaiter. "This is so cool!"

"Ring de bell, boy, so dey knowz to pull it up."

"I've never seen one in operation before," he said.

"What kinda body servant is ya?" she asked.

"I'm mostly Aleks's friend," Adam said with a smile.

Dorothy told him to get in line for dinner.

He quietly stepped into the servants line and stood behind a large black man who looked like he'd been working all day in the fields. Aunt Dorothy was kind and generous to him as she dished up his plate. One of the younger girls in line with Adam told him that his name was Big Adam and he was married to Aunt Dorothy.

"Most folks 'round here, dey don't permit deir slaves to marry, but Masser Griggs is real kind and Mrs. Griggs she says it ain't proper in de sight of God fur two people to be livin' together and not be married. Dat's right; dat's what she says," said the beautiful young woman.

"How old are you?" Adam asked.

"I's not sure, but Aunt Dorothy says I'm prob'ly old enough to marry soon," she said with a sweet smile and a wink directed at Adam. "How old is you?"

"I'm not sure, but they say I'm not old enough to marry."

"You looks old enough to me," she said.

Adam was determined to sit near Big Adam during lunch. He was huge, just like he'd been described in the stories. No one ever spoke of him being a slave. The Negro stories made him into the hero of the plantation. There was one story where Dr. Griggs had gone off to deliver a baby at a neighboring plantation. Some unwelcome guests showed up at the Griggses', knowing that Dr. Griggs was absent, and pushed their way into the house, demanding valuables—and not just the silver kind. They had intentions of taking advantage of the women. Big Adam heard Mrs. Griggs's screams from the field. He came in the house with an ax. Once the sight of Big Adam's shadow came through the front door, all but one man fled the house and dropped their loot bags in the hallway. One man remained in the bedroom with Mrs. Griggs. Legend has it that when Big Adam opened the bedroom door, he took one step toward the bed, picked up the intruder by the back of his shirt, and slung him clear out the window.

There were at least a dozen stories about Big Adam's heroism, but the best of them was the heroic tale of how Big Adam lost his leg in the Battle of West Point. Everyone always wondered how one hundred Confederates could hold off 1,200 Yanks for nearly eight hours. Everyone but the Negro community wondered because they all knew that it was thanks to the brute strength and kind heart of Big Adam. He was the gentle giant of the fort and the Rebels' secret weapon. As the Yanks tried to breach the wall of the fort, Big Adam reached out, grabbed one at a time, and threw those dirty Yanks clear to the river. They'd always add that it was a sad day for the ones who couldn't swim. Finally one of those sneaky bastards shot Big Adam right in the leg and caused him to fall into the ditch, but even his fall was not a complete loss because when he fell, he landed on at least fifty Yanks and struck them dead. Of course, through the years, the numbers of how many Yanks Big Adam killed grew larger and so did Big Adam. It was said that Adam stood at least nine feet tall; in reality, he was about seven feet. He did look to be the size of a large NFL lineman—without the potbelly.

Aunt Dorothy asked Adam to join her and Big Adam while they ate lunch. They didn't have utensils but used their fingers for the mashed potatoes. No one seemed to mind because the cornbread worked just fine for scooping and the fried chicken was so delicious that even the most polite person would have used his fingers.

"Are all plantations like this one?" Adam asked.

"Why dat's an awful strange question comin' from a boy of yur age. Is it like yur plantation?" she asked.

"Yes, ma'am … I mean, no, ma'am."

"Which is it, boy?"

"Well, it looks similar and the food is similar. We use forks and knives when we eat at my plantation," he said with a smile.

Dorothy held a baby in her arms. She told Adam that she was Sally Griggs. "Next, I promised ta give Big Adam a son so as he can has a boy to name afta him, and then dis generation of Griggs will have a son named Adam. God willin' nothin' happens to Dr. Griggs and dis plantation so dat it can be our home. God help us if we ever mus' leaves dis place. I have heard terrible things 'bout other plantation owners. Some of dem sell their slaves and separate the families. They never see each other again. Big Adam here, he had another family before us. He used ta cry at night 'cuz he was missin' dem somtin' awful. He had another child dat he called Sam. He says dat Sam was sold at the slave auction in downtown West Point. He screamed when de auctioneer ripped him clean outta his mama's arms and he and Big Adam were put up fur auction. He used ta wake up in de night 'cuz he said he heard Sam screamin'."

The bell rang for the dumbwaiter to be retrieved and lunch to be cleaned up. Dorothy handed Sally to Big Adam for a kiss before he headed back out to the fields and the baby was put down for a nap. Adam followed her from where they had sat outside into the slave quarters in the downstairs of the plantation house. The baby was placed on a blanket situated on a dirt floor. She covered her with another blanket, kissed her on the cheek, and sang her a lullaby. Baby Sally was sound asleep on the hard floor. Adam was amazed at how content she was in the midst of such bleak surroundings. She didn't know she was born to a family of slaves that would be free by the time she was five years old. She didn't know many men were about to die for her freedom or that her father would lose his leg fighting alongside the men, some who referred to him as a nigger or thought he was created without a soul. But still she slept peacefully and still her father would fight to defend the family and the home where he lived and for the only life he'd ever known. He wasn't stupid; he was loyal, and loyalty went a long way. *Loyal* was the one word that was always used to describe Big Adam. Generations of the white Griggs family always said that poor Big Adam, he gave up his leg and his life for the South and for the Griggs home.

Adam stood and gazed at Baby Sally as her mama finished her lullaby.

"Comes along now, Adam. Baby Sally must sleep. Sleep, my purty baby, sleep till Mama's work's done and Daddy comes from de fields."

* * *

Journal Entry
April 17, 2011, continued …

After dinner was finished, Mrs. Griggs situated me in what is now our dining room. It was Dr. and Mrs. Griggs's room. The room had a fireplace and the canopy bed that is now Catherine's bed. Mom had always told us that we shouldn't jump on it because it was a valuable antique and had belonged to Mrs. Griggs, our ancestor.

Mrs. Griggs said I should rest for a while after such a long journey. I fell asleep to the sound of workers singing in the fields.

> Swing low, sweet chariot
> Coming for to carry me home
> Swing low, sweet chariot,
> Coming for to carry me home, yeah
>
> Swing down, chariots, won't you let me ride? Oh
> Swing, stop and let me ride

Oh ride me, rock me, Lord
Ooh yeah, I got a home on the other side.

I learned later that the slaves were using a communication style known as the "song and response" technique. It was a method to locate family members who had been separated from each other. They sang loudly in hopes that the nearby plantations would hear. The songs were about their captivity, their homeland, and their hopes of freedom.

I slept all afternoon to their lullabies and woke up in a dark room. I jumped up from the bed in a panic, not knowing where I was or how I'd arrived. I ran to the hallway and called for Mama but was greeted by Mrs. Griggs.

CHAPTER FOUR

Fiction or Nonfiction: That is the Question!

CATHERINE WOKE UP to her mother calling from the hallway. "Catherine, get up or we'll miss our flight."

She could hear her mother say that it was the third time she'd told her it was time to get up. Pages of the journal were stuck to her face from where her drool had dried around her mouth. She'd fallen asleep toward the end of the first journal entry. *How did he get home?* she wondered. *What a silly thought; this is made-up.*

She slipped the notebook back into its envelope, checked the hallway to see if it was all clear, and then stepped lightly down to the secretary desk where she set the package next to her mother's car keys.

"Good morning, Catherine." It was her mother calling her from the kitchen.

There was no view from the kitchen to the hallway. It was part of the back addition that was added later, along with the living room and the sunroom. Catherine continued through the dining room and entered the kitchen where she found her parents sitting at the table.

"Good morning," Ivan said. "You ready to go?"

"No, Daddy, I just got up," she said in an irritated morning voice.

"What's the matter? Didn't you sleep well last night?" Colleen asked.

"I'm fine," she said.

"Go take your shower, and I'll pack a muffin for you to eat in the car. We have to leave in thirty minutes," Colleen said.

* * *

"Here's my suitcase, Daddy," Catherine said.

"You gonna give me a hug?" Ivan asked her.

"Yes, Daddy," she said with a sleepy smile. "Take good care of General. He'll keep you company."

"Don't tell, Mama, but he'll be sleeping on her side of the bed tonight," he said, and they both laughed.

General was the family's six-year-old standard-sized golden doodle. "He's about the same size as your mama."

"Hey, I heard that!" Colleen said. "I'm not even gone, and you're comparing me to the dog?" she said.

Ivan hugged Colleen, and they spoke quietly for a moment. Catherine was already in the car and couldn't hear what they were saying.

Catherine checked the time; it was time to go. She motioned for her mom to come on. Ivan opened the car door for Colleen and handed her the package with the notebook. He noticed the envelope was not fastened. It was the kind with the string that wraps around the cardboard button. "Were you reading your brother's notebook again?" he asked and handed it to Colleen.

"Bye, Daddy. I love you, and we'll see you on Monday," she said.

* * *

The Atlanta International Airport was bustling as usual. They made it to their gate with enough time to grab a magazine and some gum before boarding.

Catherine noticed that her mother seemed tired, and it wasn't long after takeoff that Colleen fell asleep with the envelope in her lap. She shifted a couple of times, her grip loosened, and soon the envelope slid to one side.

Catherine gently slid it from her mother's side. Colleen opened her eyes, smiled unknowingly at Catherine, and then fell back to sleep.

It's easier to ask forgiveness than to get permission, she thought.

* * *

You have to learn the rules of the game. And then you have to play better than anyone else.
—Albert Einstein

Journal Entry
April 12, 1862, Battle of Ship Island, Pass Christian, Mississippi

Adam and I time-traveled again! I can't believe it! I can't believe it! We did it again!

I am confident that this combination of things we used to travel is not a coincidence but a formula. My mission is to find that formula.

This time, we jumped to Pass Christian, Mississippi. My mom received a package in the mail from our aunt Ruthie. It was filled with old family photos and things that came from a scrapbook of my great-grandparents. In it were some musket shells and a letter from one of our ancestors—John Guernsey—who fought in the Civil War on a Confederate gunship off the coast of Mississippi.

Time-travel formula: railroad watch, compass, artifact, and rocks from the backyard.

Artifact signature hypothesis: artifacts have time signatures that connect to a place in time.

The railroad watch connects to the 1860s railroad. It belonged to my ancestor, a railroad engineer. Why its time signature is the rail line and not the watchmaker, I don't know. The compass—1850s—belonged to the same man.

The other piece of information to this formula is the 1850s rail line. The first tracks laid in our hometown were also put down in the late 1850s. This was the route used by both the North and the South to transport soldiers and weapons. We've time-traveled twice—both to places with the time signature of a specific artifact.

Pass Christian—Adam and I used the same items as last time, with the addition of the musket shells labeled "Battle of Ship Island" and the rocks. We stood in the same location in the backyard by the shed, behind the tree house. I leaned on the loose board on the outside of the shed, and Adam held the compass to the rock. It started to spin, and then the railroad watch started keeping time.

This time, we were both ready and waiting to observe the phenomenon. As the compass spun, the wooden boards on the shed wall seemed to turn from wood to dark glass, and then a vortex appeared in the middle. It wasn't what we had initially thought; we had thought the time window was in the location of the shed, but now we are guesstimating that it is with the combination of artifacts and the rocks.

For this trip, we both had nice-size pieces of the rocks in our haversacks. Our hypothesis was that the rock controlled the compass and the watch.

The vortex pulled us into its spin for an intense couple of seconds. Inside the vortex, we were falling and then we dropped out. The exit was a burst of light and the sound of a train, as it was before. We dropped from the spinning darkness and landed on board a train—in the 1860s.

This time, we arrived late in the day and not far from the Pass Christian harbor. The train slowed down in the middle of a thick pine forest, and we jumped off and rolled into the tree line.

* * *

"Where are we?" Adam asked. "It looks like the middle of nowhere."

"This, my friend, is a Mississippi pine forest."

The canopies of the tall, skinny long-needle pines blocked the last of the day's sunlight from reaching the forest floor, which was covered with ferns and underbrush for as far as they could see.

"Oh perfect, you can identify pine trees!" Adam said with a laugh. "We need directions to Pass Christian."

"Let's walk this way. The town is on a peninsula that is only eight square miles. We can't miss it. If we go too far, we'll have to swim," Aleks said with a laugh.

"Shhh, that sounds like a bear," Adam warned.

They heard a blowing sound followed with a clacking noise.

"There it is!" Aleks said, pointing at the black bear that was walking toward them. "Looks like she has cubs," he added.

"We need to speak calmly, telling the bear we are here while we back away," Adam explained. "Chances are she'll leave us alone."

The bear swayed from side to side, snorting and clacking her teeth. With every step the boys took backward, the three-hundred-pound sow took five in their direction.

"We are not going to hurt your cubs," Adam said.

"Please God, keep this bear from killing us," Aleks said, trembling as the bear came closer.

The boys took bigger steps backward. The bear kept coming, and they kept talking to her.

"I've heard that if we lie down and don't move, she'll maul us, but afterward she'll leave and we can get away before she comes back," Aleks said.

"No, that's not true," Adam said. "A brown bear mauls you later, a black bear eats you right away."

Their brows were covered in sweat, and their breathing was shallow.

"Let's keep walking," Adam insisted.

"We could try to go home," Aleks said.

"*No,* it would take us too long to get out our artifacts. The bear runs too fast, and we'd be attacked. We must be in her territory that she's marked off," Adam said.

"I'm sorry I talked you into this," Aleks said.

"Not necessary. I'm here because I wanted to come," Adam said. Trying to get both their minds off of their immediate crisis, he told Aleks about a rhyme that had popped into his head that morning.

"Point the compass on the rock; timepiece turns, tick-tock, tick-tock," Adam said.

"What was it?" Aleks asked.

And so Adam repeated it several times, and soon they were both reciting it over and over again as they stepped backward through the forest.

After at least a mile, they were relieved to come to the edge of the woods and step into a field.

"Do you think we're safe from her now?" Aleks asked.

"Once we are out of her territory, she won't feel threatened and we are safe," Adam said.

"How do you know that about bears?" Aleks asked.

"My father told me. There are bears where we camp," Adam said.

They heard one final blow and clack from the bear, who was standing at the edge of the woods, and that sent the boys running.

Adam looked back to see that the field was clear. The mother bear was satisfied with their retreat.

The boys checked their compass and walked south toward the harbor. On their way, they asked for directions from a farmer who was out checking on his crops.

"Excuse us, sir, which direction to Pass Christian?" Aleks asked.

"Why, that's an easy answer, young man; all roads lead to the pass. Keep going in the direction you are headed, and you will arrive in town. I'm not sure you know what you are gettin' into. The Union is threatening to take over our town. Those damn Yankees looted everything of value—and will be back for my crops when they're ready. All that's left is our devotion to our beloved Mississippi."

The boys politely backed away from the farmer. "Thank you, sir!" Aleks said, and they ran in the direction of the fight.

They entered Pass Christian, a beautiful town, still young in 1862. Large antebellum homes with rosebushes lined the boulevard facing the Gulf of Mexico.

"The houses look a lot like your home," Adam said.

"They were built in the 1850s too. That was only twelve years ago. They look amazing!" Aleks said.

The boys stopped near the harbor and looked at the family letter and their map.

"According to this letter, my ancestor's name is Guernsey. He is enlisted on the Confederate gunboat *Carondelet*, and it is going to attack the Federals on the island tonight."

The boys made their way toward the water; they never gave a thought to the dangers. This was not a reenactment where the bullets were blanks and the cannons fired empty shells; this was war. They read the names of each ship. The sun was at the spot on the horizon when its light blinds, and the glare coming from the water made it almost impossible to read the names on the three Confederate boats.

"Adam, this is taking too long. It's going to take off before we can board."

"Excuse me, sir," said Adam. "Can you point us in the direction of the *Carondelet*? It's the Confederate gunboat out of New Orleans."

The man dressed in gray looked suspiciously at the boys. "What do you two men want with a Confederate ship? Tell me your unit, or I'll take you with me right now and put you in the stocks."

Aleks shouted, "My name is John Guernsey, and I enlisted in New Orleans as an able-bodied seaman at eighteen dollars a month on the Confederate gunboat *Carondelet*. My fellow soldier and myself came ashore for a quick visit to my grandmother's homestead. After drinking a few jiggers of rum to keep our courage up, we became disoriented and unable to find our gunboat, sir!"

Adam let out an affirmative, "Yes, sir!"

The Confederate gave out a bit of a chuckle. "All right, my brave young man and your equally brave body servant, come with me; I will show you the way to your vessel. We have to be quiet because this area is overrun with Union."

Ship Island was one of the largest lumber-shipping ports in the world, according to his ancestor's written account. When the war broke out, the Confederates occupied the island. They blew up the lighthouse and left the island, and then the Federals took possession of it. On April 12, 1862, the Confederates made an attack on it with three gunboats to regain possession.

The boys approached the harbor, and their eyes widened at the sight of at least fifty vessels, including some from different countries.

"Over to the right," the officer pulled out his telescope and handed it to Aleks. "Look more toward the right; it's about four hundred yards from the vessels in the harbor."

"See that small boat there; it's used to transport men to their ships. Tell the soldier on it to take you to the *Carondelet*. Tell him your kinfolk's name, and he will take you to it," he said.

The boys entered the boat with a group of soldiers who were being transported to the ships. There was such chaos, and nerves were so high that when asked his name and ship, Aleks said again that he was John Guernsey and he was stationed on the *Carondelet*.

"There are three boats in this fleet, Adam, which one was it again?"

"It's this one. We are practically on board!"

And with that, the two were told to make haste and to fight the Yanks. They were swept up with a few other seamen and landed on deck.

The boat was newly built, armed with seven guns, forty-eight-pounders. There was white sand covering the deck.

"What's this sand for?" asked one seaman.

"To take up the blood!" said another.

Aleks's eyes filled first with intrigue and then horror, for everything was happening exactly as he had read in the letter. Approaching the young man who had just inquired about the sand, he said, "John Guernsey? I'm Aleks Ness, a cousin of yours." Adam watched nervously but was ready to help if necessary.

"Ness? Never heard that name before." The young man seemed distracted but interested. "How are we kin?"

"We are both related to the Dietz family," Aleks said.

The maiden name of John's mother was confirmation enough for him. John accepted the kinship with a handshake. After all, this was 1862—no Internet, twenty-four-hour news, or cell-phone service. Aleks knew the Dietz name from the letter John wrote to his niece. The letter ended up in a family scrapbook and was currently in Aleks's pocket.

The boat left port and sat about twenty-five minutes from the island. At two in the morning, everyone was called to quarters.

"Line up!"

"For what?" Aleks inquired.

John motioned to the boys. "We are getting rum."

"Why?" Aleks asked.

"To stimulate our courage," John said.

"You know we'll get arrested for underage drinking," Adam whispered.

"There is no age limit on drinking here. Just hold it in your mouth and spit it out when no one is looking."

The gunship left Pass Christian at two thirty in the morning and sailed with the other two Confederate gunboats.

The boys positioned themselves near their gun. Adam slept off his rum, and John told Aleks about their family in Indiana. He talked about how his parents had died and the children were placed with other family members. That was how he came to live in Pass Christian and fight on the side of the South. He also told Aleks about his brother who was fighting on the side of the North.

"You lived most of your life in the North. How come you are fighting for the South?" Aleks asked.

"I am fighting for the people who took me in after my parents died. I am fighting to protect their home and the people who live here."

They arrived near Ship Island before daybreak.

"Adam, wake up!" He was passed out, snoring.

There was a midshipman in charge of their gun dressed in a fine uniform, a blue-gray stripe down his legs and gold braids on his arms and shoulders. He pulled the lanyard and fired the first gun.

"He looks so skeered," whispered John.

Aleks's gaze shifted from the exploding cannon to the midshipman. All that seemed to support the young man was the stiff wool of his uniform. His teeth were chattering.

"Elevate seventeen hundred yads." He was so scared he couldn't pronounce *yards*. When he saw the flash of the enemy's gun, he dropped behind the gun. John was behind him, and Aleks dropped behind John. The others fell in behind him, strung out like the tail of a kite. They followed that up until one of the officers, seeing what they were doing, told the midshipman that he was not setting a good example before the men. After that, they all stood up; their shots went clear over the island, a mile high. The enemy made the same mistake.

Theirs was the first gun fired.

"It woke them up," said John. "They were asleep, not dreaming an enemy was near. The roar of that gun was enough to wake the dead. It woke them and stirred up a hornets' nest."

* * *

"Mama? Mama? *Colleen*!" Catherine said as she patted her mother on the arm.

The flight attendant was telling Colleen to put her seat back in the upright position for landing.

"Catherine!" Colleen said, looking crossly at the notebook open on Catherine's lap.

Her mother's revelation startled her, and the notebook flew up out of Catherine's hands and back down into her lap. She quickly picked it up and handed it back to her mother.

"Did you take the notebook and read it while I was sleeping?" Colleen asked.

"I was bored, Mama," she said. "I didn't write anything in it. Mama, you should look at it. It is disturbing."

Catherine was known for being dramatic, so this comment did not cause alarm.

"Oh my goodness, Catherine, what on earth can it be?" she asked.

"There's information about Adam in here. Aleks explains the cause of Adam's disappearance as a complication of their time travel," Catherine said. "Point the compass on the rock; timepiece turns, tick-tock, tick-tock. Jumpin' the rails on the track; all wheels turn, click-clack, click-clack."

"That's cute. Where did you get that?" she asked.

"Aleks's notebook," she said.

"None of this makes any sense to me," Colleen said.

The plane was taxiing to the runway, and a message came through Colleen's phone. It was Aleks. He was at the baggage carousel waiting for them.

"Your brother has some explaining to do," Colleen said.

"But, Mama, if you ask him, then he'll know we looked at his notebook and he told us not to open it," she said.

"*We* didn't read it; *you* did," she said with a wink and a smile. "Don't worry, sweetheart; I'll handle it in a way that I won't tell on you. No more snooping, but when you do, keep me informed if it's something that I need to know to help your brother."

"You sound like you want me to snoop," Cat said with a nervous laugh.

"There are more serious things than privacy," Colleen said. "Do you have your library book from the seat pocket?"

"Yes, ma'am."

CHAPTER FIVE

Boston and the Notebook

THEY ARRIVED AT her brother's apartment, and in the excitement of seeing him, Catherine prattled on and on about her friends that he knew back home and nearly forgot about the notebook—that was until Aleks asked for it.

Colleen handed it over to him and asked the question burning in Catherine's mind, "What do you need with this old Einstein notebook?"

He flipped it open and without making eye contact with either of them, said, "I was wondering if it was still at home. I thought I'd brought it with me when I moved but couldn't find it. Thanks for finding it for me."

Then he switched topics to where they'd sleep in his one-bedroom apartment. It wasn't even a one-bedroom; it was more like one room that was divided by a bookshelf. On one side of the bookshelf was his bed, and on the other side was his living room and kitchen. There was also a small bathroom with a standup shower.

The couch folded out into a sleeper, and Aleks put some sheets on it while they got ready for bed. As soon as Colleen shut the door to the bathroom, Catherine started with questions.

"Don't you think he's acting odd?"

"I don't think he's been himself since Adam's disappearance. So, no, I don't," Colleen said. "Get changed so we can get to bed. I'll talk to him tomorrow."

They came out of the bathroom with their pajamas on and found Aleks sitting on their bed reading his notebook. He glanced up when he heard the door open and shut the notebook.

"I thought we'd go to the museum tomorrow." He popped up and gave Colleen a hug and then kissed Catherine on the head. "Good night! I'm so glad you're here. Love you, Mom. Love you, Cat."

"Well that was strange," Catherine whispered to her mom.

"Go to sleep, sweetheart," Colleen said, patting her on the arm.

Catherine couldn't sleep for thoughts of the stories she'd read the previous night and on the plane. A light came on and shined through a crack in the bookcase, lighting up the darkness of the living room ceiling in the shape of the bookshelf cracks. *Looks like Aleks is awake,* she thought.

She slid out of bed, slowly, so as not to disturb her mother, who was obviously sleeping, Cat decided, from the sounds of her snoring.

She peeked around the bookshelf. Her brother must have heard her coming and looked over the top of his laptop.

"You couldn't sleep either?" he said in a weary voice.

"No, Mama is snoring too loud. Whatcha doin'?" Catherine asked.

"I had some reading to finish up before Monday. I thought I'd get some of it done now."

"How's school going?" she asked.

"Pretty well," he said.

"Umm, are you studying the Civil War?"

"Not now. Why?" he said.

"We are studying it in Mr. Nolen's class. I noticed that the notebook that you asked us to bring looked like it was about the Civil War," she said.

She had done it! She had told on herself, and she didn't mean to tell on herself. She was a teenager now and was trying to shake the reputation of being the "little sister," "tattletale," or "pest" who "can't keep a secret to save her life."

"Catherine, I asked you not to open it to look at it." He sounded cross.

She blew her lips in frustration. "How do you know that I looked in it?" she asked.

"Because there's no way you'd know that there was anything about the Civil War without reading it," he said.

"Why would you write made-up stories about Adam's disappearance?" she asked.

"That's not why I wanted the notebook. It's the formulas in the front," he said. "Would you like some water?"

"Are you trying to change the subject?" she asked.

"No, silly, I'm being a good host," he said.

"Since when do you treat me like a guest?" she asked.

"Since you came all this way to visit me."

"Come on, buddy; tell me what you're up to with the notebooks and maps in this book," she asked, handing Aleks the hollow book from her suitcase, which was sitting next to the bookshelf. She hadn't planned on this interrogation, but it was going well, she thought.

Catherine sat down on her brother's bed, and he closed his laptop with his notebook pressed inside of it. It was his Einstein notebook. He hadn't been reading for class. He didn't want her to know he was reading it.

She tilted her head, her eyes filled with concern for her brother, and she began her counseling session. "Listen, Buddy, I know that you are blaming yourself for Adam's disappearance, but no one blames you, not even Adam's parents. I did look at your notebook. I dropped it in the attic, and it fell open to an entry. Well, that's not exactly how it happened, but the important thing is that you know that we love you. Don't be ashamed of your writing. I keep a journal, and sometimes I make things up. It's called creative writing."

"Thanks, Cat! I love you too," he said with a knowing smile.

"So, please don't be mad at me. I didn't mean to read it," she said.

"You're right, Cat. Writing is good when you're trying to sort things out, and I have been trying to sort out what happened to Adam, but I needed the notebook for the formulas," he said. "In my lab, we are looking at the chemical compounds found in cannons. Cannons were used in the Civil War; therefore, part of my research includes the effects of cannon fire on the surrounding countryside."

"I know what the effects are: people die. Sounds like a silly study to me."

"Yes, that would be silly. No, what we are studying are the chemical compounds. Here's an example for you. Remember the story about our house on the day of the battle? The roses were not blooming when the battle began, but by the end of the battle, the roses were in full bloom."

"Oh, I see. That's interesting," she said with a tone of disbelief. "You know what I heard? Adam's missing person case has been reopened."

"Have the police been in touch with Mama and Daddy?" he asked.

"Not that I know of, but I did overhear Daddy saying something about them questioning Van."

Van was their older cousin from New York who'd lived with them during his last two years of high school. His mother had passed away from cancer, and her dying wish was for her brother to finish raising him since Van's father was estranged.

"Is he okay?" Aleks asked. His head dropped into his hands.

"Daddy said he didn't want to tell you because he didn't want you distracted from your studies. He said you couldn't do anything about it and that he was contacting Van's attorney," she said. "I'm sorry. I shouldn't have told you. Daddy will be mad at me."

"Don't be silly; I would have found out."

Van had finished out his senior year of high school in Georgia but after graduation he was sentenced to a year in prison and five years of probation for a felony.

The entire school community was devastated when he was arrested and convicted of vandalism of a historic site. The crime occurred when Van and a group of his friends congregated at an old barn one Friday night after football season was finished. The weather that night dictated the use of coats and scarves. It was a mix of boys and girls, all leaders in their school. A girl in their group was shivering; she'd insisted on not wearing her coat that evening. Van was chivalrous and gave her his coat, but it wasn't enough for the young lady; she insisted he build her a fire.

He was smitten with her. Who wasn't? She was Miss Everything at their school. Hoping to win her affections, Van and the other boys gathered kindling and broke up some limbs that had fallen from a tree outside the barn. They all worked on building the fire, but then Van took the lighter from his car and put it to the wood, starting the fire. The fire burned hot. They put more limbs on the pile and sat for hours talking, laughing, and listening to music.

After a couple of hours, the fire had burned down to nothing but glowing embers. When Van left to take home some of his friends who had early curfews, he asked a couple of the guys to stomp out the embers and throw some water on it before they left the barn.

Apparently his friends didn't throw any water on the embers, and when the night wind kicked the red-hot ash into the dry air, it caught the draft that blew through the barn and landed on the dry wood, igniting the barn. The entire structure was burned to the ground when the farmer discovered the smoke and fire in his field the next morning.

Van wouldn't reveal the names of his classmates. He took the fall for the entire group. He said he had lit the fire and was responsible.

The DA had made an example out of him and prosecuted him to the fullest extent of the law. Ivan felt he'd failed his sister and blamed himself for Van's trouble.

* * *

"I overheard the police talking about Van when they came to our house the other day to speak with Aunt Mary," Catherine said. Aunt Mary was Adam's mother and worked as the housekeeper for the Ness family.

Adam was the only child of Mary and Asa Griggs, and they were devastated by his disappearance.

"Mrs. Mary cried and cried and told Mama that her heart was broken for them to still think our family had anything to do with Adam's disappearance," Catherine said.

"I didn't, Cat, and I'm going to prove that I didn't," Aleks said. "He was my best friend."

"I believe you!" Catherine said.

"I know you do," Aleks said. He looked at his phone, sitting on the shelf next to his bed. "It's late, Cat; we can talk more tomorrow. You better go to bed. If I remember correctly, you get crabby when you don't get enough sleep," he said with a smile.

"Good night, Aleks."

"Good night, Cat."

For as long as she lay awake, the light was on in his room. She wasn't certain what time he'd finally gone to sleep.

* * *

The three of them whiled away the day, browsing the streets of Watertown, Boston, and Cambridge. "After we make the pilgrimage to Longfellow's resting place, can we stop by Russo's in Watertown?" Catherine asked. "I read about it on a Boston website," she added.

"What's that?" Colleen asked.

"Oh, Mom, you'll love it," Aleks said with a smile. "It has everything. Sort of like a Fresh Market but with pastries right from France, flowers from Amsterdam, and fruit from Hawaii. If it wasn't so cold in the winter, this would be the perfect place to live."

When their day in the city came to a close, they had spoken of everything but Adam, and the tension stayed where they had left it last—with all the unanswered questions.

* * *

"Good morning!" Aleks said. "Mom, I have a coffee ready for you. Would you like any sugar?"

Aleks sat down at the foot of the hideaway bed.

"No, sugar," Colleen said. "Thank you, sweetheart."

"I was thinking we'd catch the 11:00 a.m. service at the Old North Church, have lunch at the museum café, and then visit the museum. After the museum, I'd like to take you to Harvard Square and show you around, and then we'll have dinner at the oldest tavern in the country," Aleks said.

Catherine sat up and wiped the sleepers from her eyes. "That sounds great," she said.

"I've got some bagels for breakfast, but, Mom, you have to promise not to count the calories. They are the best, and you have to try the cream cheese too," he said.

"When in Rome!" she said with a laugh.

While Catherine was in the bathroom getting ready, Colleen and Aleks sat at his small table next to his window overlooking rooftops and chimneys and shared some small talk until Colleen brought up Adam and what she had read in his notebook.

Aleks was visibly nervous and remained reticent. He avoided eye contact with her and after several minutes changed the subject.

"You're not going to discuss this with me, are you?" Colleen probed.

"No, ma'am," Aleks said.

"Are you in trouble?" she asked.

"I am telling you the truth. I don't know where Adam is or why he disappeared. I am doing everything I can to find him."

"What does your notebook have to do with all of this?" Colleen asked.

The bathroom door opened, and Catherine stood in front of them and twirled around in her new dress. "What do you think? Is it perfect for today?"

"It's perfect, Cat!" Aleks said. "Mom, why don't you take your shower next? I'll finish up my reading for tomorrow's chemistry class."

Aleks went into the bedroom and left his mom's questions hanging.

Catherine followed her mom into the bathroom. "Did you talk to him?" Catherine whispered.

"Yes, and I will talk to him some more later, but I don't think he is going to confide in me," Colleen said.

* * *

After taking in the beauty of Boston's oldest surviving church building and the Episcopal service, they enjoyed a lovely brunch at the museum and then wandered around its halls and found their favorite masterpieces.

"Look at this Claude Monet!" Catherine hollered.

"Shhh, Cat, you are supposed to talk quietly in a museum," Aleks said.

"She knows that; she's just excited," Colleen said.

"It's the *Water Lilies* by Monet," Catherine said.

"I know. Isn't it beautiful?" Colleen said.

"This museum has one of the largest Monet collections outside of France," Aleks said.

"Wow, Aleks, you've learned a lot since you've been here," Catherine said.

"It says it right here in the pamphlet," he said with a laugh.

* * *

After several hours looking at art, sculpture, and a special exhibit of Gordon Parks's photography, Aleks offered to show them the shops around Harvard Square.

"Bookstores! Aleks, take us to some bookstores!" Catherine begged.

"You'll find plenty of bookstores where we are headed," he promised.

* * *

Catherine browsed the Harvard Bookstore until her mother told her it was time to check out and head to dinner. She had collected at least five books that she thought she could not live without.

"Pick three of them, and put two back," Colleen told her.

"Oh, Mom, let her get them all. Besides, how often does she get to shop at Harvard Bookstore?" Aleks said.

"Oh, all right, but you are going to carry them. I'm not carrying them," Colleen scolded.

Catherine never left a bookstore empty-handed, and her bookshelf told of it because her room looked like a library with numerous classic novels and modern young adult series.

"You happy now?" Aleks asked.

"Of course I am!" Catherine said.

The Bell in Hand Tavern was about a fifteen-minute ride back across the Charles River into Boston. Aleks hailed a cab and mentioned for the first time that there was a young woman joining them for dinner.

He had asked Martha Shakespeare to meet them for dinner. The irony of it was that Miss Shakespeare was a descendant of the great writer, but she herself was doing graduate work in physics at MIT.

"Are you dating her?" Catherine asked.

"We are good friends, and I like her," Aleks said.

Colleen didn't ask any more questions; she just smiled at Aleks.

They arrived at the oldest continually operating tavern in Cambridge. They stepped out of the taxi, and Aleks greeted the young woman waiting at the door. She had aviator sunglasses perched on top of her head, holding back the sides of her long, thick blonde hair. It was the color of honey, and it fell around her shoulders and down the middle of her back. She broke all the rules when it came to the stereotypical female science major—at least as far as how Catherine thought they were supposed to look.

"Mom, this is Martha," he said. "And, Martha, this is my sister, Catherine."

"It's so nice to meet you," Martha said.

"Are you from England?" Colleen asked.

"Yes, near Oxford," she said.

Aleks requested a table for four, and the group enjoyed polite conversation while they had dinner together. Catherine and Colleen both told Martha how happy they were that Aleks had a friend.

"They make me sound like I don't normally have friends," Aleks said with a laugh.

"No, it's just that you are in a new place, and it makes me feel better knowing that you have a good friend like Martha," Colleen said. "Your father is going to be so jealous. We met Martha, and we ate at the oldest tavern in the country," she said. "Martha, I hope you'll come visit us in Alabama sometime."

"Yes, I would love that. Aleks has told me so much about your home. I love Southern history."

Martha excused herself from dessert because she had research to finish at the physics lab. "I'll see you there later?" she asked Aleks.

"Yes, I'll see you about seven," he said and walked her the short distance from their table to the door.

"Wow! He has a girlfriend, and he didn't even tell us," Catherine said. "I wonder what else he's not telling us."

"Not exactly a girlfriend," Aleks said, overhearing his sister's comment as he walked up behind her and sat back down at the table. "She's a girl, and she's a friend, so if that qualifies, then yes, I guess I do," he said, poking fun at his sister.

"She's a beautiful girl, and she must be extremely bright too," Colleen said.

"Why's that?" Catherine asked.

"Because she likes your brother. I can tell by the way she looks at him and smiles," Colleen said.

"Thanks, Mom! She is super smart. She is studying quantum mechanics as a graduate student at MIT. She is actually my GTA for one of my engineering courses that I am taking this fall."

"What are you doing at the lab with her tonight?" Catherine asked.

Aleks mentioned the cannon study but was saved from answering further questions because about that time the server delivered their dessert to the table.

"Look, Cat, your favorite, cheesecake," Aleks said. "New York cheesecake is the best."

"But this is Boston," she said.

"Yes, but we are close enough that it is fresh daily," he said.

"Aleks, didn't you say it takes about ten minutes to get to the airport from here?"

"Yes, ma'am."

"I hate to interrupt this sweet time together, but it's six thirty, and we have to be at the airport in thirty minutes," Colleen said.

* * *

“Mama, are you crying? We’ll see him at Christmas,” Catherine said as they waved good-bye to her brother.

Her mother wiped her tears with a tissue and looked up at the flight departure board. “Oh gosh, Cat, our flight to Atlanta is boarding.”

They ran through the first-class preapproved security entrance to their concourse and then to their gate. The flight had boarded, but the gate was still open. The gate attendant scanned their tickets, and they walked down the boarding gate and onto the plane.

Colleen gave out a sigh. “We made it! Will you message Aleks and let him know?” she said.

They settled into their seats, 2a and 2b.

“I wonder what he is doing with the notebook,” Colleen and Catherine said simultaneously.

“Jinx!” Catherine said.

“He told me last night that he is researching the effects of cannons on the surrounding countryside,” she said. “That he needed the notebook for the formulas, but I don’t believe him.”

“Did your brother answer any of your questions about his notebook?”

“No, but I have pictures of his journal entries if you want to see them,” Catherine said.

“Okay, I would like to see the pictures and I would like for you to tell me about what you read,” she said.

“Well, in it, he mentions Adam. He makes it sound like he and Adam traveled back in time several times. The third time they time-travel, it’s to Gettysburg, and Adam gets stuck there. That’s where he is now. Sounds crazy, doesn’t it?”

“What were the dates of the journal entry?” Colleen asked.

Catherine showed her mother the pictures of the journal that she’d taken on her phone. Colleen loaded them onto her tablet and read during the flight.

CHAPTER SIX

Gettysburg

Once we accept our limits we go beyond them.
—Albert Einstein

Journal Entry
August 5, 2013

ADAM HASN'T MADE it home from Gettysburg. I've tried to access the time line, but I can't get back to July 1863 and now I'm afraid to travel to a new place on the time line—afraid I won't return.

This is my worst nightmare! Two weeks ago, Adam was declared a missing person and the search for him went nationwide. My family was placed under surveillance, and I'm part of an investigation for Adam's disappearance. The FBI questioned me for twenty-four hours last week. I almost broke down and told them the truth, but if I had confessed then they'd have declared me insane.

I've spent hours reviewing the facts of our exit from Gettysburg. It was like any other July 4 week at our house; friends come over and we play football, horseshoes, and badminton, and then we have BBQ.

Adam and I were overly confident that we understood time travel. We'd traveled back and forth twice.

We planned this trip like we'd normally make plans for going to the movies or a football game. Only this time we'd stay a couple of nights, but we'd follow the same pattern and travel on the 1860s rail.

It was July 1, 2013, and we were taking a break, having a Coke on the balcony, when I came up with the idea to travel to Gettysburg.

* * *

"Hey, Adam, you know what this week is?"

"Of course I do! It's the Fourth of July, you dork."

"Let's go to Gettysburg!" Aleks leaned in and looked for Adam's response.

"Aleks, you're crazy, man!"

"We can camp out at Gettysburg. My pa camped there during the Boy Scout Jamboree of 1957," Aleks said.

"This sounds way too dangerous," Adam said.

Aleks shared with Adam that on July 1, Lee's men had ridden into Gettysburg, captured Union troops, and held them captive in the church. Some of his other troops were pillaging Northern farms for food and supplies.

On a lighter note, he told him the story about the bacon. "Guess how much bacon the Rebs demanded from the town of Gettysburg?"

"I don't know. How much bacon did the Rebs demand? Is this a joke?"

"No, it's not a joke. They demanded six thousand pounds of bacon. I swear it on my Pa's Bible."

"Thanks for the history lesson," Adam said.

"Tell me this, if we get captured, what's our story?"

"We are looking for my father."

"But your ancestor served in the Thirty-Third Alabama," Adam said.

"We know that, but they don't. There is no Internet; men riding on ponies deliver mail, and besides that, the telegraph lines are down. We can tell them anything we want as long as it makes sense to them. Come on, man. We have to do this. Can you think of a better way to spend our last bit of freedom before our senior year? We only have a few weeks before football practice. We won't have time for time travel again until Christmas break," Aleks said.

After a day and a night, Aleks finally convinced Adam to pack his haversack.

They'd even come up with a story for their parents. They said they would be camping at Lake West Point for two nights. They'd both been through Boy Scouts and had camped there before with the troop.

Their parents agreed to let them have the camping trip under one condition: they had to arrive home on Thursday morning in time to shower before the picnic.

Their mothers were surprised to see them in their reenactment clothing with their haversacks on their backs.

"We want our campout to be authentic," Aleks said. "It's the anniversary of Gettysburg."

Adam slapped him on the back. "We better head out and pitch our tent before it gets dark. We won't have electricity," Adam joked.

The boys jumped into Aleks's truck and drove in the direction of the lake; when they were out of their parents' view, they soon turned down a side street and then parked in a spot on the back side of the fort. It was the road leading to the back gate, which was only used for special events or by the grounds crew. The overgrown trees and shrubs on either side of the gravel road would keep the truck safe and out of sight.

Aleks put his key under the tire and locked the door. They climbed over the back gate of the fort and ran around the back side. The fort was all clear. They quickly climbed over the chain-link fence between the fort and Aleks's house.

Something was breaking branches in the woods in front of them. It was General. "Who let General out?" Aleks said. "I just put him up," he whispered to Adam.

Adam reached into his haversack and pulled out a piece of beef jerky. He placed it under the fence, just out of the dog's reach.

"General's going to dig a hole until he gets to the jerky," Aleks said with a laugh. "Good thinking."

It was about ten steps from the fence to the shed—an area covered with vines, trees, and thick underbrush. Once they made it to the shed, they positioned themselves on the large boulders.

"It's go time!" Aleks said as he held tightly to the railroad watch.

Adam popped the top and pointed the compass to the rock. They had musket shells from Gettysburg. It was a novelty item that Ivan had found years earlier at a coin show. Aleks hoped they carried the time signature of the battle.

It happened again. The boards on the outside of the shed looked like a dark liquid glass, and then a vortex formed in the center. They were sucked through the vortex and landed on a locomotive.

They found themselves in between two box cars. They looked around for hostiles, climbed onto the outside of the train car next to them, and pulled open the side door. They couldn't believe their eyes; they'd found Napoleons.

"Look at these cannons, Adam! They are monsters!"

Aleks jumped on top of one like a horse. Adam stuck his head curiously inside the barrel and took a deep breath, inhaling the residue of the last shots fired.

"Wow! That smells like it's been fired recently!" Adam said. "Look at this! I found a description!" He read aloud, "Property of the United States of America."

The boys jumped down from the cannons and made a run for the door. Union weapons meant Union soldiers; they were wearing the wrong color.

The boys rifled through their bags for a pair of binoculars and pulled open the train door to take a look.

Aleks looked out the door and then looked ahead at the smoke on the track. The train was coming to an early stop because of a fire that had burned Rock Creek Bridge. Confederate General Jubal Early and his men were the ones who had set fire to the bridge. They had defeated the Yankee militia in Gettysburg almost a week earlier.

"Adam, we have to jump, now! The line we are on is about to cross a bridge that's been burned."

"We're idiots!" Adam hollered.

They jumped just in time, for the railroad bridge was one hundred feet ahead. The two rolled down the bank as the locomotive's wheels screeched like an Alabama owl and fire spit from its brakes.

"That was way too close. Let's forget this and go home!" Adam said.

"You're right. Let's go back!" Aleks said. "You'd think we'd learn our lesson," he added.

They sat out of the way in a thick wooded area with their artifacts set for travel. They watched the compass, but it didn't spin; instead, it gave the direction, like a normal compass.

"Point the compass on the rock; timepiece turns, tick-tock, tick-tock." Adam repeated it over and over again, quietly to himself.

"I know you're scared, so am I, but we have to keep clear heads. If we panic, we'll defeat ourselves," Aleks said.

The boys sat leaning up against trees with their heads in their hands. They were in disbelief that they couldn't get home at will. This was not at all part of their plan. They had all the usual artifacts for travel, including the rocks. With the destruction of the rail line through Gettysburg, their travel had stopped. Aleks rubbed his head, pulled out his notebook, and began problem solving. He'd come up with a new time-travel theory that now included a working rail line as part of the time-travel equation.

They looked around, just in case any soldiers had lingered in the area. Looming over them was the worry that Adam would be mistaken for a runaway slave—the punishment for which was hanging.

The boys looked around and found a barn that seemed unoccupied. The covering muffled the sounds of war. They kept themselves occupied with the idea of getting home.

"We'll locate the Alabama Fifteenth and travel south with them to the nearest working rail line," Aleks said.

"Why do we need the Alabama Fifteenth?" Adam asked.

"Since our original plan has been messed up by the rail line, I think we'll be safer traveling with them than on our own."

"What about north?" Adam asked. "Why not head north?"

"I don't know enough about the area to feel comfortable with heading north. I think we should stay as close to home as possible," Aleks said.

Adam argued that they were better off traveling by the Underground Railroad. He shared the knowledge that had been passed down to him from his grandmother. She had told him what all the people who worked it were called and what their job was for the group. Adam started with the conductor and went through all the terms used for the Underground. "A conductor was a person who escorted the escaped slaves from one station or safe house to another," he said. "I used to get so annoyed when my granny would talk about this," he said with a laugh.

"It feels like forever until the sun goes down," Aleks said, changing the subject.

"Yeah, I know. Is it possible that time moves more slowly here?" Adam said.

Next the boys did some role-playing as a master and slave.

"We're not very good at this, are we, Aleks?" Adam said with a laugh.

"No, we definitely suck," he said.

Aleks pulled out his tablet from his haversack. "What'd you bring that for?" Adam asked.

"I don't know; I stuck it in at the last minute," he said. "My mom has tons of books downloaded on here. Maybe we can find something there," Aleks said.

His mother had *Uncle Tom's Cabin*, *Gone with the Wind*, and Shelby Foote's *Shiloh*.

Adam pointed to Uncle Remus and asked Aleks to open that one.

Adam read aloud, "'Didn't the fox never catch the rabbit, Uncle Remus?' asked the little boy the next evening.'

"'He come mighty nigh it, honey, sho's you born—Brer Fox did. One day, atter Brer Rabbit fool 'im wid dat calamus root, Brer Fox went ter wuk en got 'im some tar, en mix it wid some turkentime, en fix up a contrapshun w'at he call a Tar-Baby, en he tuck dish yer Tar-Baby en he sot 'er in de big road, en den he lay off in de bushes fer to see what de news wuz gwine ter be.'"

"Here, let me try," Aleks begged. "'En he didn't hatter wait long, nudder, kaze bimeby here come Brer Rabbit pacin' down de road—lippity-clippity, clippity-lippity—dez ez sassy ez a jay-bird…'

"This is how Negroes speak in this time period?" Aleks asked.

"Yep, we always laugh about it, but I guess this was the beginning of my people learning English."

"My people, your people, when did we become so different?" Aleks asked.

"We've always been different. We like to pretend our differences don't exist," Adam said with a smile.

The boys practiced speaking like Uncle Remus until they fell asleep for a few hours.

* * *

"Mawnin'! Masser Aleks—nice wedder dis mawnin'," Adam said with a chuckle. "Ef you don't get up, I gwine ter bus' you wide open. That's pretty good, don't you think?"

Aleks let out a moan.

"Masser Aleks, we's gots ta get a-movin' fer wes gets found out."

CHAPTER SEVEN

Second Day of Gettysburg

THEY WOKE UP early on July 2 to the sound of voices in the distance. These were men who lived 150 years before their own time. The boys were both excited and terrified.

"Aleks, wake up. Wake up! We have to move before sunrise."

Aleks groaned and rolled over at the sound of his friend's cheerful voice.

"Hey, buddy, I've got a plan!"

Aleks sat up straight, his eyes wide. "We aren't camped out at the lake, are we?" he said.

"No, that was a cover story for our parents, remember? I was thinking of something my grandfather told me. When the Southern men went off to fight in the war, some of them brought body servants with them," Adam said.

Aleks thought it was a great idea. Adam explained that a body servant was an honorable position because body servants were the most loyal and respected of the servants. They usually grew up with their masters and formed a bond from childhood.

They often went off to war with their masters to take care of cooking and cleaning, and some even fought side by side with them. They also cared for their masters when they were injured, buried them if they died, and delivered the news to the plantation.

These men were trusted and respected, and they loved the Confederate States of America (CSA) because it was their home too. When captured by the Union and offered their freedom, they often refused and accepted the same punishment as the captured Confederate soldiers.

Calling Adam the body servant was a great plan and would work unless he and Aleks were separated. The boys decided that Adam also needed free papers so he could prove he was not a slave.

Adam knew of a place not far from where they were at Rock Creek that was known to be part of the Underground Railroad. "It's called Dobbin House Tavern … or at least it is called that now. This family who helped runaway slaves built it in 1776. It has a slave hideout," Adam said.

His parents had taken him on a trip to Pennsylvania, and it was one of several sites they had visited in the area. They'd even eaten dinner there.

"Can you remember at all what else was around Dobbin House, the battlefield, or the names of roads?" Aleks asked.

"Yeah, I do. I remember it overlooked the site where Lincoln gave his Gettysburg address."

Aleks retrieved his map of Gettysburg and found the location on the map. "Oh my gosh, look at this! It shows everything!"

The Dobbin House was clearly marked, but so were the locations of the troops for the battles. "It looks like we have to cross Union lines to get there," Aleks said.

They planned to do all their traveling at night. Most of the troops would be in their camps and resting. They used their compass and headed north. Adam remembered it was about a thirty-minute walk.

"Let me look at your map again," Adam said.

Aleks stretched it out on the ground and retrieved his flashlight for Adam.

"Look here … You see that, McAllister's Mill? That's part of the railroad too. It was one of our stops along the way, and it looks like we'll pass it." He had visited this location on the Underground Railroad walking tour with his family and knew it was near Rock Creek.

It was a mill near the water. Stories told that the boy at the mill would bring people in and hide them under the wheel. Aleks agreed that it was best for them to try to get help there first.

It was three in the morning, and the boys headed for the abandoned mill near Rock Creek. "Look! There it is," Adam whispered.

Moonlight lit up the roof of the brick building, lending it an ethereal quality. "Looks like God is guiding us," Aleks muttered.

Adam stayed near the river, keeping himself out of sight while Aleks headed toward the building.

As Aleks approached the mill, he went to the wheel and saw the boy sitting outside a few yards from it.

“I come in peace. I’m a shepherd for my body servant,” Aleks whispered.

The boy looked around cautiously and then motioned him under the wheel.

Astonished by the foolish bravery of the young man, a white woman who appeared to be the leader of the outlaws grabbed a rifle. She held her gun and her gaze on Aleks and began questioning him about what business brought him out in the middle of the night.

Voice quivering but still deep and strong, he explained, “A friend of a friend has sent me.” This was the password, and their jaws dropped in astonishment to hear the young man say it. They asked him a few more questions before welcoming him into their secret place.

“Where are you headed, boy?”

“We are headed to the River Jordan,” Aleks said.

“Are you traveling alone?”

“I have one piece of baggage,” Aleks said.

“Where is your baggage?”

“It’s down by the river,” Aleks said.

With the nod of the stationmaster, Adam was brought up from the river to the brick building where the meeting was being held. For the first time, the best friends saw into the desperate lives of enslaved people.

“That lady looks like a zombie,” Aleks whispered.

“What did you say?” asked the man standing next to him.

“I said that lady looks tired.”

“She is desperate to save her youngest child from tomorrow’s auction block,” the man said.

Their shepherd’s name was Harriet, a freed slave who worked on the Underground Railroad. For a moment, the boys thought they had met the famous Harriet Tubman, the woman who started the railroad; they later realized that by this time in history, Tubman had already retired.

The boys convinced her to give Adam papers.

She whispered to a black man sitting at a table in the corner. She motioned for the boys to come over to the table and introduced them to Basil Biggs. “He is a free negro,” she said.

Adam’s face lit up. “I learned about him during our tour,” he said to Aleks. “He’s a veterinarian who helped with the Underground Railroad.”

“What did you say, boy?” Basil asked.

“Nothing, Sir,” Adam said.

"Is this boy keeping you against your will?" Basil asked.

"No Sir," Adam said. "We are friends," he added.

He gave Adam papers and directions for the next station.

They shared a prayer with the group and then went along with the ones headed to the next station.

The lady told the group to move on and to "keep movin' along the rail. There's a conductor up yonder who will take you to the next depot in Chambersburg."

The boys slipped toward the back of the group and hid in the woods until the others had traveled on and it was all clear.

"That was like a chapter out of *Uncle Tom's Cabin*," Adam said.

"I've never read it," Aleks said.

"You've never read *Uncle Tom's Cabin*?"

Aleks shook his head no. "I don't know anyone who's read it except my mom," he said with a laugh.

"Abraham Lincoln credited the woman who wrote the book with starting the Civil War. She was an abolitionist, and her writing addressed the issues of slavery and the Underground Railroad. Uncle Tom was the main character. It's an awesome book. You have to read it. It will help you understand my people better."

"There you go again with your 'my people' stuff!" Aleks said.

The boys walked north, toward Dobbin House, until sunrise, finally resting in a group of trees.

* * *

"Did you hear that?" Adam asked.

Shelling had begun. The cannon fire sounded like lightning strikes, and it shook the ground where they sat.

"Is that the Alabama Fifteenth?" Adam asked.

"No, it's too early. They haven't arrived with Longstreet. The fight on Little Round Top doesn't occur until later today," Aleks said, climbing up the nearest tree with his binoculars in hand. "It must be Union," he said and stopped halfway up the tree. He checked his compass and reached for the next branch. *What's that sound?* he thought. There was a rustle on the forest floor beneath him. He ducked behind some branches, but it was too late. He was in a tête-á-tête with his worst fear.

The Union soldier's head swung like a pendulum and locked onto Aleks's gaze. "Boy, with what company are you?" The low voice of the man dressed in blue was all Aleks heard; he might as well have been speaking a foreign language because Aleks was so panicked that all he heard was the pounding of his own heart. "Come down!" the officer commanded. "State your name, rank, and company."

Aleks shimmied down the tree, eyes wide like a boy caught with his pants down. He had been captured by the enemy and had no plan for escape and worse, no weapon.

"What's your name, son?"

"A-A-A-Aleks," he stammered.

"Hello, Aleks. I'm Union Chaplain Jeffrey Wall of General Meade's army."

"Nice to meet you, sir. I'm a civilian, and we are looking for the Alabama Fifteenth."

"Why are you dressed like a Confederate?"

"We have a package from home for my father, Dr. Griggs. I thought it best to dress like a Confederate so we didn't get shot."

Chaplain Wall told Aleks to take off his jacket, and he searched him from head to toe.

"Now, let me see what you have in your haversack. Is that where you are keeping your package for your father?"

Aleks slowly opened the haversack, wondering how he was going to explain the tablet and the phone. He took out his notebook first, and then his pencils and pen. The chaplain was taken with the pen. He opened Aleks's notebook and looked through the front. The theory of relativity, explained by Einstein, appeared to amuse him. "An hour sitting with a pretty girl on a park bench passes like a minute, but a minute sitting on a hot stove seems like an hour." He read it out loud and chuckled.

He and Aleks shared a smile.

He took the pen and held it up. "What's this?" he asked.

"It's a pen. It's ink that I use to write on paper," Aleks explained.

The chaplain tried to use it with the cap still on. "Hmm, doesn't seem to work well for writing."

Aleks asked to show him, and he took off the cap and then let the man write with it on his notebook.

The chaplain wrote his name on the back corner of the inside page of the notebook.

"This would work well for writing my sermons," he said. "Where can I find one of these?"

Aleks offered to let him keep that one and gave him the three other pens he had in the side pocket but explained that the ink would run out.

Other items in the haversack included the rock, the railroad watch, the compass, musket shells, a cup, a toothbrush, some food items, a blanket, and his electronics.

The chaplain took his time looking at each item. The musket shells raised his suspicions. "Who shot these shells?" he asked. "And why do you have them?"

Aleks explained that his father had given him the shells on one of his visits home. He had unintentionally left them in the haversack.

The chaplain seemed to warm up to Aleks as they spoke. He was lifting up the tablet when Adam made a noise not far from them.

"How many others are traveling with you?" Wall asked, sounding cross for the first time.

"I'm alone," Aleks said.

"Now, I'm going to ask you one more time, who is traveling with you?"

"No one, sir!"

The sound of a bobwhite whistled through the trees. That was their code. Aleks knew Adam had seen what had happened.

"Is that no one?" Wall asked.

"What?"

"The whistle I heard is a signal." Wall bent down, grabbing Aleks's shirt. "If you care about your friend, you will tell him to come out of hiding."

Looking at Wall's large stature and considering he was outweighed by at least seventy pounds, Aleks abandoned the plan and called for Adam to come out of hiding.

"Don't be afraid, boy; I'm not going to hurt you."

He had dropped the electronic tablet and drawn his musket when Adam made the disturbance.

Wall looked directly at Adam. "Are you a runaway slave?"

"No, sir, I's gots my papers right here. I'm Masser Aleks's body servant. It's miz duty to go wit' him to gives dis package to hiz fader."

Wall instructed Aleks to pack up his haversack. "I'm taking you both with me. General Meade is a fair man; he'll listen to your story, and we'll keep you with us until we send you back to Alabama. Your story is a bit far-fetched, and your accents are strange, even for Southerners. You must have mothers praying for you because most of the men in my company would have shot you just for lying."

"Yesa, masser, our mamas pray together," Adam said.

"I've heard that before, that some slaves are treated like family," Wall said. "Although, I can't imagine how anyone justifies owning another person," he added. "Listen, I'm going to bring you to my company where you'll be safer than out here in the woods. I want you to walk in front of me and to the side. That way, you can keep track of me and I can watch you."

* * *

After a good hike down Taneytown Road, they arrived at a small, shabby town house. "This is General Meade's headquarters," Wall explained.

Anxious officers paced back and forth in front of the commanding officer. They pointed at maps and said an occasional expletive. Meade glanced up and caught sight of Chaplain Wall.

"General Meade, sir!" Chaplain Wall said.

The chaplain and two boys snapped to attention.

"Please excuse my language, Wall! The goddamn Rebels are cutting us off from Washington and stopping our supplies. Chaplain, I need you to pray!"

"Right now, sir?"

"No, not right now, goddamn it! First tell me what you scouted and then explain who your friends are and why I shouldn't shoot them on the spot."

"Sir, Confederate lines were seen west and northwest of town, on Seminary Ridge, a half a mile away from our lines.

"And the boys?" Meade asked.

"These boys are civilians and have a package for his father, sir. His father is a doctor with the Fifteenth Alabama."

"Why should we believe them?" Meade asked.

"Sir, they look far too healthy and their clothes too clean to be soldiers for the Rebs," Wall explained.

"Search their packages. If you find anything suspicious and have any doubt that they are not who they say they are, then my orders are to send them up north after the battle," Meade said.

"Sir," the chaplain said quietly to Meade, "what if they look to be harmless?"

"Then find them blue coats and put them in the back of our line. Keep a close watch on them, and when this hell is over, we'll send them back to Alabama."

July 2 in Gettysburg was scorching hot, and Aleks and Adam were left in the sun as a means of intimidation. The aide to Meade tied them to a tree with their hands behind their backs. Aleks and Adam watched as some of the eighty thousand Union covered the area as far as they could see in every direction.

They were on Cemetery Ridge with views of the rolling green hills of Southern Pennsylvania. The land consisted of fields with outcroppings of rocks and patches of trees and orchards.

What seemed like a day later but was only an hour, the aide returned with their haversacks and threw them on the ground next to the boys.

"I don't know what you did to bribe that chaplain, but he's vouching for you two with his life. Meade has a guard on him, and if you two end up being spies for the Confederates, we have orders to shoot him and then both of you."

Next the aide threw blue coats at each of them, hitting them in the face. One of the buttons hit Aleks's eye, causing his contact to fall out and scratching his cornea, a condition that wouldn't bother him for several hours but would result in excruciating pain that would last at least a day.

"Excuse me, but could you untie us so we can put on our jackets and take our positions in the back?" Aleks asked.

"What's that, Rebel?" the aide asked.

"I was wondering if you could untie us," Aleks asked again.

The aide spit in Aleks's face and then looked at Adam, asked what he was looking at, and called him a name that until then Adam had only thought was spoken by uneducated Southerners.

Adam looked down at the ground. The salt from his tears burned his eyes. It hurt to cry, but he couldn't stop himself.

"I have something in my haversack that I can trade for you cutting us loose," Aleks said.

The Yank was certain that no Reb could possibly have anything he'd want but went ahead and looked anyway. He tossed the contents of Aleks's haversack on the ground. Out fell the iPad and phone along with their artifacts and other items.

"Which one you trading?" the aide asked.

"You may take one item, either this one or that one," Aleks pointed his foot to the blanket and then to the iPad.

The exchange caught the attention of several other Union soldiers. They gathered around the haversacks, emptied Adam's too, and then each took their pick. "You think I'm a fool, boy? I don't want no piece of glass," he said and whipped the electronic tablet down, shattering the screen. "I should shoot you for offering me a worthless trinket. I'll take the blanket."

The aide took his knife and cut Aleks's hands free from the rope and the tree. The ropes had rubbed his wrists raw.

"What about my body servant?" Aleks asked.

The boys in blue laughed and told him he'd have to figure out how to free his own slave.

The Union aide walked off with the others. Aleks had silently watched as first one and then another picked through his belongings. The railroad watch and compass were picked up and examined, but showing no movement, they were repeatedly slung down, considered broken. Adam kept his eyes closed and prayed silently.

Aleks could see the chaplain in the distance coming toward them. He came with two soldiers, and a third one was carrying a drum. The drummer was told to cut Adam loose. "You boys okay?" Chaplain Wall asked.

Aleks asked for water to wash off his hands. He needed to replace the contact in the eye hit with the button from the jacket. Adam's wrists were bleeding from the rope that had been tied too tightly around his wrists. "We are fine, sir," Aleks said. "Thank you for the water," he added and then washed off Adam's wrists. "Do you have bandages, sir?" Aleks asked. "I'd like to wrap Adam's wrists."

Chaplain Wall instructed them to put on the jackets and stay with the drummer toward the back of the regiment. The chaplain was going to the hospital tent for bandages.

The drummer took them around the back of the Union formation and lined up with the others who might have been a year or two older than the time travelers. They stood next to the flag bearer. The drummer told the flag bearer that the two rebels were under their guard until further notice, according to Meade's orders. From there, they could see the fighting at Little Round Top. Amid the hissing and bursting of shells, they could hear a band playing.

"Let's sit under the shade of this tree," said the drummer. "Everyone else has a shelter tent up." It was ninety degrees in the afternoon sun, and the lines of soldiers waited with tents on top of their sabers to ward off heat stroke.

The boys introduced themselves to the drummer and flag bearer. John was thirteen. He had joined up without his family knowing it. His mother had said he was too young to fight, but he went anyway. Now, he was hoping to write them a letter to explain where he was and that he had been given the honor of being a drummer for Meade's unit.

"I didn't think we'd be in a fight so quick, and now I fear I may not make it home," John said.

Aleks retrieved a pencil from his haversack. "Here, you can use this to write your letter," he said. "And I have paper too."

The flag bearer, who introduced himself as Joshua snatched the paper and pencil from Aleks's hand, threw them down, and yelled in Aleks's face, "We don't need your hand-me-downs! It's thanks to you that our country is in this mess."

John swooped down and picked up the pencil and paper. He sat with his back to the others and took a moment to write a letter to his mother.

Joshua exaggerated the Northern victories, their superior generals, and their more advanced weaponry. Aleks likened the Yank's rant to an Alabama Crimson Tide fan. Nobody in the SEC wanted to listen to them except another Tide fan.

Unable to keep quiet for any longer, off Aleks's tongue and out of his mouth rolled the craziest things the young Yanks had ever heard.

"The South should have won!" Aleks hollered.

Adam's head dropped to his hands. Aleks knew he'd said the wrong thing, not only to the Federal but also to Adam.

"Won what?" Joshua asked.

"This disagreement between the States!" Aleks said, wishing he could stop the conversation.

"You're out of your mind," the Yank said.

Adam jumped to his feet. "Yousa right, he be talkin' crazy from de heat! Masser, doz ya need water? Ya gots heatstroke!"

"You're right; this boy is so tired he sounds like a fool," said John, throwing Aleks's pencil at his feet.

"You're rude," Aleks said. He'd had enough of the Yanks and their pompous attitude; after all, he'd given John his pencil and then he threw it back at him. "You're a fool for being a Yank!" Aleks shouted and added, "We beat you and your sorry General Sideburns at Fredericksburg!"

"His name is Burnside," John said.

"I believe Lincoln said it would have been easier to take hell than to take the Confederates at Fredericksburg," Aleks said.

"You're right. Fredericksburg was a victory for the Rebels," John said.

"And let's not forget your Union general Fightin' Joe Hooker and his great loss at Chancellorsville. He should be nicknamed 'Retreating Joe,'" Aleks said.

It seemed once Aleks started he couldn't stop himself, and he grabbed one of the drummer's sticks and threw it into the ground where it stuck straight up.

The drummer boy swung at Aleks with his other stick.

Aleks blocked it just before it struck him. With the other hand, Aleks pushed him against the tree. The drummer let out a high-pitched yell.

"You holler like my sister," Aleks said.

"I'll shoot you," Joshua said. "Keep your hands off of him!"

"You gonna shoot me with your stick?" Aleks laughed and peered closer at the long strand of hair exposing itself from under the blue hat. "You're a girl?" Aleks said quietly. "What's your name?"

The scuffle caught the attention of a group of soldiers at the back of the line. One large man grabbed Aleks by the back of the jacket, pulled him off his feet, and threw him backward. Aleks hit the ground hard, striking his head on a rock. Another Yank swept down and busted Aleks across the face with the butt of his rifle. Aleks rolled over with his face in the dirt, his nose bleeding and his head pounding. Next came a kick in his back from another Yank who said he'd been waiting for a piece of a Reb.

Adam picked up a rock and threw it at the attackers. It hit one of them square in the forehead as he turned around. The young Yank made a run toward Adam. All attention was now on the Negro, giving Aleks an opportunity to crawl up on his knees and wipe the dirt from his eyes. Adam was going to be killed if God didn't intervene.

All Aleks saw were three Yanks with Adam hog-tied, and they had every intention of stringing him up in the tree.

God answered Aleks's prayer; there was no other explanation for who arrived back on the scene next. "Tell me what's going on here," Chaplain Wall commanded as he came upon the fight.

The drummer glared at him. "Your prisoners here are starting fights. He and his Negro need to be sent north."

"There's not time for that now. General Meade has called the troops to attention," Chaplain Wall said. "Untie this man and get into formation now or you will all be put in the stocks tonight. I'll see to it personally."

The time travelers were covered in bruises, sweat, and their own blood. They'd learned a valuable lesson, but Aleks wondered if it was too late.

* * *

The fight raged on all sides—to the north on Culp's Hill and along Cemetery Hill. By afternoon, the ground at the Wheatfield, Devil's Den, and the Peach Orchard was red from the blood soaked into its soil, and there were puddles of blood on the rocks. They heard the moans of the dying soldiers with missing appendages, shattered skulls, and bullet wounds—all lying side by side with their enemy.

They stepped reluctantly toward the conflict with zombielike creatures. Most of the men had beards. They marched alongside men with hollow eyes and no light, no emotion, only movement. Their zombielike appearance was from lack of nutrition and sleep. Now, the scorching heat and heavy humidity caused the men to labor in their breathing. Each step brought the twenty-first-century boys further into the nightmare. The air smelled of death, clouds of smoke blocked the sun, and Aleks saw shadows leap across the field. Looking up, he saw that his fear was true. Carrion circled the battlefield, waiting for their feast.

Aleks stopped, holding his head, moaning in agony.

"What happened? Are you hit?" Adam asked.

“It’s my eye. It feels like it’s been cut,” Aleks said.

He couldn’t open it. Adam tried to look at it, but his friend couldn’t open his eyelid. Aleks took his fingers and pried it open, and there was no visible injury though it looked red. It was the corneal abrasion he had received from the coat button earlier that day.

He was in so much pain he’d lost his ability to keep up with the back of the line. Adam hung back with him. John, the drummer boy, alerted the chaplain of the Reb’s strange behavior.

Chaplain Wall escorted Aleks and Adam back to camp. Aleks was in bad shape from the fight earlier. They took him to the hospital tent, and he waited on a cot beside men who were in line to have limbs amputated. Adam sat on the floor next to the cot and held his ears and kept his eyes on the floor. The patients’ screams were deafening, and the pile of limbs outside was stacked higher than a nearby field wall. Aleks decided nothing was so wrong with him that he needed to stay in the hospital. He told the chaplain he thought resting inside a dark tent would help him the most.

The chaplain put a guard outside the time travelers’ tent with strict instructions to shoot them and ask questions later. He made sure he gave the orders loud enough for the boys to hear it.

CHAPTER EIGHT

Under the Cover of Night

"TODAY, LONGSTREET NEARLY captured the high ground at Little Round Top, and then he almost captured Culp's Hill."

"I's too tired to speak, masser," Adam said and finished with a swift kick to Aleks's shin. "Shhh," Adam tried to hush him. "The guard's gonna hear you."

"What do you mean, Little Round Top? There's no such place—there's only a Big Round Top," said drummer John as he entered the tent.

"You don't know where Little Round Top is?" Aleks scoffed at the drummer.

"Are you talking about Sugar Loaf? We beat your Rebs to the top of Sugar Loaf."

Aleks had forgotten that he'd read an account of the Alabama Fifteenth at Gettysburg, and Little Round Top was known as Sugar Loaf until many years after the war.

"I heard General Warren beat your Alabama boys to the top of Sugar Loaf using hand-to-hand combat," John bragged. "Looks like we are faster and stronger than you."

Aleks's face was red, and his eyes were filled with rage. Before Adam could stop him, he spewed, "Really, faster and stronger? Your General Warren scurried up the side of Little Round Top all right, but he only beat the Alabama Fifteenth by minutes. Did he tell you there was enough blood spilled on both sides to call it a tie? As we speak, your generals are talking about how today was a huge loss for the Union and they fear General Lee will cut off their supply lines. Your leaders are in a panic. They are swearing and hollering at each other as they point at their maps and decide whose fault it is that they have Lee sitting between them and Washington."

Fear filled Adam, as he knew that Aleks had surely done it again. He whispered, "Shut up."

It was too late. Any hope of peace inside the tent was gone. The drummer erupted, "It won't be long before we free your slaves, like your friend here who's too ignorant to know his master is neither his friend nor his family."

"Mark my words, Drummer, our real glory comes tomorrow. Pickett lost the first time, but I assure you he won't make the same mistake twice," Aleks said.

"The same mistake twice? You're crazy! I don't have time for this nonsense; I'm going to see General Meade," John said.

The tent was quiet. Aleks knew he'd made a mistake by saying too much about Pickett. The two boys lay there for hours—worried and unable to sleep. Aleks was thinking about Pickett and all the soldiers who would die the next day. Was this the reason they discovered time-travel? It was what every Southern boy dreamed of—stopping the slaughter of six thousand Confederates—stopping Pickett's Charge.

"They don't know," he whispered.

"Know what?" Adam asked quietly.

"If I can get to Pickett tonight and explain the outcome of the charge tomorrow, then those men won't die. Faulkner wrote about this moment that we are in now, how every Southern boy thinks of this moment on July 3, 1863, in Gettysburg when it's not yet 2:00 p.m. It hasn't happened yet! Adam, we have a chance to do something bigger than time travel. We can stop Pickett's Charge. If we can do this, what other great things can we accomplish? How about Lincoln's assassination? We have a chance to change everything!"

Adam sat quietly, partly for fear of the guard waking up and hearing their conversation and partly because he thought he and Aleks had agreed not to make any more changes. During their visit to the Griggs House in 1861, Aleks had dropped some hints to Mrs. Griggs about her family getting involved in the textile business when farming was no longer lucrative. She had apparently listened because upon their return to 2011, Aleks's family name was on several of the textile mills throughout the Chattahoochee Valley. They both agreed afterward that it felt like cheating to manipulate fate and they would not use time travel for personal gain.

Aleks didn't see how that compared to saving six thousand lives from a horrific fate.

"I'll admit that it seems noble and like the right thing for us to do. When you first mentioned it, I was thinking we should do whatever we can to help those men. Then, I started thinking beyond tomorrow and what kind of effect we'll have on my people—150 years from tomorrow."

"Geez, man, it's not all about your people!" Aleks said harshly.

Aleks could tell from Adam's reaction that his words were offensive, but still he didn't understand how Adam could be so cold and uncaring about the six thousand.

"Let me explain it to you this way," Adam said, trying to keep his talk at a whisper. "It's more a question of ethics and consequences. We just studied this in our government class. The Trolley Problem goes something like this: there is a runaway trolley on the railroad track. You see a lever, and if you pull it, then the trolley goes off into a sand pit and the five people onboard are saved," Adam said and paused.

"Yes, that's it! I want to pull the lever for the men in Pickett's Charge," Aleks said.

"Yes, but pulling the lever has consequences," Adam said. He explained that in the Trolley Problem when the lever is pulled and the trolley switches tracks, the trolley then hits and kills the person walking on the other track.

"So in this instance, the trolley is Pickett's Charge, and we have to decide if we are going to pull the lever," Aleks said. "That's an easy decision."

"What are the consequences?" Adam asked, looking his friend in the eye. "I have an idea that this war would be extended and even more people would die on both sides. I won't let you do this!"

The guard looked in the tent and informed them that his orders were to keep them quiet and in the tent. "General Meade's aide has advised us that you caused trouble with the drummer and we are to watch you more closely. Word has it that he plans to send you up north to the prison camp. So I'd be quiet if I were you."

Hour after hour passed into the night, and neither boy could sleep. They had to escape before daylight, or by the sound of it, they'd be prisoners of war.

Aleks contemplated their escape and what he and Adam had spoken about earlier. Who was on the other track? The nation was on the other track, but couldn't they save the nation too? Why not? Was that crazy to think they could stop Pickett and save the country?

"Hey, Adam," Aleks said quietly. "Are you awake?"

"Yeah," Adam said.

"Our guard is asleep. I'll go out. If it's safe for you to come, I'll make a bobwhite call. Then, meet me at the group of trees, the ones where they had us tied up earlier."

The guard snored like he'd never wake up, and it was an easy escape for the time travelers. They met at the tree directly behind the tent and then retreated from the camp.

"We should just head for the rail line and forget meeting up with the Alabama Fifteenth. It's too risky," Adam said.

Aleks disagreed even though he knew it was risky. He felt it was a calculated risk and one worth taking; for them to travel alone in this area was even riskier.

* * *

They walked for a half an hour and found shelter in an orchard. They were both exhausted and decided to rest.

"I think we took a wrong turn," Adam said. "I don't remember seeing an orchard in this direction. Wait a minute! That looks like an encampment up ahead. Stop! We've gone the wrong way," he said.

"Adam, I'm sorry. I meant to go this way. I can't let these men die. Not when it's within my reach to save them," Aleks said.

"I'm a moron for trusting you," Adam said.

Aleks had guided them south of Gettysburg but then west through the peach orchard. When they came out of it and headed north, they were heading smack dab for the Confederates and not too far from Pickett.

Adam pushed Aleks back into the orchard, threw down his haversack, and dove for Aleks's knees.

Adam got the advantage with a headlock that was cutting off Aleks's windpipe. "We are going to leave this place without you saying a word to Pickett or to his men. Give me a thumbs-up if you agree with me.

Promise that we'll head home now, and I'll let you go," Adam insisted. "No more interfering with history!"

Aleks agreed, and he gasped for air as he listened to Adam explain how none of Pickett's men or the entire Confederacy for that matter would be aware that their fate had been changed. He told Aleks that if the Confederates whipped the Union at Gettysburg that they would think that God was on their side and that they were right about everything, including slavery.

"Have you questioned how a Southern victory here would possibly affect slavery, our nation, or world history?"

Aleks was rubbing his throat. It was still sore from the headlock. He shook his head no.

"Slavery would continue, for who knows how long, and our nation would stay divided. As a divided union, which is an oxymoron, it would be of little help in defeating Nazi Germany and helping many other nations, not to mention how ineffective we'd become at protecting our own borders against terrorism," Adam said.

The boys had come to an agreement, which was forced upon Aleks, and were both ready to head home. Aleks helped Adam pick up his things that had fallen out of his haversack when he'd thrown it down on the orchard floor.

"You should have five rocks," Aleks said.

"I did have five but can only find two of them. I have everything else. Does it matter how many I have?" Adam asked.

"I'm not sure. We've had the same number each time. I am afraid to test it, kind of like my lucky boxers that I wear for every wrestling meet," Aleks said. "I'm not sure if they're lucky, but I don't want to test it!"

"That's way too much information," Adam said, throwing a peach and hitting Aleks in the chest.

The sun was beginning to peek over the horizon, and the boys decided to seek shelter in a home they had spotted not too far from the fighting. They'd begin their journey again at nightfall.

CHAPTER NINE

Gettysburg, July 3, 1863

IT WAS EARLY July 3, the day of the greatest artillery bombardment of the war and the day of Pickett's Charge. The boys pressed their binocular scopes firmly against their faces.

The area between them and the house on the edge of the field was all clear. "I'll run to that tree; wait for my signal, and then you come," Aleks instructed. They made it to the farmhouse door unnoticed and knocked desperately.

"What if they shoot us?" Adam asked.

"Have faith," Aleks said.

"I wonder if any of the dead men who fought at Gettysburg had faith. I bet they were thinking, *Yep, sure didn't see that coming*," Adam said.

The farmhouse door opened, and they were greeted with the barrel of a shotgun held by a middle-aged man with a round face and a stout body. His beard went nearly to his chest, which seemed normal now, but had looked odd when they had first witnessed all the unshaven soldiers at Gettysburg.

The boys held their hands up, and Aleks did the talking—telling their names, that they were unarmed, and how it was they were captured by the Union.

The man lowered the shotgun, nodding at the boys and gesturing for them to come into the house.

"I'm Mr. Bayly," he said. "I'm not sure I believe all that, but you certainly don't look like soldiers. Come on in! Let's get these boys some dinner, Mrs. Bayly."

They passed the modest parlor and found a woman as old as Mr. Bayly standing in the kitchen, staring out the window toward the battlefield. Smoke was visible from the window.

"This is my wife," said Mr. Bayly. "We have a boy your age, name of Billy. He's around here somewhere," he said.

"He's in the attic, getting a better view of the battle," said Mrs. Bayly. She turned now and got a good look at the boys. "Why, they're just kids, Papa! Put that shotgun away. Don't frighten them any more than they already are."

Aleks interrupted. "Hello, ma'am, we are thankful for your generous offer to come into your home. We'll head home tomorrow but were afraid we'd be recaptured if we traveled south today."

"Shhh!" Mrs. Bayly hushed him. "You are too upset and tired; tell us more after you've eaten and had time to rest," she said.

There was stew on the fire, and bread was baking in the oven. The boys were starving. The last time they'd eaten was almost twenty-four hours earlier. This meal would not be a large one, but it was appreciated by all partaking. It also would be shared with the wounded soldiers lying in the back rooms of the house.

Large areas of blood, some dried, covered the floor in the entry and trailed down the main hallway. The wounded men were convalescing in the back of the house. These soldiers were on their way to the fight when a caisson exploded and they were thrown and landed near the Baylys' field. One man lost both his eyes and the other an arm.

Mr. Bayly served the time travelers at the kitchen table, which sat under the window overlooking the field. A patch of trees blocked the view, allowing only the smoke to be seen from the window.

Mrs. Bayly said her son Billy had eaten his dinner upstairs; he was so fixated on the war that she couldn't stop him from watching long enough to come to the table. She said the view of the battlefield was perfect from up there. The strange thing was even though the house sat only a few miles from the battle, there was an eerie silence. Aleks explained to her that this phenomenon was known as an acoustic shadow.

Billy's curiosity finally got the best of him, and he came downstairs to see who was talking to his parents. The tall, thin blond-haired boy of fifteen came into the kitchen and his mother introduced him to the time travelers. She asked him to show the boys the attic and to get the beds upstairs ready so that they could sleep up there that night.

"I ain't never seen you 'round here before," Billy said. "Have you boys been in the fight?" He asked as the time travelers followed behind him up the stairs.

"Yes, but only because we were forced to by the Union, but now we are headed home."

"Look at this!" Billy said excitedly, pointing out the attic window.

"Billy!" his mother called. "Come on! Let the boys rest a spell. Pa needs your help in the barn."

It was two in the afternoon, and neither of the time travelers could sleep. Instead they pressed their binocular scopes hard against their eyes and watched from the attic window as Pickett and his men came out from the woods.

Adam glanced at Aleks and noticed him grinning.

"What did you do?" he asked suspiciously.

Pickett's men were not taking their famed march through the open field toward the Union Army.

"I swear I didn't go to Pickett's camp! While you were asleep in the orchard last night, I heard someone walk near us. It turned out to be one of Pickett's men. He pulled his gun, and out of fear for our lives I told him we were from Alabama and were on our way home. He said he didn't want any trouble. He'd come to get some peaches. We had a friendly exchange, and for those thirty minutes he wasn't a soldier at all but a scared teenager like us. He's already married and only wants to go home to his family.

"I told him that we'd been captured by the Union, and he asked if we knew any of Meade's plans for the next day of battle. I couldn't let him die. He has an infant son at home, a mother, and a younger brother. His father was killed two days ago. He buried his father at Gettysburg. He dug the grave himself. I confided in him that Meade already knew of Pickett's plans for the next day. I told him his only hope of surviving was to escape.

"He said that all the men thought the plan was a bad one because it only made sense that when men march into an open field they have no advantage. The enemy would only have to open fire on them, and they would be like sitting ducks," Aleks said. "I had to tell him. You would have done the same thing."

The boys watched Pickett's men change directions from the well-known Pickett's Charge and march south and then east, coming around and surprising Meade's troops from behind.

At first, it seemed to be an effective strategy but what the South didn't plan for was the Union to flank Pickett. He ended up surrounded on all sides.

"It's worse than the first Pickett's Charge. They are being slaughtered on all sides," Adam said.

The boys watched the green fields turn red.

"The end is the same for both; right or wrong, they are all dying," Adam lamented.

They watched through the sunlight's blinding bursts off the sabers. An occasional Rebel yell still gave hope, but the sight through their scope was gruesome and they knew the cause was lost.

Aleks's message to the young Confederate had done nothing to help the Confederates, and worst of all for Aleks—he had betrayed his friend's trust.

They heard later that Pickett met with General Lee and pleaded for him to change the orders, and he agreed to change their plan and attack Meade from behind.

Finally, a green flash shot across the horizon signaling the sunset and an end to the day's fight.

That night, Mrs. Bayly worked by lantern light placing extra blankets on the spare bed upstairs in the one-room attic. She wished the boys a good night, and the light from the whale-oil lamp disappeared down the steep, narrow staircase. The boys took their places: Aleks on the spare bed with his back against the wall, Billy facing him on the opposite wall, and Adam on his palette on the floor in the five feet of space between the twin beds. The boys talked and laughed in the darkness, and during those wonderful hours there was no right or wrong side and skin color seemed to vanish, Aleks thought.

* * *

The front door of the house slammed as it closed. The loud sound woke the boys.

Aleks sat up; his hair and body were soaking wet.

Billy looked at Aleks and laughed. "You're supposed to sleep on the wire mattress underneath. It's cooler," he said. "Sorry about that, I guess my mama forgot to take off the feather mattress when she made the bed last night."

Billy stood on his bed and looked out the attic window. "My parents are leaving. I'll return in a minute after I speak with them."

"Hey, Aleks," Adam whispered.

"Yeah?"

"You didn't sound like yourself last night when you were talking to Mr. Bayly."

"Oh, I was speaking like a person from this time period. I was speaking like someone from *Gone with the Wind*."

"You need more practice. You sounded like a girl. Was it part of your plan to sound like Scarlett?" he asked with a laugh.

Aleks threw his dirty socks at him, hitting him in the face. "You know any girls who smell like that?"

"Yeah, your sister!" Adam laughed.

"Cat's gonna kill you when she hears what you said!"

The boys stopped their horseplay at the sound of footsteps.

"Hey!" Billy said. "Here are some clothes to put on." He threw some clothes at Aleks and then Adam. "Come on downstairs after you're dressed, and we'll have breakfast," he said. "My parents have gone to help the wounded."

* * *

"Happy Fourth of July," Aleks said, as he sat down at the table.

"That's right. Today is July 4. We all have that in common," Billy said.

"We thanks you furs invitin' us to break bread with you," Adam said.

"A Yankee boy feeding two Confederates; this never happened in the history books," Aleks said with a smile.

"What do you mean 'history books'?" asked Billy.

"He means that in the South, it's uncommon for a Yank and a Rebel to be guests in each other's home."

"You don't sound like a slave," said Billy.

Adam had forgotten to use his Uncle Remus dialect. The boys glanced at each other. Aleks thought of something quick.

"Yes, that's right; he's my body servant. He was raised on my plantation, and we are like brothers."

"Brothers? That's not what I've heard about slaves. They get treated like animals. They are whipped, they can't read or write, and they have no rights. My parents say that's the reason we fight this war. I've seen Negros with big scars—scars because their owners whipped them."

"Adam knows how to read and write and he has free papers. Show Billy your papers."

He fumbled in his pocket. "They are in my Union jacket."

"Oh no, my mama washed your clothes this morning before she left."

"Where are the clothes now?" Aleks asked.

"They are drying on the back porch."

The boys followed Billy toward the back door. Billy gave a shout for the boys to come outside where he'd found pieces of paper in the big pot over the woodstove.

Billy took a stick used for stirring the laundry in the boiling water and with it lifted out soggy pieces of paper.

"How do we get more papers?" Aleks asked.

"My parents are friends with a local judge. He will give you papers. You don't even sound like a slave. You sound like one of those educated Negroes."

* * *

A loud knock came from the kitchen door. "Go up to the attic, and I'll give you the all-clear when it's safe to come down," Billy said.

At the door, Billy found hungry Union soldiers. "We don't have any food. We gave away the last chicken yesterday and ate the last of the eggs this morning. Soldiers came through yesterday, and my mama made dinner for them. There is nothing left to eat here."

"Who's we?" the soldier requested.

"It's just me and my parents."

"I heard something upstairs. Who you hiding here?" The soldier pushed past Billy and into the house. "You got chickens upstairs?"

"No, sir."

"Then you won't mind if we have us a look-see."

Up went the men in blue, and down they came with the boys. Aleks was trying to convince the soldier that they were not hiding.

"I know you are Rebs. I can hear it in your voice. Why are you here? You've lost the battle," he said. And then he added to Adam, "That means you'll be free soon."

Adam didn't respond; he just kept his head low and eyes to the floor.

"You afraid to speak, boy? Cat got your tongue?"

CHAPTER TEN

The Bayly Family

BILLY KNEW THESE men meant trouble for his new friends if he didn't find something for them to eat. "Like I said, we don't have much to eat but our trees are ripe with cherries. We'll pick you all the cherries you want."

And that was what they did, all afternoon.

"You look like somebody shot you!" One of the blue coats laughed as he pointed to the juice spattered on Aleks's shirt.

Aleks jumped down from the tree, wondering if this was about to turn hostile.

"You look ready to fight. We don't want to fight you," the Union soldier said.

The larger of the blue coats chimed in, "Shoot, my brother is in Mississippi and he fights on your side. Are you from Mississippi?"

"We are from Alabama, but I have a cousin in Mississippi."

The man reached into his pocket and pulled out a picture. It was two boys posed with their parents. "We are all alike; we are all Americans. We sit in our camps at night, look at our pictures, write letters to home, and pray for God to end this war."

"Why do you fight if you don't hate the South?"

"We fight for our nation. It is the only honorable thing about this fight."

"We best be on our way," he said.

The shorter blue coat said, "We don't want the Old Snapping Turtle to think we deserted."

"Who's that?" Aleks asked.

"Meade!" they said in unison.

They all had a good laugh.

"He snapped at us," Adam said.

"You sound like a white boy," the blue coat said.

"Are you a spy?" the larger blue coat asked.

"No, he's my body servant, and my mama practically raised him as her own."

"Don't let anyone else hear you speak like that. And don't think because we are Union that we all like darkies or all fight for your freedom. We have abolitionists in the North, but we also have folks who want darkies free so they won't come up north. They will just as soon kill you as set you free," he said.

"We've gotta go, Joe. Meade will have our heads," the large man said.

"Here, you can bring him some cherries," Billy said and handed him a bucket.

The three boys stood shoulder to shoulder under the cherry tree and waved good-bye to their new Yankee friends.

"Here's a riddle for you. A Yank, a Reb, and a darkie stand together under a cherry tree. All three look like they've been shot, but no one is bleeding. What happened?" Aleks asked.

"That is the worst riddle I've ever heard," Adam said, whipping a cherry at him and hitting him in the arm.

Aleks picked up a handful from the ground, hit Adam's leg, and nailed Billy in the arm. Billy joined in, and all three were in one big cherry fight. For a moment, nothing else mattered.

Billy was a good friend, but it was time to find their way home.

"Billy, we need a favor," Aleks said. "We need a map of the best route south across the Potomac and into Virginia."

Billy interrupted. "What about papers for Adam?"

"How long do you think it would take?" Aleks asked.

"I heard my mama say one time it took about a month, depending on the situation. They have to prove that Adam is not a runaway, that there isn't a bounty hunter looking for him. She said it's because no one wants to take someone else's property."

"The longer we stay here, the greater our risk of being stranded. We have to leave at dark and can't wait for the papers," Aleks said.

It was midafternoon, and the sky looked like rain. The boys took baths, prepared their haversacks, and filled their canteens. Billy's parents had returned a short time earlier from helping with the wounded near Cemetery Ridge.

"Here are your coats, boys. I am frightfully sorry about Adam's papers," Mrs. Bayly said.

"Mother, there is something we can do," Mr. Bayly said. "We have two horses hidden by our back barn. The Union and Confederate soldiers took our other animals, but they've not spotted these or the barn because of the woods. Billy and I can ride with you to the point where you meet up with the Alabama troops, and then we'll ride back home. We heard that Lee is still on Seminary Ridge."

"Thank you, Mr. Bayly, we would be forever grateful to you and your family for helping us," Aleks said.

They loaded the horses, thanked Mrs. Bayly, and headed through the fields and toward the forested area. They followed closely behind Billy and his father because they were in danger of losing their way from the heavy rain. Visibility was low. It was difficult to see even a few feet in front of them.

They found it impossible to ride clear of all the dead, and the stench from rotting flesh took their breath. They kept from breathing it in by pulling up their undershirts and covering their mouths and noses.

There were some fifty thousand dead bodies, black and bloated from the sun. It was the most unimaginable and hellish of scenes.

Along their route were mass graves and a scene of the living ravaging the dead for their boots, coats, and weapons. Men were desperate for supplies since the supply routes had been blocked and supply wagons looted.

As Mr. Bayly and the boys drew near to Seminary Ridge, they spotted the Army of Northern Virginia retreating on its own terms. At this point, the time travelers prepared to part ways with the Baylys.

The boys left their blue coats and the horse with Billy and his father and walked the rest of the way. They carried a red flag Mrs. Bayly made from a handkerchief. She said the Rebels would show them Southern hospitality at the sight of the flag.

"Hey! Hey!" Aleks waved his handkerchief.

"Sing 'Sweet Home Alabama'! They'll love it," Adam spurred him on.

"That song hasn't been written yet."

"You've got a point, whistle 'Dixie'!"

They were trying to get the attention of some Confederates on Seminary Ridge. Lee was holding his position there.

And so he whistled the tune that had even charmed Abraham Lincoln. They came upon a group of men, and one of them was speaking German.

"Guten Morgen?" Aleks's salutation stuck in his throat like a cat with a hairball. He was so nervous his lips were quivering. "Guten Nacht?"

The man turned to him and said in broken English, "No, it's not a good night to be in this army, *junger* man."

"Thank you, sir! You are right. It is not. We are looking for the Alabama Fifteenth. Could you point us in its direction?"

"I'm Colonel Oates. You are in the right place," said the man, who was wearing a red shirt, a gray coat, and a hat with the letters "HP."

Aleks noticed the secession badge and couldn't help but read it aloud. "Liberty, Equality, and Fraternity." He looked at Adam's reaction after he read it. He looked stoic, but Aleks knew Adam must be seeing the irony in the motto of their hometown boys. *They wouldn't know equality at this time in history if it looked them in the face,* he thought.

"You boys with a company, or are you new recruits?" Colonel Oates asked.

"No, sir, we've traveled from Alabama to bring supplies to my father. We lost our way after being captured by Meade's army but managed to escape. We are supposed to meet my father and then take the train home to Georgia."

"What is your father's name?"

"Dr. Ness, sir."

"I'll do my best to help you find him. I'm the commanding officer of the Alabama Fifteenth. Hmm, thought I knew all the doctors in our infantry. I don't recall a Dr. Ness. Are you boys certain he's with the Alabama Fifteenth?"

"It's an honor to meet you! Are you *the* Colonel Oates?" Aleks asked, snapping to attention.

The officer nodded his head yes. "Why?" he asked.

"Your attack on the Union is legendary," Aleks said.

"Thank you, son, but you are premature in calling it legendary."

"Yes, sir, what I meant is that we admire your courage against the Union. You beat them to the top. Without water or food, in the scorching heat and humidity of the day, your men marched twenty-five miles to Little Round Top, some without shoes, climbing to the top as they fought the green Union sharpshooters. Your men never gave up!"

Adam elbowed Aleks in hopes he'd shut up. Oates and his men were flattered but became suspicious as he rattled off details only known by the men who fought on the "big hill" that day. "And I'm sorry about your brother," Aleks added.

Once again, he had given away more than he'd intended. However, the last comment had apparently fallen on deaf ears because the colonel interrupted him with a question. "How long has your father been a war surgeon?"

"Two years and I have my mother's letter here telling us which regiment."

Aleks fumbled for the papers in his haversack and then in his pockets.

"Masser, here's yur ledder."

"It says the Thirty-Third, not the Fifteenth," Aleks said.

"I's so sorry, Masser Aleks." Adam kept his eyes low. "I was 'fraid to tell you after wez captured by the Yankees."

"When we get home, Mama will ask what took us so long. She will wonder why my father didn't get his supplies."

"Pleaze, Masser, pleaze don't tell. I's so sorry that I cause such trouble. Don't whoop me, Masser. Don't whoop me."

The boys both knew Aleks's ancestor served with the Alabama Thirty-Third and that his company was not at Gettysburg. They had used it as their cover story for this trip. The only problem was that Aleks had made a mistake and changed their story by referring to his father as Dr. Ness instead of Dr. Griggs. Dr. Griggs was a Civil War surgeon for the Thirty-Third. Aleks recognized his mistake, but it was too late to change his story and say he had told them the wrong name.

"You boys may still be at the right place. Come on; we'll check in with General Lee's command and find the location of the Thirty-Third."

The boys were beside themselves with fear and bouts of excitement as they walked toward Lee. President Lincoln had first asked Lee to command the Army of the Potomac for the Union. Lee declined and sided first with his state of Virginia and then with the Confederacy. Aleks couldn't believe he was so close to this great man.

CHAPTER ELEVEN

The Long Journey Home

THEY CAUGHT A glimpse of General Lee as he met with officers to discuss their retreat. He ordered the wounded to be transported out first with Longstreet, Ewell, and Hill, and then the rest of the army had orders to join them at Williamsport, near the Potomac. Maps were spread out on the tables as the commanders planned their routes across the river.

The officer informed the boys that the Thirty-Third was not at Gettysburg but was reportedly in Tennessee. They offered to let them travel with the wagons toward Chambersburg and continue south from there until they had reached a working rail line.

They remained there for a moment, watching the interactions of the generals and their aides. Aleks noticed there was a short sword lying on the table closest to him and Adam. No one was looking. Everyone's back was to them. Those who were facing the time travelers were on the opposite side of the head table, and the people standing around the table in front of them obstructed their view.

This was his chance to be armed. He justified the thievery by telling himself it was for self-preservation. *Do or die,* he thought. He slid the sword off the table and into his haversack. It was open on the top and easy access for him to conceal it.

"Let's go," Aleks said softly.

On their way out of the commander's headquarters, Aleks slid his phone out from his pocket and snapped a few photos from his side hoping to capture Lee and his men in the shot. Aleks quickly put his phone away, noticing he'd caught the attention of the German general.

The German followed them from the tent, but they managed to slip into the cloud of chaos left from the battle and eventually lost sight of him in the crowd of soldiers.

They caught up with the Confederate wagons and traveled with them toward Chambersburg, Pennsylvania. Heavy clouds overhead continued to deliver a cleansing rain to the bloodied battlefields. The soil refused more water. The dirt turned to mud, and the puddles turned to ponds. In some areas, the water was so deep it came to their armpits.

The seventeen-mile wagon train was escorted by more than two thousand cavalry and drudged along at two miles an hour. From Chambersburg, they headed south in the direction of the Potomac hoping to cross at Williamsport, Maryland. At one point, the entire wagon train came to a halt when the soldiers and officers on horseback fell asleep in their saddles.

Few words were spoken between the boys on the journey; their thoughts were filled with the voices of those around them. The wounded men sang a song of sorrow to the rhythm of the rain. It was a never-ending song, for when one man died there was another who took his place in the chorus of the suffering. The song served as a cadence for the five thousand who marched by their side.

There was no end to the rain. It continued all day, all night, and into the next day. The men and horses trudged along in the muck and mire, finally reaching the shore on the afternoon of July 5.

Aleks and Adam overheard some soldiers discussing how the heavy rains had made the river impassable.

"Are you telling me that we marched through hell and can't cross over? If only this was the Chattahoochee River. I'm sick of being treated like a slave. There is something worse than being black in America; it's being a slave in America. One Yankee asked me, 'What you lookin' at, boy?' I was looking at his uniform. You know, before this trip, I believed the North fought to free black people from slavery. I believed that if my parents had moved north that my life would have been better. Can you believe some of the Yankees have treated me worse than the Rebels? I was a fool to think that anyone fought for us."

"My dad says people fought to end slavery, but it was mostly fought over economics and states' rights. Slavery was the best place for black people at the time," Aleks said.

"Please explain this to me," Adam demanded.

"General Lee once said that he didn't believe in slavery, but it was the best place for the black man at the time. Your ancestors were in for execution in Africa or slavery in America," Aleks said.

"Easy for you to say, white boy!" Adam said with clenched teeth. "Tell me about how good slavery was for us and how far we've come. Please explain how I am better off with my family as housekeepers and yardmen for you. Damn it! I'm tired of you making this okay."

Adam pushed Aleks down, and he slipped in the mud, landing on his back. Aleks stood up in a flash with a kip-up. Adam swung his fist, hitting Aleks in the chest. Aleks dove at Adam's knees, lifted him over his head, and flipped him on his back. The fistfight had turned into a wrestling match; it ensued until both were muddied to their eyeballs, and Aleks had him pinned in a half nelson.

"I win this time," Aleks said. "I'm sorry that I made you angry. I didn't mean to …" he said and looked up to see a Confederate soldier looking down at them both with suspicion.

"Is this Negro messin' with you?" asked the man in gray.

"Oh, I'm sorry, sir. We were just playin' around. This is my body servant," Aleks said.

They jumped to their feet and faced the soldier. He waved his rifle at Adam.

"Just 'cause the president of the Northern states says you's free don't mean nothin' to me. We shoot disobedient niggers 'round here."

Even the chorus of the dying paused to hear the outcome of the skirmish.

"This is no time for playin'. We is under orders from General Lee to transport these wounded across the river. No more horseplay or you'll both be shot for insubordination."

"Yes, sir!" Aleks said.

"Since you boys like messin' in the dirt, you can assist the burial squad. That'll sober you up!"

The boys helped dig shallow graves and place the bodies. The graves were scattered and poorly marked, but there was not enough time to do anything more.

When they finished with the burial squad, they were ordered to load the flat boats with wounded. For two days, they worked at the river, sending the wounded to the other side.

"This is the last group. We'll be the next group to cross the river," Aleks said.

Afterward, they crowded in with other soldiers around a fire near the banks. They warmed their hands and dried their clothes. Aleks thought this was surely the coldest July day he'd ever experienced.

Aleks had not calculated correctly; he and Adam were told to stay toward the back and cross with the burial crew. That way, if anyone else died they could take care of them before they left the area. The boys waited and waited for their turn to cross the river; they waited so long that the water became too high to cross and then came the terrible news that the bridge up the river at Fall Waters had been destroyed by a Union raiding party.

"What do we do now? We are stuck here, and you know the Union is on its way," Adam said. "I overheard one man say it could be a week or more before the river is crossable."

"We can't wait a week. We can build our own boat and cross the river, or we can go back into Maryland and find another route out of here," Aleks said.

"Let's build a boat. Wasn't your pa a canoe builder?"

"Yes, and he taught me a few things. Sure wish Pa was here now; sure could use his red canoe."

After dark, the boys left camp and scouted some old barn boards that they twined together with some rope Aleks had in his haversack. It wasn't enough so he snuck back to camp and untied some of the boats, leaving them tied up only on one end. He was certain the boats were better off now than before because he'd secured the boats by changing their slip knots to square knots.

The boys put in the water about a mile downriver from the Confederates' camp. The water was freezing cold compared to the bathwater temperatures they swam in down South. The rough wake knocked them around like a mechanical bull, but they were in this to win. They held tightly to the rope, knuckles white, flat on their stomachs, hoping the current would soon land the raft on the other side. Finally the wake settled enough that Aleks took a board and started paddling. Adam stayed flat on his stomach. He was frightened. Aleks knew it was because Adam wasn't the best swimmer. To put Adam at ease or at least relieve his terror, Aleks took a piece of rope and tied Adam to the raft. Finally, near sunrise on July 8, they made it to the banks of West Virginia.

"Am I hallucinating, or are there two horses over there?" Aleks asked.

"No, you're right, bro; those are horses. I bet their owners are not far from here," Adam said. "Let's go see if they'll let us ride them."

The boys approached the two black horses. Pleasant and happy for companions, the horses allowed the boys to mount them and they rode in the direction of Gordonsville, Virginia.

* * *

Traveling through the rolling hills of the Piedmont Region, Aleks was enamored with the spectacular views of the Blue Ridge Mountains.

Adam woke him from his daydream. "I've been thinking a lot about what you said—how slavery wasn't the main reason for the Civil War," Adam said.

"You shouldn't take it personally. It's what history says, not what I say," Aleks said.

"Let's say you're black. Would slavery be the most important issue of the war?" Adam asked. "I want you to answer but only after you've thought about it. Consider all we've seen and talked about since we started these trips."

The boys rode in silence for an hour. Adam broke the silence with talk about the weather, and soon they were talking about the first thing they'd do when they arrived home—sleeping in their own beds was high on the list—and what they were going to tell their parents. Serious conversation gave way to normal joking, but still Aleks felt the tension that had been building since their first trip.

The trip took a day for having to rest and water the horses, but late in the day, they rode into Orange, Virginia.

They were exhausted and famished. All the provisions given them by Mrs. Bayly were depleted. The Episcopal Church of St. Thomas was their first stop in Orange. It was their best chance for food and shelter.

"A man of God won't turn us down; isn't there scripture about feeding the hungry?" Aleks said.

"You won't go hungry here," said the lady standing at the entrance of the church. "Hitch your horses to the locust tree and come inside."

They walked past the stately white columns in the main entrance, a door through which Jefferson Davis and General Lee would also pass.

The time travelers noticed more bloodstained floors—it seemed almost normal to them after Gettysburg—and the pews were filled with injured and dying soldiers.

The same welcoming voice from the church entrance beckoned them to come further down the main aisle. It was the minister's daughter. They learned her name was Margaret. She told them her father served with a unit from Virginia and her mother was at home caring for the younger children. As the eldest child, she was caring for the church and allowing it to be used as a hospital. Margaret was tall, thin, and blonde. Her day dress was torn and dirty, and her face had years of worry already written upon it.

She paused from her work, took out her handkerchief, and wiped the sweat from her brow. She said, "We need extra hands to help with these wounded. Would you be willing to work for food?"

"Yes, we are desperate," Aleks said.

"You may be in need, but you are not desperate. Look around you; these men are desperate, and we are unable to care for them because there are too many of them and not enough of us," she said.

"I'm sorry, ma'am. What can we do to help?" Aleks asked.

"You had to ask, didn't you?" Adam said quietly.

The boys moved those who'd already passed away to an area outside of the church.

"Seeing guys our age mortally wounded or dead, it's sobering!" Aleks said.

"I know. Look at this guy here," Adam said, pointing to a young blond guy who favored Aleks. He'd only recently passed away. "If I saw him alive, I'd think he was like you—had everything in the world—but look at him now; he has nothing. It's sad," he said.

Margaret called them to come back inside the church. She needed their help with bathing the injured. First she had them haul water from an outside well and then wash the soldiers. She was so thankful. Without the time travelers' help, it would have taken all night.

Aleks had never washed the family dog, much less another human.

The time travelers thought it couldn't get worse, but it did when Dr. Banks, an elderly surgeon, asked the boys to assist him in amputation and bullet removal.

It was the worst thing the boys had witnessed up close to this point. They had seen the pile of limbs at Gettysburg, but assisting in the actual removal of a limb meant blood everywhere.

First, the doctor administered chloroform by dripping the liquid onto a cloth held so that the patient inhaled the vapors. Then he used several tools to remove the limb. He cut the skin and muscle with a two-edge knife, sawed the bone with a tool that looked like a small handsaw, and then tied off the arteries.

Adam passed out at the sight of blood spurting from an artery and rested a few minutes before helping with the next surgery. From then on, the doctor told Adam to hold the patient down but to look away.

The blood did not bother Aleks. The doctor thought it was because Aleks's father was also a doctor, but it was more likely because he had taken a swig of whiskey while they waited for a patient's chloroform to take effect—that and he secretly imagined the blood was ketchup. He gave Adam the same advice, but it didn't work for him.

The doctor finished up with his final patient of the day. He told the boys he'd be back the following day and that he sure could use their help tomorrow.

"I'm sorry, Dr. Banks, but we are heading back home to Alabama and can't stay," Aleks said.

"Well, I sure am sorry to hear that. You boys were a great help to us here," Dr. Banks said. "Have a safe trip home, and come see us if you are ever back in these parts."

The doctor left, and the boys stepped outside to the well. They washed off the blood that had spattered on their clothes and bodies. The boys discussed leaving right then and traveling in the dark.

"Why should we wait till morning?" Adam asked. "There is barely enough food to feed the wounded."

"You're right; our chances of getting food are better in the woods. Between the two of us, we can catch something. Remember that time we cornered and trapped the groundhog?" Aleks said.

"Are you serious? Neither one of us has ever hunted, and the only reason we caught that was because your dog cornered it first and it ran into the trap to get away from General," Adam said.

"You're right; even if we don't find anything in the woods, the sooner we get home, the better," Aleks said. "Let's go!"

"It's better if we don't go in and say good-bye to Margaret. If we do, we'll feel guilty about leaving her with all the injured and dying. So it'll be easier if we just leave," Adam said.

"But wait! We need to go back in and get our haversacks," Aleks said.

"I'll go in and get them. If you go in, Margaret will talk to you," Adam said.

Adam went back in the church and straight to the corner where they'd laid their belongings earlier that evening.

Meanwhile, Aleks went to the horses, offered them each a drink, and checked them over. They looked rested and ready to ride.

Everything was quiet around the area of town near the church. Aleks thought this would be the perfect time to leave—that is until a group of young ladies walked around the corner by the church. In their arms were baskets filled with chicken.

"Can I help you?" Aleks asked. He wasn't sure where his sudden impulse to show hospitality had come from but figured it probably had something to do with his stomach and the aroma from the baskets.

"Yes, have you seen Margaret?" asked a petite blonde in a blue-striped day dress and white bonnet.

"She is in the church," Aleks said and smiled.

"Hi," she said. "I'm Susie, and these are my friends: Mary Elizabeth, Virginia, and Caroline. We are friends of Margaret and told her we'd bring supper for the Alabama gentleman and his body servant. You haven't seen him, have you?" she asked, blushing.

"I'm Aleks from Alabama," he said.

"Well, of course you are," Susie said.

The smell of the chicken and bread clouded his mind, and he forgot about the plan to stay out of the church. Away he went inside.

"Hello!" Margaret said. "Thank you for bringing dinner for our guests."

"Margaret, you said he was nice-looking, but I think you've been modest with your description. He is handsome indeed," said Mary Elizabeth.

"Listen, Mary Elizabeth, your Johnny is still fighting for you," Susie said. "You know, my Bobby died for the cause, and I am a young widow. You leave this lonely handsome gentleman to my care," she added.

"Here comes dessert," Adam said with a smile.

Two girls with pies swished their way toward the Alabama boys.

"Would you like peach, apple, or cherry?" Virginia asked.

Aleks blushed. "I think I'd like to try a piece of each one. I bet they are all good," he said.

"Some folks say all the good men are gone to war, but that's a lie because you are right here," said Caroline. "Have you seen the war?" she asked.

"Yes, ma'am, we were at Gettysburg and are heading home to Alabama tomorrow."

"Tomorrow? You can't leave tomorrow; you just got here. Margaret needs your help in the hospital. And, well, we have a charity ball planned for tomorrow night and there are not enough men for our dance cards. Please don't leave tomorrow. Oh, you must stay," Caroline begged.

"I'll try," Aleks said, knowing they were leaving for the train station at first light if not sooner.

* * *

The ladies, including Margaret, all left the church after tucking in the wounded and promising them biscuits and jam in the morning.

The time travelers wouldn't be there when the ladies arrived back in the morning. The young ladies would look for them in the church and outside, finally discovering the boys' borrowed blankets in the corner where they'd slept and a thank-you to Margaret and the other four ladies.

The boys had snuck out before sunrise, leaving the local Southern belles heartbroken upon the discovery that more good men had left town.

* * *

"I can hear the train. We must be getting close to Gordonsville," Aleks said.

"I have never been so happy to hear a train," Adam said. "At home, when I hear a train, it normally means we are going to be late for school because we have to wait for it to clear the railroad crossing."

"Look over there!" Aleks shouted. "There's the depot, and next to it is the Exchange Hotel."

The boys tied their horses to the nubby-looking hitching post and looked around at the busy train depot and the hotel that was being used as a hospital for the wounded veterans.

"I learned about this in my Civil War history class," Aleks said. "After the war, it was used for newly freed slaves."

"That's cool," Adam said.

"Let's go take a look before we get on the train. It won't leave for another thirty minutes," Aleks said.

"I swear! If you go in there, I'm going to beat the crap out of you." Adam couldn't believe his eyes, considering how far they'd traveled to get to the train.

"Stay here if you like, but I'm heading over to the depot," Aleks said. He was enraptured by the history and missed Adam's outrage. "Adam, what do you think of this place? Kind of reminds you of my house, doesn't it? It was built one year after the old Griggs Home, in 1859."

"Right you are, son. Who's Adam?" the older gentleman said with a laugh. "Would you like a biscuit? My wife packed me a little extra, and I'd be happy to share with you."

Aleks whipped around, looking everywhere for Adam. In a panic, he thanked the gentleman, took a biscuit, and stuck it in his pocket.

The main staircase from the exit was filled with people coming and going. Aleks checked the balcony height. *It's no higher than the one at home,* he thought. He climbed over the balcony handrail and jumped twelve feet to the ground outside.

As his boots hit the ground, he startled some ladies standing nearby and they let out shrill screams as if the young man had personally attacked them. This in turn caught the attention of a chivalrous guard who had nothing more exciting going on than to chase down a balcony jumper.

Aleks outwitted the guard by ducking under a train car. He held tight to the underside of the car, holding his body off the ground and out of sight from the guard.

For what felt like an hour but only lasted ten minutes, he hugged the underside of the train. When he saw the man's shoes disappear into the crowd, he rolled out from under the train. No one seemed to pay him any attention. He looked around the depot area and spotted Adam being questioned by a hostile-looking well-dressed white man.

"Excuse me. May I help you?" Aleks asked the man.

"Well, not unless you are the owner of this slave. You see, he fits the profile of the one accused of stealing Farmer Murphy's pig."

"I can assure you that he is not, for this is my body servant and we are headed home from making a delivery to my father who is a Confederate doctor."

"Well, you wait right here. I'm going to get that wanted poster, and we'll decide if you is going anywhere." The overweight Southern aristocrat spoke with a sternness that would have made most people stay put—but not Aleks. He grabbed Adam's arm, and they ran for it.

The boys ran through the crowds of friends and family who were waving farewell to their loved ones leaving for the war. They jumped on the train before the aristocrat returned and found his accused was no longer captive.

"Get back here, thief!" he hollered and shook his fist in the air.

The boys were safely on board and found a quiet spot after the train started moving. They were standing on a platform between two cars.

Aleks pulled out their time-travel artifacts and pointed the compass on the rock.

"You've got everything, right?" Adam asked.

"I'm almost certain we could travel from anywhere near here as long as the rail line is working," Aleks said.

"Why didn't we?" Adam asked.

"I didn't want to risk something going wrong, but it definitely makes sense. We can talk more about the formula when we arrive home."

Adam nodded and said, "Jumpin' the rails on the track; all wheels turn, click-clack, click-clack,"

Aleks responded. "You ready?"

The compass was spinning. The watch started keeping time, and the door of the train turned to dark glass. The vortex formed, and that was when it happened.

* * *

"Mama, what are you thinking?" Catherine asked.

"Your brother either has an overactive imagination, or he has discovered time travel," she said. "I don't know what to think."

"Do you think he's doing the cannon studies?" Catherine asked.

"I don't know why he would lie to us about that," Colleen said.

* * *

Colleen and Catherine drove up to the gate and into their driveway. They were back home at the Griggs House.

"We're home," Colleen said as they entered the house.

"Hey!" Ivan said, and he greeted them with hugs and kisses. "How was your trip?"

"It was nice but always hard leaving our boy," Colleen said.

"What did he say he's doing with the notebook the two of you kept snooping in—you know, the one from the attic?"

Cat listened hard from her bedroom as her parents spoke quietly in the living room. She only gathered a few words here and there but could tell it worried them. Her father's final words about it were that he had faith in Aleks and that when Aleks needed his help, he would ask for it. Her mother argued with him. Then he said what he normally said when he wanted Mama to quit talking. "That is the final word!" But Catherine knew as well as her father that even though her mother walked away quietly and chose not to argue this time, Colleen was the one in charge and she would keep looking for answers and a way to help their son.

CHAPTER TWELVE

Eureka!

MARTHA MET ALEKS at the first-floor elevator with her access card. She pressed the button for G2; this took them to the basement. The doors opened, and a few feet in front of them stood a large chain-link fence that stood from floor to ceiling and surrounded the entire basement floor. The gate to enter the area required a key card and an access code. Martha pressed the four-digit code and slid her key card, and the electric gate creaked as it opened into the underground lab of the MIT Green Center for Physics.

Freshmen were permitted on all floors of the Green Center except the basement. It was for the restricted theoretical nuclear and particle physics studies.

Aleks had befriended Martha the first week of school. They had met at the Area Four Coffee Shop and Restaurant, the one near the Kendall Hotel at Technology Square in Cambridge. He was at the counter ordering a double espresso with extra milk and asked her about the book she was holding. It was a freshmen-level physics book. They had a brief exchange, but she hurried out of the coffee shop with her coffee. He was taking the class and thought she was also a freshman. He found out the next day that Martha was not a classmate but his GTA (graduate teaching assistant), and a friendship of common interests and attractions began.

Martha was allowing him to use the lab when she was doing her graduate research. She told him that she recognized his passion for physics. He kept to his tables with his artifacts and used the large magnets under her supervision, but he didn't share with her the details of his research and why he was fascinated by the properties of the rocks.

* * *

Fall semester was filled with countless hours in the lab, including weekends and occasional weeknights. Aleks's social life was Martha in the lab and conditioning for wrestling season; otherwise, he was in his dorm room studying. He didn't have time for a sport or a fraternity, but he felt pressured to fulfill the commitment he'd made when he applied to MIT saying he would wrestle. The fraternity he'd pledged, TKE, barely initiated him because his attendance was low, but they accepted him anyway because he was a legacy.

The Christmas holidays came, and he stayed at school to do research. He'd also made the starting wrestling team, and meets had already begun. He was relieved to find Martha stayed in Boston for the holidays as well. She had too much research to finish to travel to England and back. This would be his opportunity to confide in Martha about his time-travel research. He wasn't making any progress on his own, and her knowledge would be valuable. It was finding the right time to speak with her about it that was the real problem.

She received special clearance from the school to be in the lab during their winter break, which wasn't difficult for her to obtain because of her graduate status and research, and she managed to get Aleks hired as her undergraduate research assistant.

"Aleks, I can't believe you are not coming home," Colleen said. He recognized the disappointment in his mom's voice.

"I promise I'll see you soon," he said. "Besides, Martha went to a lot of trouble getting me the research assistant position. It's an amazing opportunity."

"Would you like us to come to Boston?" she asked.

Ivan took the phone. "Hey, Buddy, your Mama still thinks you are her little boy. She treats me like a child too," he said with a laugh. "Listen, we understand if you need more time to study and hang out with your GTA. We didn't have good-looking girls at Tech, much less good-looking GTAs. We went to Auburn for pretty girls." Aleks knew his father was jesting about the girls. His dad loved to talk about the Auburn girls because Colleen was an Auburn alumna. "Listen, we are proud of you. Let us know if you need anything."

* * *

Christmas break came and went, and there was never a good time to talk to Martha about the research. Every time he was ready to bring it up, they'd get interrupted or he couldn't find the right words. They wouldn't come out. How could he make it sound credible?

He rang in the New Year, 2015, alone in his dorm room. Martha was busy with her own research, and she no longer able to grant him access to the lab because it was under heavy surveillance. The research performed in the back room was so secretive that she didn't know of anyone involved in it. A retinal scan was required to confirm identity and gain access to the room.

* * *

Spring was approaching, and Martha managed to break away from her studies and attend Aleks's last wrestling meet of the season.

Aleks had not seen Martha since Winter Break. He was surprised to see her at the meet. He saw her when he glanced up at the student seating area in the stands, and she was in the front row, smiling and waving at him.

This is it, he thought. *Tonight after the meet, I have to confide in her. I'm desperate.*

Aleks was desperate not only to save Adam but also to save himself from what was brewing in his hometown. Racial tensions were on the rise nationally; in some areas, it had not been this bad since the 1960s.

The national media was reporting on every incident that appeared to involve race. The heightened coverage of racial issues and crimes gave momentum for the media to revisit West Point for a follow-up piece on Adam's disappearance. Almost two years had passed with no new leads.

The media coverage caught the attention of the NAACP, and it in turn ignited a fire under the DA to make an indictment in the case. Aleks was the only suspect. The newspaper reported that the missing boy's backpack had been found in Aleks's bedroom. It was the only physical piece of evidence that connected him, but it was enough for most townspeople to convict him.

He'd heard from his family attorney, who said that the DA was itching to name him as a person of interest in the disappearance of Adam. The DA also claimed to have submitted new evidence to the judge and expected to bring charges—possibly obstruction of justice—within the next month.

* * *

"Good match!" Martha said, giving Aleks a high five.

"Yeah, thanks! Thanks for coming," he said.

"You were brilliant out there. I could see your strategy," she said.

"To not be pinned," he said with a laugh.

"No really, Aleks, you are quite good," she said, blushing.

Aleks gave her a hug and apologized for smelling like an athlete. He offered to get cleaned up and take her for a late dinner.

"I would love to. We have a lot to catch up on," she said.

"You have no idea," Aleks said.

"What do you mean by that?" she asked.

Aleks told her that it would take a while so he hoped she didn't have to be anywhere too early the next morning.

She sat on Aleks's couch and looked through some of his coffee table books while he showered and changed. She'd also found a small photo album of childhood photos. There were pictures of his Alabama home, his parents, his sister, high school wrestling, and his friends.

As he was coming out pulling a clean shirt over his head, Martha asked him about the album. "This is sort of who you are in a nutshell?" she asked.

"I wish it told the whole story," he said with a laugh. "Let's go to the Waffle House. I haven't been there since I was back home. Is that okay with you?" he asked.

"Yes, of course. I've never been to one before. I'm assuming their waffles are amazing," she said.

* * *

Aleks knocked the slush off his tennis shoes as he held the door for Martha to enter the restaurant. "It is too cold to live here. It's supposed to be sunny and seventy by April," he said.

"Not in England, we have blustery weather there in the spring too."

They ordered waffles and hot chocolate and talked about everything but what Aleks needed to discuss with her. As he was taking his last bite of waffle, she asked him what was different about him. She told him that she noticed he seemed pensive, unlike himself or at least the Aleks she had known fall semester.

This was it, his opportunity, and he had to jump. Another hour passed as Aleks explained why he was doing research on time travel and about Adam's disappearance. He showed her the most recent letter from his attorney. The look on her face was at first one of disbelief and then of shock and urgency.

"If you want me to take you home now, I will," Aleks said, looking down at the table. "I know this is not your ordinary problem, but if you could … trust me, grant me access to the lab, and help me test the properties of the rocks, I promise that what I'm talking about is real."

Martha agreed to take him to the lab but only for a few hours. Aleks was no longer approved for access since his limited teaching assistant position had expired. If she was caught taking an underclassman into the restricted area, she'd be disciplined and possibly lose her teaching position.

They left Waffle House and dropped by Aleks's apartment to pick up his backpack before going to the lab. Martha also had to stop by her place for her lab key card.

They arrived at Aleks's apartment. There was a note on his door that he had a package in the office.

"It says it's perishable. I better go check it out; my mom said she was going to send cookies."

Aleks ran downstairs to the office to pick up his package and then back up the three flights to Martha, who was standing by his door. "I'm sorry; that was rude of me not to let you in," he said. "How about a cookie?"

"Not now, but at the lab. I have some tea at my desk, and you know what the English say about tea," she said.

"No, I don't," he said.

"A cup of tea makes everything better," she said with a smile.

"You don't believe me, do you?" Aleks said.

"I didn't say that. I'm waiting for you to show me what you have before I come up with my theory about time travel and your story," she said. "I do believe you are a good person. Let's say that's why I'm granting you access to the lab."

Aleks was more thankful than Martha knew. Honestly, most everyone in his hometown believed he at least knew what happened to Adam, and at this point, he was uncertain what his own parents thought about it. He knew they worried about it and grieved for the Griggs family's loss.

* * *

He used a knife from the lab table to open the package from home. "Here they are, the best chocolate chip cookies you've ever had," he said.

There was a note at the bottom of the box. It was from his mom saying how much she missed him and to enjoy the cookies.

"Thanks, Mama," he said to himself. He placed his research objects on the lab table and sat looking at his formulas and his hypothesis, but still there was nothing new.

"Let's start by looking at your magnetic rocks with this machine." Martha was referring to the large machine in the corner of the room. "I've assisted with research on this machine but haven't used it by myself."

Aleks thought she was amazing. She had it up and running within thirty minutes and started analyzing the rocks. What she found out about the rock was different than what he had initially thought. He'd surmised the rocks were highly magnetic, but the machine detected something different. It showed properties known as tachyons.

"I thought tachyons were only science fiction," Aleks said.

"They're not pure fantasy anymore," she said. "In fact, this rock appears to be emitting a huge number of tachyons."

Writing feverishly, Aleks added the discovery to his notes.

Martha went through the time-travel formula with Aleks and formed a hypothesis.

If her hypothesis was accurate, then their time travel required the rocks to emit a certain number of tachyons to transport a certain amount of mass: the greater the mass, the greater the number of tachyons required.

Martha had an idea; they'd transmit something small with a small number of tachyons.

She took two cookies from the box, placed a rock inside the box with the cookies, and told Aleks to follow his normal formula for time travel. "According to what you've told me, the cookies should travel to your house in Alabama," she said.

"Point the compass on the rock; timepiece turns, tick-tock, tick-tock," Aleks said.

The compass on the rock began to spin, and the watch began to move. This time, instead of having the rocks on him—in a pocket or in his backpack—the rocks were in the item being transported, the box of cookies.

Martha's eyes filled with awe as the table beneath the box turned to a liquid glass and the vortex formed; within seconds, the box was gone and everything else was back to normal. The table was solid, and she and Aleks were still in the lab.

"Do you know what this means?" she said, jumping with excitement. "You are one of the great scientists of all time!"

"That sounds nice," Aleks said.

"Let's have some tea and cookies!" she said. "Thank goodness I took two of the cookies out before we sent it back to your mum." Martha started her electric teakettle and pulled the cups from her desk. "Would you like sugar or cream?" she asked.

"Thank you, Martha, but I'll get a Coke from the vending machine. Where I'm from, we drink Coke," he said.

His phone rang. "It's my mom," he said. "Oh, hey, Mama … Cookies?"

"Listen, Buddy, that's why I'm calling. The strangest thing just happened. I was outside, and General came from behind your tree house. In his mouth, he had the package of cookies I swear I overnighted to you yesterday. Sounds crazy, I know."

"That's crazy!" he said, smiling ear-to-ear and giving Martha a wink. "So, how did General end up with my cookies?" he asked, giving Martha a thumbs-up. "I promise I'll give Martha some cookies when they arrive tomorrow," he said.

"What's remarkable is that there are ten cookies and several rocks in the box. I put a dozen into the box. General must have eaten the other two cookies, but how on earth he opened the box so neatly, I have no idea. He usually makes such a mess out of packages when he finds them at the door before I do," she said. "I have no explanation for the rocks."

"Listen, Mama, can I call you later? We are right in the middle of some intense research. Love you, Mama."

"I love you too, Buddy," Colleen said.

* * *

"It's all about the number or size of the rocks!" he hollered. "Adam didn't have the same number of rocks on the way home from Gettysburg as he had on the way to Gettysburg," he said.

He'd discovered the rocks' magnetic qualities years earlier while playing with a magnet in his yard. Once he found one magnetic rock, he and his father had looked for others, testing each one with a magnet from an old school science experiment. They discovered that some rocks in the yard had magnetic properties. He and his father theorized that the rocks were meteorites, possibly rare meteorites, billions of years old.

* * *

Aleks grabbed Martha and kissed her.

"Oh my goodness, Aleks, you were one of my students. This is certainly a boundary violation," Martha said.

"I'm sorry," he said. "No, I'm not!"

They both laughed, and she was blushing.

"This is a brilliant discovery!" Martha said.

"Yes, Martha, I can never thank you enough for what you've done to help me and my friend," Aleks said.

The two scientists sat down together at the lab table. Aleks was writing down their findings, and Martha could not stop smiling.

"Now that I understand why he didn't come back, I'm not afraid to travel back to get him."

"How do you know where he is?" Martha asked.

"He left a message on an old table that's at my house. It'll take me awhile to explain this to you, but I will. I am almost positive he is at my house in 1865."

"What can I do to help you?" Martha asked. "How can I help you find your friend and get the DA off your back?" she asked.

CHAPTER THIRTEEN

International Threat

MARTHA HELPED ALEKS as he hurried to pack up his backpack. They stopped and looked at each other; they'd both heard someone or something moving in the back room. *No one else should be in the lab at ten o'clock,* Aleks thought. "Maybe it's a rat," Aleks said. "We are in the city of Boston."

Martha pointed to the back of the lab. She quietly whispered to him that lights were on and that was where she thought the movement was coming from. She warned Aleks to pack up his artifacts quickly, as she was shutting down the machine. "Come on," she whispered. "We need to leave immediately."

The back room door squeaked and creaked as it opened and then slammed shut. Brisk footsteps started toward them. "Keep your head down, and let me do the speaking," she said.

The footsteps stopped. Aleks gave a sigh of relief. The footsteps started again, and now it sounded like more than one person. *There,* Aleks thought, *I'm all packed.* He looked up to see Martha by the door, waiting for him. He bent down to pick up his backpack, and upon standing up, he heard his name spoken by a man with a German accent.

"Are you Aleksandr Ness?"

"Excuse me!" Aleks said, ignoring the men and pushing past them. The two large men in dark suits backed up and stood directly in front of him.

One man looked familiar to Martha; she'd seen him entering the lab before. The other man looked like Aleks, only older.

"I'm Kyle Killar," said the man who looked similar to Aleks. And then he introduced the man with him as Hans Spangenberg. Hans had brown hair, looked to be the same age as Killar, probably mid-forties. He came to Killar's shoulder; he was about five feet eight inches and looked in good shape. My great-great-grandfather wrote about you in his war journal, and we followed you here last fall," Killar said.

Killar explained how he and Hans were tracking Aleks's time travel and were interested in the research Martha allowed him to do in the lab.

"You have me mistaken for someone else. I haven't even been to Germany," Aleks said.

"Aleks is merely a freshman student. I'm a GTA, and he's been working as my lab assistant," Martha said.

The men seemed unconvinced by their denials. They put their hands on what appeared to be pistols in their pockets and ordered them to sit down; they were insisting on showing them something.

Aleks took a seat, but Martha stood with her hand on the door.

"Tell your friend by the door to sit down. We'll let her know when we are finished," Killar said.

Martha sat down by Aleks.

"This is my great-great-grandfather's journal," Killar said. "He was General Schmidt from Germany, and he shadowed General Lee during the Battle of Gettysburg."

"I'm not your guy," Aleks said. "Now if you're finished, I have studying to do for tomorrow."

"Stop! I will tell you when I want you to speak," said Killar. "Look here … He logged the visit that you and your body servant had with Colonel Oates of Alabama. According to my grandfather, you were there to find your father, Dr. Ness, and you had modern-day devices. He recorded everything about you and your friend. Look here at this picture he drew of your cell phone. How else can you explain the Apple symbol in 1863?" Killar asked, pounding his finger on the sketch in the journal.

"I believe it was Benjamin Franklin who said that 'Historians relate, not so much what is done, as what they would have believed.' Your ancestor was mistaken, Mr. Killar. We both know time travel isn't possible. If it were, I'd be using it to make stock buys that were going to pay off well in the future," Aleks said with a nervous laugh.

"Your fancy quote and your stock market joke do not fool us," Killar said.

The Germans glanced around the lab. "What do you have in your backpack?" Mr. Spangenberg asked.

"My books," Aleks said.

"Hand it over," said Spangenberg. "We want to take a look."

He pulled items from the backpack as he questioned him. "What are you doing with a piece of a cannonball, musket shells, and a railroad watch? Explain these Civil War artifacts," Killar demanded.

Aleks stood red-faced and speechless. He was frightened. His heart was pounding, his palms were sweating, and his head felt hot. He patted it as if putting out the flames.

"Your black friend, the one my grandfather wrote about in his journal, is he the same teenager missing from your hometown? Is he the one you need to rescue?" Killar asked. "Well, good luck on going back to get him," he said with a sadistic laugh and added, "The Confederates have a bounty on your head."

Aleks swallowed hard. *A bounty, why do I have a bounty on my head?* he asked himself. There was nothing he could say. These internationals must have had listening devices in the lab and possibly on his phone, although he didn't know when they could have had access to his personal items unless they'd been in his apartment.

Aleks looked at the lab door, and to his surprise, there was Joe, the security guard. He felt relieved to see him enter the lab.

"Mr. Killar, are you a professor here at MIT?" Aleks asked.

"Don't try to change the subject, Mr. Ness," said Killar.

"I was wondering which classes you teach," Aleks said.

"Do—"

Joe interrupted. "Is everything okay here?" He was a huge man in every sense of the word. He was tall and slightly overweight for his frame and had a buzz cut. He had a deep voice that projected well and made the area around him shake when he spoke.

"Hey, Joe, we were just leaving. We'll walk out with you," Aleks said, picking up his backpack from the floor where the Germans had dropped it after going through it.

The two men followed behind them and left the parking lot in a 1956 Chevy.

"What's the story with those guys?" Joe inquired.

"I'm not sure. They came out of the back area of the basement lab," Aleks said.

"They must be researchers," Martha said.

"Why do you say that?" asked Joe.

"No one else is allowed in that area. It takes a retina scan for access," Martha said.

"Have you been back there?" Joe asked Martha.

"No," she said.

Joe entered Kyle Killar into the school's database from his car computer. "No matches found," Joe said.

"I didn't think he worked here. I know all the researchers in the graduate school," said Martha.

Joe took Martha and Aleks to the campus police station to wait while he checked out the lab. "From the sounds of it, they were threatening you. Is that right?" Joe asked.

"Yes and I'm sure they were armed," Aleks said.

"You two will be safe in my office. Stay here. The assistant will take your statements for the complaint. Give her all the details about them threatening you. I can arrest them on that charge alone, but it seems we have them on trespassing as well," said Joe.

He used the office phone to call for backup and then drove back to the lab. He took four officers in with him and had another car with two officers wait outside.

* * *

Joe returned an hour later with no new evidence. He told Martha and Aleks that he wanted them to spend the rest of the week and weekend at home with their families.

"Martha can come home with me to Alabama. There's no way she'll get a flight out to London tonight, and she shouldn't go back to her apartment," Aleks said.

"I can't leave. I have a research paper due tomorrow," she said.

"I'm sorry, Martha, but Aleks is right. You may not be safe on campus. I'll feel better if you go home with Aleks for the weekend."

"What? But I can't! This paper counts for 30 percent of my grade," she said.

"It's okay, Martha," Joe assured her. "First thing tomorrow morning, the campus police department will send an e-mail to your professors. This will be an excused absence."

They gave their official police reports to Joe and received a police escort to their apartments where they packed.

They stopped to fill up Aleks's red GMC truck and started their drive to Atlanta.

"How much petrol does your tank hold?" she asked. "I will give you some pounds for the trip."

Aleks laughed out loud. "I doubt your pounds will spend well here."

"Oh my goodness, I'm exhausted! I'm not thinking straight. I can't believe I said that. I meant to say gas. How much *gas* will it take?" she said.

"I'll take you up on your petrol offer when we are closer to Atlanta," he said and smiled.

He assured her she could rest while he drove, but she couldn't sleep. She worried about her classes and the Germans. When she got nervous, she talked a lot.

"What did the German mean when he said you had a bounty on your head?" she asked.

"I think someone is offering a reward for me," Aleks said.

"That's rubbish! How could someone from the past possibly have a reward for your return?" she asked.

"The only thing that I can come up with is that I borrowed a short sword before I left Gettysburg. I took it off a table in the general's tent because Adam and I were unarmed. After I returned home, I noticed that it had General Oates's name on it. He is a well-known general of the Alabama Fifteenth and later became the governor of Alabama."

"Where is the sword now?" she asked.

"It is in the safe in my parents' home. I gave it to my dad as a gift. Told him I found it at an estate sale. He said the person couldn't have known its value," Aleks said. "I felt bad for lying to him, but there was no way I could be honest about it at the time."

He watched a steady rhythm of light snow hit the windshield. "This reminds me of the song, 'Sometimes It Snows in April.' Do you know it? It's an old Prince song," he said.

"If I didn't know better, I'd say you are trying to change the subject," Martha said. "And no, I don't know that song. Now, why didn't you tell me about your time travel sooner?" she asked.

"I thought you would think I was crazy and not have anything else to do with me," he said.

"No, that wouldn't happen. You are one of the nicest crazy people I've ever met," she said with a laugh. "What about those German researchers? Do you think Joe has found them?" she asked.

"Would you mind searching them on the web?" Aleks asked.

Martha searched Kyle Killar first and then Hans Spangenberg. "I don't think I'll be able to sleep tonight," Martha confessed. "These German guys sound like they are capable of murder."

CHAPTER FOURTEEN

Sweet Home Alabama

THE ROAD TRIP took twenty hours, two Big Gulps and talks that covered the Civil War, modern-day racial issues and why being an American, as Maya Angelou once said was "complicated."

They drove into downtown historic West Point, Georgia. It was a four-street town with a main street that held the three restaurants between an old depot on one end and the town bank on the other end. He stopped at the Irish Bread Pub to use the restroom. When he walked inside, he found a couple of familiar folks sitting at the bar.

"Well, well, look who the cat dragged in. Welcome home, Mr. Ness! I heard you left us stupid Southerners," one man said.

Aleks slapped him on the back. "You know y'all are the smart ones. There's still ice on the Charles River in Boston."

"Really?"

"It's still cold there. When we left Boston, it was snowing," he said, sitting down at a high-top table near the bar.

He pulled his cell phone from his pocket. His mother had taught him to announce himself before driving up into someone's driveway. He never did that at his own home until now; he'd come too far, and it was too unexpected.

"Hey, Mom?"

"What's going on, buddy?" she asked.

"Are you busy?" he asked.

"No, I'm here talking to Daddy. We were just sitting in the rose garden. What is it? Are you okay?" she asked.

"I'm in town," he said.

"You are in town!" she hollered with excitement.

"Yes, ma'am," he said. "It's me and Martha, my friend who works in the lab. We are down the street at the Pub. I wanted to call before we drove up."

"Come on home," she said.

In the few minutes it took for them to drive around the corner and up the hill, Aleks filled Martha in on how his dad would talk her ear off. "Boy, is he going to like you," he said with a smile. "There they are up in the rose garden," he said, pointing at the backyard.

It was as Aleks had described. The house stood majestically on a grassy hill with two fifty-year-old oaks on either side. The home's square columns and pitched roof were a perfect example of Greek Revival architecture along a river that once spoke to passersby of a community's wealth and strength. Aleks told Martha that once this quiet place was so busy, pedestrians covered the sidewalks and carriages went up and down the street. "There was even a large hotel on the corner where train travelers spent the night when switching between the Montgomery and Atlanta rail lines."

By the time they'd parked, Aleks's parents were waiting at the car to greet them. "Martha, this is my father, Dr. Ness."

"It's a pleasure to meet you. Aleks has told me so much about you," Martha said.

"So tell me about your research. Aleks tells us that you are working on your masters," Ivan said.

Colleen interrupted and told them to come in the house. "Martha, it's so nice to see you again. Are you hungry? Would you like something to drink? Coffee or water?" Colleen asked.

Aleks glanced at Martha and laughed.

"We are fine, Mama. I warned her that you'd try to feed her and talk her to death."

They entered the sunroom, passing by the cannon-marked limestone walls and Civil War artifacts. The living room was next, and they all followed Colleen in and sat down.

"Catherine, would you get them some water?" Colleen asked.

The fireplace mantel was marble, and the ceilings were at least twelve-feet high. It reminded Martha on a smaller scale of the queen's salon rooms in Buckingham Palace. The grand piano took up a small portion of the room, and then there was a bookcase, a secretary, wonderful porcelains, and an antique mirror above the mantel. The Oriental rug was full of warm, welcoming hues that accented the walls, furnishings, and ornate curtains on the four large windows that reached from the floor to the ceiling.

"Have you heard of Tara?" Martha asked.

"The house in *Gone with the Wind*," Colleen said with a smile.

"Your home is beautiful! It reminds me of that house," she said.

"Thank you," Colleen said. "Aleks tells us that your last name is Shakespeare, but you are a scientist."

"Yes, odd, I know," she said with a laugh. "Aleks said you have a degree in English literature," Martha said.

"Yes, I studied at Auburn University," Colleen said.

"Do you teach?"

"No, I worked as a journalist and in public relations before having a family, but now I write as a hobby." Colleen smiled. "Martha, why don't we get you settled in the guest room. Catherine, please show her the way and make sure there are towels in the bathroom."

The guest room was everything one would expect from a historic nineteenth-century Southern home. The bed was a mahogany four-poster dressed in a chintz pattern of hydrangeas. In front of a marble-front fireplace sat two chairs on either side of an antique porcelain table.

"This is the only original fireplace left in the house. The others were closed up. Well, except for the one downstairs in my dad's office—that was the slaves' kitchen," Catherine said.

"Oh," Martha said, startled by Catherine's choice of words. "I don't know that I'd ever be comfortable with the word *slave*," she said nervously. "Are black people embarrassed by it? It seems to me like it would be a sensitive topic."

"I don't know," Catherine said. "We never mention it and either does Aunt Mary. She is a black lady who has worked for us my whole life. I don't even know if her ancestors were slaves. I've never thought about it before."

"My mom spent her early childhood in a small midwestern town—my grandfather had to move north for 10 years to oversee one of our family's mills and then he moved back to take over my great-grandfather's farm—anyway that small town didn't have black people. When she moved back to the South in middle school, she says she had no prejudice toward people of different races because she had not formed any as a child," Catherine said.

"She says she learned quickly that there were certain lines in the south that could never be crossed—if she wanted to be accepted. And it figures that my mama crossed the lines. You know what she did? She danced with a black boy at her first school dance, and she was ridiculed for it," Catherine said, eyebrows raised as if she still couldn't believe her mama had done such a thing.

"Have you ever danced with a black boy?" Martha asked.

Catherine, with her head stuck in the linen closet, said, "Yep, you have plenty of towels and washcloths in here." It seemed that Catherine had answered the question by not answering it. The truth was that changes occurred slowly when it came to racial issues, and not much had changed in this small area of the world for the past thirty years.

Catherine left Martha to settle in to the guest room and to freshen up for dinner.

Martha sat at the marble vanity in a gold chair with the initial N embroidered on the back of it. Her view from the vanity was out a bay window that overlooked a brick courtyard filled with white roses on a wrought-iron fence and the promise of hydrangeas and crape myrtles later that summer. A lion fountain nestled in shrubbery peeked out from the back corner, and an arbor seat covered in small pink roses was picture perfect. Martha called her mother to tell her where she was staying for the next few days.

"Mum, I can practically see women in beautiful ball gowns. This place looks as if it's straight from a storybook," Martha said. She told her mother that Aleks had invited her home to meet his family. She left out the real reason for their trip. *It would be too upsetting for my parents and would take too long to explain,* she thought.

"I can't believe it. I had no idea you were planning to make this trip. Do you think he's too young for you, a freshman?"

"Mum, I'll call you later. We are about to have dinner," she said and ended the call before she had to answer more questions.

CHAPTER FIFTEEN

The Proof is in the Pudding

"DAD, CAN I speak with you and Mom in private?" Aleks asked.

"Of course, let's go downstairs to my office," Ivan said.

Aleks followed his parents downstairs. The three of them sat down—Aleks and his mom in the tufted leather wingback chairs on the opposite side of his father's mahogany desk. Ivan sat down.

"I need to tell you everything," Aleks said.

"Does this have something to do with Adam?" Colleen asked.

"Yes, it has everything to do with him. I know where he is, but I need your help getting to him."

"Why haven't you told the police? You know they've reopened the case," Ivan said.

"I haven't told anyone—except for Martha. I told her yesterday. I haven't told the police because they wouldn't have believed me. The last time I was with Adam, we were riding on a train."

Ivan interrupted. "We knew that already."

"I know, but it was a train in another time line. It was 1863, and we were headed home from Gettysburg."

Ivan swallowed hard and said, "Okay, Buddy, you have my attention!"

Aleks spent the next hour telling his father about the past five years.

"Aleks, if what you are telling me is true, then you have discovered the dreams of Einstein, H. G. Wells, and Stephen Hawking. You have made a discovery that changes our understanding of the world as we know it. Early Christians were burned at the stake for less than this," he said with a nervous laugh.

"Really, Ivan? Burned at the stake? Must you be sarcastic at a time like this?" Colleen was upset at Ivan's choice of words.

"You don't believe me, do you?" Aleks said. "I knew you'd have this response. That's why I haven't told you," Aleks said.

Aleks started pulling out artifacts and placing them on his father's desk. "This is how it works. I place this compass on the rock, at which point the railroad watch begins to keep time. I use an artifact with the time signature of our destination, and the vortex opens and we arrive at the location by train," Aleks said.

"You know this sounds far-fetched," Ivan said with a laugh.

Aleks was frustrated. His own father didn't believe him. Of course he wouldn't; he wouldn't believe it himself had he not done it.

"Ivan, don't make fun. He is serious," Colleen said. "Why didn't you tell us about Adam? Why didn't you tell his mother?"

"I planned to fix it," he said. "That's why MIT was my first choice for studying quantum mechanics. I knew it had the best labs and the brightest minds. If it could be solved, it would be there. Let me get Martha down here to help explain what we found in the physics lab," he said.

Aleks found Martha upstairs with Catherine. They were in the guest room talking. "Hey, I need your help to explain what we discovered in the lab," Aleks said.

"Can I come too?" Catherine asked.

"Of course. Tell me this, how much of my notebook did you read before you arrived in Boston?"

"Enough to worry about you," she said.

He gave her a "love you" pat on the head. "That's what you get for snooping," he said with a wink.

The three of them went down a flight of stairs to the first floor and back through the doorway into their dad's office.

Martha sat down with Colleen on one side of the desk, facing Ivan on the opposite side. She in all seriousness explained her findings of the tachyons and the displacement of the cookies from the lab back to the house. Colleen confirmed that everything she said about the cookies was true. "They were certainly the most delicious cookies I've ever tasted," Martha added.

Colleen was visibly pleased with the compliment. "I'll have to make some while you are here," she said.

"I'm going to play the devil's advocate here. What real proof do you have that you traveled?" Ivan said. "You could end up with charges against you in the disappearance of Adam, and if all we have to go on is your word that he was left in a different time … Aleks, I don't have to tell you that a jury is going to laugh you off the stand."

"I know, Dad. You're right," he said.

"I didn't believe him either. When he first told me, quite frankly, I thought he had lost his marbles," Martha said. "But, the proof was in the pudding, when he showed me …" She stopped talking in midsentence. "That's it! Let's show them. You have plenty of rocks here to travel to and from without any problem," she said.

Martha and Aleks made preparations to travel back to 1865, take a picture in downtown West Point, and then travel back to 2015.

Martha slipped on one of Colleen's reenactment day dresses. Aleks put on a button-up shirt and a pair of khakis, and they headed to the backyard.

"Now, be careful; don't stand too close, because I don't know how far-reaching the suction of the vortex is on the area around it," Aleks warned his family.

* * *

Ivan watched with his binoculars as Aleks went through the formula, and the two vanished into thin air.

Ivan told Colleen and Catherine to stay back, and he went up and inspected the area where the two had been a few minutes earlier. "They are gone."

Ivan inspected every inch of the ground around the tree house, the large outcropping of rock, and the shed where Martha and Aleks had stood moments earlier. The gravity of the situation had left him without words. Colleen kept asking him questions, but he didn't answer.

"Ivan, are you okay?" Colleen asked.

Catherine saw her father's face as he walked from behind the tree house and down the hill by the rose garden toward the back kitchen door. He looked stunned.

"They're gone. They're gone," he said and held his hands up in disbelief, coming into the house past Colleen and Catherine. He took a seat at the kitchen table. "Do you know what this means?" Ivan asked.

"Would you like some coffee?" Colleen asked.

"No, I'm going down to my office to read some of Aleks's journal entries while we wait for them to return," he said. Ivan got up slowly from the kitchen chair as if in a trance, walked from the kitchen into the short hallway, and glanced up at the mural depicting the day of the Battle of West Point. It covered the entire wall that separated the living room from the short hall that extended between the sunroom on one end and the kitchen on the other. This entire section with the three rooms—sunroom, living room, and kitchen—was added in 1951. He turned to the left and walked slowly down the fifteen-foot main hallway that ran the length of the original part of the house and took the staircase that was situated about midpoint. The stairs were divided; one flight went up to the third floor, and the other flight took him to the first floor, where there was a small foyer and two rooms, a den to his left and on the opposite side of the foyer his office.

Catherine tiptoed behind him. She stayed in the foyer and sat on the settee, which was out of sight from the office. She could hear her father talking to himself, and she peeked around the corner to look.

He sat at his desk, surrounded by the warmth of memories in the form of family pictures, collegiate memorabilia, and books all situated on mahogany-paneled walls and bookshelves.

Ivan surveyed his desk. "I wondered where these musket shells and pieces of cannonball had walked off to," he said to himself, leaning back in his office chair, flipping a musket shell between his fingers.

He shook his head and then settled in and read from the notebook.

* * *

The downstairs entry door opened with a creak, and the slam of the antique hardware against the limestone wall woke up Catherine. She'd fallen asleep waiting for her brother and spying on her father.

"They're back!" Cat hollered. "What took you so long?"

Ivan rushed out of his office and into the foyer. Colleen came downstairs from the kitchen and met them in the entry. The group hugged.

"We were gone"—Aleks checked his phone—"an hour and twenty minutes. Cat, that's not bad time considering we traveled back 150 years."

"Martha, are you okay?" Colleen asked.

Martha said, "Yes, we're fine. It was an incredible journey that never in my wildest dreams did I think was possible."

Ivan stood with his arm around Aleks. "I'm sorry for doubting you, Son," Ivan said.

"It's okay, Dad; I wouldn't have believed you either," Aleks said with a laugh.

Colleen invited everyone to sit down in Ivan's office to talk. Ivan took his desk chair, Colleen and Martha sat opposite the desk in the leather chairs, and Aleks grabbed a chair from the den and placed it between his mother and Martha.

"Where am I going to sit?" Catherine asked.

Martha scooted over and patted the seat of her chair. "I'll share with you," she said with a smile.

"Aleks, this will clear your name," Colleen said, wiping away the tears on her cheeks.

"Yes, if we can get Adam back home," he said.

Aleks noticed his dad had the notebook in his hand and it was opened to an entry.

"Which one are you reading?" Aleks asked.

"Your first trip with Adam to 1861," Ivan said.

"Have you gotten to the part where I'm in Dr. Griggs's office?" Aleks asked his father.

"No, I'm at the part where you wake up from your nap, Aleks. We'll talk about that in a minute. Show us your pictures first," Ivan said.

Aleks pulled out his phone from his pocket. "Here's the one of Martha and me on the train, and here we are in front of the depot," Aleks said and smiled. "See, there it is," Aleks said, pointing to the words on the side of the train car—Atlanta & West Point

Ivan took the phone, expanded the photo, and shared it with Colleen. They looked in amazement together at the pictures as they paged through the photos.

"What was it like?" Colleen asked.

Martha, excited to speak, responded first. "It was dark when we arrived, and the town was quiet. The roads were all dirt. See, my shoes are filthy," she said, holding up her foot to show the bottom. "I would love to study a sample of this dirt."

Catherine jumped up and ran upstairs. She came right back with a sealable plastic baggie. "Will this work?" she asked.

"Oh, to save a sample?" Martha said. "It's worth a try. Do you mind if I borrow a pen or something to push off a sample for the bag?"

Aleks took a pen from his father's desk and used it to push some dried mud from Martha's shoe into the baggie.

"What picture are you looking at now?" he asked his parents.

"It's the one of the house," Ivan said.

Catherine looked too and spotted the differences in the house from the current version.

"When we ran up the hill by the house and stopped to take this photo, a man hollered at us from the street and asked us what business we had at the Griggs Plantation. We ran to the back, near the rocks, and came back home. I didn't want to take any more unnecessary risks," Aleks said, looking down.

"This is a wonderful thing that you have discovered," Ivan said.

"Yes, but now I think of it only as how Adam disappeared. I am responsible for Adam jumping the time windows in the first place, and because of that, I am responsible for his disappearance."

"Did you force him to go?" Colleen asked.

"No, ma'am, he wanted to go, but I encouraged him to keep jumping even when he didn't want to anymore. He didn't want to go to Gettysburg."

Ivan sat quietly.

For the first time ever, it seems, the man who has a thirty-minute answer for everything that perplexes most is mute, Aleks thought.

"Ivan, should we tell him about my ancestor's letter?"

"Not now," he said, dismissing her question. "I don't believe this is a bad discovery. I believe that God created everything and that in your naïveté, Aleks, you put Adam in danger. Please explain how your jump from Gettysburg back home differed from the other times."

Aleks explained the theory that he and Martha had arrived at in the lab—basically, that after they had lost all but one of Adam's rocks in the orchard, he did not have enough tachyon-emitting rocks to bring them both back home.

"Why did Adam's haversack return?" Ivan questioned.

"Again," Martha interjected, "Adam's haversack contained one rock. It had enough tachyons to transport the mass of the haversack but not enough for Adam."

"Have you worried about transporting only part of a person back?" Ivan asked.

"That's a good question," Martha said. "We haven't done enough research to explain it any more than we already have," she added.

"I may know where Adam is right now. He left me a message on the table by my tree house. This message was from a year ago. I'll go get it to show you," Aleks said, running out of the room.

Aleks returned a few minutes later carrying the old wooden treasure that he'd saved from the junk pile.

He turned the table to its side and pointed to the initials and dates.

They all marveled at the marks on the bottom of the table.

"He was here a year ago, but how do you know he's still there?" Ivan asked.

"I don't know and won't unless we go back," Aleks said.

Ivan nodded in agreement and set his elbows on his desk, bringing his hands together in a steeple. "There's another problem too. We have to find him before you are indicted. I heard from Judge Hooper last week, and he said that the DA is eager to indict someone in Adam's case and you are still the only one connected to it," Ivan said.

"Is it safe for Aleks to be home? Will the DA rush for an indictment if he hears Aleks is home?" Colleen asked.

"I don't think it'll matter," Ivan said. "They could serve him papers in Boston just as easily."

"Oh great! Seems I'm a wanted man in two time lines and by internationals," Aleks said, sighing heavily and rubbing his head.

"What do you mean by that?" Colleen asked, looking and sounding alarmed.

"Well, we had a run-in with some German scientists in the lab, and that's what brought us home for this surprise visit."

Aleks explained how the German scientists found a Civil War journal with indications of a time traveler from the future. He explained that within the same entry, it noted that he was the son of Dr. Ness of Alabama and the men located him at MIT.

"They found articles about my acceptance to MIT and Adam's disappearance. It interested them enough to search me out, and when they did, they found I matched the description in the journal."

"What do you think their intentions are?" she asked.

"Their intentions are to use time travel to steal the Mexican silver speculated to have been buried by the Confederacy in Danville, Virginia, at the fall of the Confederacy," he said.

"So these German scientists are treasure hunters," she said.

"How do you know this?" Ivan asked.

"They didn't tell me; it's speculation, but from research Martha did on Kyle Killar on our drive here from Boston, I think it's valid. Killar is a direct descendant of British aristocracy and under investigation for a robbery at Blenheim Palace. The items stolen had previously belonged to his family's estate—all coins and precious metals. He was accused of other robberies as well, but there's not enough evidence to arrest him or his accomplices."

"What is his connection to Germany?" Ivan asked.

"The English Crown denied support of his family estate in the 1850s, and one of his ancestors fled to Germany. The ancestor became a part of the German army and married a German officer's daughter. A century later, Kyle was born from this English-German line. His father was a scientist who devoted himself to the study of cold fusion. Kyle spent time in the lab with his father. He was touted a genius, sent to the best schools and universities, and recently rumored to be stealing back his family's fortune—with intentions of reclaiming the family's English estate, or should I say, *castle*."

"Yes, it is a castle in Branbury," Martha added.

"That sounds familiar. Is it near Oxford?" Colleen asked.

"Yes," Martha said. "It is not too far from Oxford."

"What makes you think they are after the Mexican silver?" Ivan asked.

"Kyle and an accomplice were arrested for digging on Federal property in the Danville cemetery," Aleks said.

Martha added that the article quoted an anonymous source that revealed an independent contractor was hired by the city to use deep-seeking metal detecting equipment on the entire area. The City of Danville denied the claims; however, according to the source, Killar and his friend worked directly with the contractor and were given the exact location of the silver. The source also claims that the city is in cahoots with the Germans," Aleks said.

"Why would Danville be working with a couple of Germans?" Ivan asked.

"Seems the city's budget was in need of the silver, but since it is buried in a cemetery, there is no politically correct way to access it," Aleks said.

"That's right," Ivan said. "I recently watched a History Channel special about it; there are believed to be 160,000 8-reale coins buried, and because of a smallpox epidemic and the Union soldiers occupying the town, theory has it that no one reclaimed the silver. Do you know how much the 8-reale coins are worth in today's market?"

"No, but I bet you do," Aleks said with a laugh.

"Let's see, 160,000 ounces of silver is worth about $3.2 million in actual silver, but these coins are worth a lot more because of their numismatic value. One piece of eight is worth a couple thousand dollars," he said. "So the value of the missing silver is close to $320 million."

"Oh my goodness, I forgot dinner in the oven. I put it in while you and Martha were gone. Let's talk about this more over dinner?"

"Yes, of course," Ivan said. "We can work on a plan over dinner."

* * *

They entered the dining room; its walls were warm and rosy and its cathedral ceiling was half the shade of the walls.

"Everything in your home is a wonderful mix of family and formality," Martha said. "It is brilliantly done."

"I love your word usage and your beautiful accent," Colleen said.

Martha and Ivan went into the kitchen with Colleen. Aleks and Catherine sat across from each other.

"You better be careful," Catherine whispered.

"About what?" Aleks asked.

"Mama likes Martha, and she loves anything English. She'll have you married off faster than you can say 'fish 'n' chips,'" she said giggling.

"You better watch out, or I'll tell everyone who you like at school," Aleks said.

"You don't even know," Catherine said.

"Know what?" Colleen asked as she brought in the chicken potpie.

"Oh nothing," Catherine said.

Martha followed in behind her, carrying the rice, and Ivan came in with a pitcher of water for the table. He sat down at the head of the table near the kitchen.

The crystals on the antique chandelier scattered light spectra across the room, over the formal place settings and the breakfront that sat against the wall opposite the kitchen.

"This is my favorite," Aleks said. "You make the best chicken potpie. Thanks, Mama."

Colleen took the chair between Catherine and Ivan, and then Ivan blessed the food.

"Aleks, I have a confession to make," Colleen said. "I was reading your journal on the plane."

"Really? How surprising!" Aleks said and smiled a sweet grin. "You did this on your way to Boston?"

"No, it was on the way home," she said.

"Mama!" Catherine said sternly under her breath, bumping her mom under the table.

"How was that since I had my notebook?" he asked.

"Please don't be upset with your sister," Colleen said. "She was worried about you and took pictures of a few pages with her phone before we left home," she explained.

"It's okay. I would have told you earlier but didn't expect for anyone to believe me," he said. "Dad, what did you read?"

Ivan had been listening to the confessions and enjoying the food. "I read your entry from the Griggs House 1861," Ivan said.

"Did you read the part about the rocks?" Aleks asked.

"No, I don't remember anything about rocks in that entry," Ivan said.

"I found something while I was in Dr. Griggs's office in the house."

"What was it?" Ivan asked.

"Well, I was examining a rock on his shelf when Mrs. Griggs came in and sternly asked me not to touch anything. She said that she wouldn't want me to get hurt by one of his surgical tools. At the time, I thought it was odd that she would be concerned, because I wasn't near the surgical tools and clearly had a rock in my hand. Anyway, I asked her about the rock. She said it was from her childhood home in England. What is even more interesting is that it was situated next to another rock. When I asked her, she said the other one was from her yard, back where our present-day shed is located. She laughed politely, saying her husband was like a little boy about his rocks. No one was allowed to touch them."

"Did the rock from England look similar to the ones in our yard?" Ivan asked.

"Yes, and I managed to bring a small piece of the rock from England back with me. I didn't intend on taking it. I had dropped the rock before she entered the room. When it hit the floor, a piece broke off. About that time, I heard her coming down the hallway, and I panicked and stuck the piece in my pocket," he explained.

"Does the rock from England have the same magnetic properties as the rocks from our yard?" Ivan asked.

"Yes, and other properties as well," Martha said. "I tested it in the lab."

"Have you taken any trips to England?" Colleen asked.

"No, I haven't explored the capabilities of that rock. I put it aside, but I've wondered about it and Dr. Griggs and Mrs. Griggs. Have you heard any stories that would make you think they time-traveled?"

"There is a letter that I was given—" Colleen started.

"We'll show him that later; there's not time now," Ivan said.

Colleen started cleaning up dishes, and shortly after, the girls joined her in taking them from the table to the kitchen sink.

She reentered the dining room through the swinging door from the kitchen. "Ivan, I've been thinking that with what's come up with Aleks that we should cancel the fundraiser this weekend."

"Absolutely not!" Ivan insisted. "If we cancel, it looks like we think Aleks is guilty and draws suspicion. It's better for Aleks if we continue as if everything is normal."

"You're right," she said. "Well, Aleks, would you and Martha join us? Mrs. Nancy has a dress she can borrow for the event."

"We need to wait and see on that," Ivan said.

"What do you mean?" Colleen asked.

"It depends if we can clear Aleks of anything related to Adam's disappearance before then. I don't want to have him arrested at the party," Ivan said.

"Ivan!" Colleen scolded.

"I'm sorry," Ivan said.

"It's okay, Mom. Dad's right," he said. "We'll definitely come if we can."

It was nearing ten o'clock, everyone went to bed except for Ivan and Aleks. They stayed up to talk for a while.

CHAPTER SIXTEEN

The Mystery's Missing Pieces

ALEKS AND HIS father convened to the living room where they pored over historical documents and photos, looking for something that gave a hint of Adam's whereabouts. It was late but an emergency, so Ivan contacted a couple of close friends who were members of the Fort Tyler Board and lived and breathed local history.

Within thirty minutes, there was a soft knock at the sunroom door. The men entered with several large folders and a box. Ivan brought them into the dining room.

The men were brothers but as different in their looks and mannerisms as Gregory Peck and Mark Twain. "I'm not sure what you're lookin' for or why, but here it all is. To be honest, we have a whole closetful back at Raymond's office. We weren't sure exactly what you needed so thought we'd start with this," said William, the one sporting the Hawaiian shirt and Mark Twain mustache and hair.

His brother, Raymond, a retired attorney and DA, always looked formal, like he was wearing a suit even when he had on a T-shirt and jeans. His hair was perfectly placed, he wore round-rimmed glasses, and he kept a stately air about him.

"Would you like us to help find whatever it is you are looking for?" Raymond asked Ivan and Aleks.

"We'd better do this on our own," Ivan said. "I know you still accept cases from the DA, and we wouldn't want to put you in a bad light with him."

"Then, I won't ask you if this has anything to do with Adam's disappearance," Raymond said.

The brothers shook hands with Aleks and patted him on the back. They'd known Aleks his entire life. When his parents terraced and landscaped their backyard and dug down ten feet to mix and move the old dirt around, the brothers, then in their fifties, came over with their metal detectors and invited ten-year-old Aleks to join them in their Civil War treasure hunt. They found buttons of uniforms, part of a cotton scale, and some musket shells. Some of these items were donated to a local museum; however, young Aleks kept a few and lined them up on the bookshelf in his bedroom. Several years later, after the time-travel discovery, he and Adam had secretly planned to use them to witness the Battle of West Point.

The brothers had always shown an interest in his athletic and academic pursuits. When Aleks was mentioned as a suspect in the disappearance case, both of them came to his defense in the community. Now, bringing these documents and photos over late in the evening, after only a call and no real explanation as to why, they'd again shown their support.

"We'll do anything we can," William said.

"We sure will," his brother agreed, and with that said, they left the house.

* * *

"Look at this, Dad!" Aleks must have said that twenty times. There were copious amounts of fascinating documents, but nothing they found in the files or the box amounted to a clue about Adam's location.

"Have you searched the sunroom folders yet?" Ivan asked.

"No, not yet," Aleks said.

The curio in the sunroom had three wide shallow drawers that were filled with folders holding newspaper articles and historic documents that were passed down from Colleen's ancestors.

* * *

About three in the morning, Colleen looked around the house to find Ivan and Aleks asleep on the sunroom couch, both with papers in their hands. There were papers covering the top of the curio-style coffee table, papers scattered on the floor, and papers on the couch between them.

"Did you find anything?" she asked Ivan, patting his shoulder.

"Not yet," Ivan said, barely opening his eyes.

"Let's get some coffee, and I'll help you look," she said.

Aleks woke up and joined his parents in the kitchen. The three of them made coffee and returned to the sunroom.

Colleen paged through the unopened folders tucked in the bottom drawer of the curio. She was reading newspaper articles about reunions of the veterans who fought at Fort Tyler and accounts of the battle from her ancestors. It was interesting, she thought, but it was like finding a missing diamond in the grass; it seemed impossible and quite possibly was.

Aleks sat between his parents on the white tufted couch that sat against the wall of windows facing the backyard rose garden. He rubbed the sleep from his eyes and picked up another folder.

"Look, here is Dr. Griggs's patient ledger," he said, showing his parents. "He was paid two chickens when he treated this patient."

"Did you know his office was in the house?" she asked. "That's right; of course you knew that."

"Are the Griggs family photos in here?" he asked.

Ivan pulled out an old scrapbook. Aleks looked through it with them, and he was able to name family members.

"Here is Dr. Griggs, and that's Mrs. Griggs, and look at this one; that's Persia and J. W. They were nice people and good to Adam and me. You would have loved Mrs. Griggs. She is—I mean *was*—a lot like you, Mom. She was kind, and she helped everyone."

"Here are photos of their slaves," Ivan said, handing the book to Aleks.

"Oh, I hate hearing that word; it seems *house servant* or *field hand* would be better," Colleen said.

Ivan leaned over to look at the scrapbook, and in the pages were pictures of Big Adam, Jim, Dorothy, Mammy, and Sally. There were other black people he didn't recognize because they were field hands and he had little to no interaction with them.

"Some of those guys would have been good defensive backs," Ivan said. "Look at their size!"

"There doesn't seem to be anything here," Aleks said, setting it on the edge of the coffee table. "I'm getting another cup of coffee. Would either of you like one?" he asked, standing up and hitting the scrapbook with his knee, pushing it off the table and onto the floor.

"Dang it! I'm sorry," Aleks said.

"It was an accident," Colleen said. She helped him pick up the photos that had fallen out onto the floor and under the couch and curio.

"That's all of them," he said and set the scrapbook back in the top drawer of the curio.

* * *

"Look who I found in the kitchen," Aleks said, entering the sunroom with Martha. "She's going to help us search."

"Good morning, Martha. How are you this morning?" Colleen asked.

"I'm fine, thank you," she said and flashed her beautiful smile. "Have you had any luck?"

"No, I'm afraid not," Colleen said.

"Hand me a folder, and I'll get started," she said.

"This is the last folder," Colleen said.

Martha sat in the large overstuffed chair across from the couch.

"Your rose garden is absolutely beautiful," Martha said. "How many plants do you have?"

"There are thirty-two bushes and six varieties," she said. "My grandfather raised roses when I was a child."

"They are beautiful," Martha said.

"Look at this!" Aleks said, holding up a photo from the table.

"Who is it?" asked Colleen.

"It's Adam with Dorothy and that must be Sally on his lap!" Aleks said.

"What does this mean?" Colleen asked.

"This means that he is there. At least I think that's what it means," he said, examining the photo.

Colleen and Martha sat down on either side of Aleks to see the photo.

"That's Adam," Colleen and Martha said in unison.

Martha had seen pictures of Adam in Aleks's photo album.

"He looks older in this photo than he did two years ago. I can also tell by the photo of Sally. She was a baby when Adam and I were there in 1861, and in this photo, she looks about five."

The sunroom door opened, and in walked Catherine, still in her pajamas.

"What's going on in here? I could hear Aleks hollering," she said.

"I found a photo of Adam at the Griggs House, and it's not from when we were there the first time," he said. "Looks like he is there now."

Colleen was picking up papers and placing the documents back in the folder. Aleks and Martha helped straighten up, and Catherine sat in the rocking chair, looking at the papers left on the table that sat against the limestone wall.

"What are you reading about, Cat?" Aleks asked.

"I want to help solve your mystery," she said.

"I appreciate your enthusiasm, Cat, but I think it is solved," Aleks said.

"Here's a list of those who fought in the Battle of Fort Tyler, and here's another one of those who died in the battle," she said, handing it to him.

He read off the first two names, "General Tyler and Captain Gonzales … I don't see anything here that we didn't already know," he said.

"How about this letter from Mrs. Griggs?" she asked.

It was a firsthand account of the day of the battle. He scanned over the letter, which told of General Tyler ordering her to vacate the house because he was certain it would be demolished. After they left the house, the Union soldiers took it over.

"Look at this," Aleks interrupted. "Mrs. Griggs said that a chest of silver was lost on their trek across the wagon bridge to West Point. I wonder if it was recovered. Just one piece of this silver would guarantee our entrance."

"I've heard stories about that but thought it was contrived. No, I don't believe any silver was ever recovered," Colleen said. "If it had been, we would have it because everything was passed down to me."

Aleks couldn't believe what he read next. His eyes rested on the name of Adam Griggs IV. "Oh God! No!" Aleks shouted.

He jumped up from the couch and paced back and forth, talking to himself and running his hands through his hair. Colleen picked up the letter and read it.

"'He received a fatal wound at the end of the battle while he heroically cared for the men who defended the fort.' It also says he was a slave on loan from Aleks Ness, his master, who was away at Gettysburg but had not returned to claim him. It goes on to say that on the day of the battle, Adam defended her home as if it were his own."

"If we don't get to him before he's killed, then we can't save him. Oh my God, what have I done!" Aleks said.

CHAPTER SEVENTEEN

Down Yonder in the Chattahoochee

"LET'S GO!" IVAN said.

"It's not that easy," Aleks said. "We have to go scuba-diving first."

"For what?" Ivan asked.

"For an artifact that connects us to the day of the battle," Aleks said.

"We have musket shells. Why can't we use those?" Ivan asked.

"We can, but they've gotten mixed up with the shells from other battles. We don't have time to figure out which ones are from that battle," Aleks said.

"And we have time to scuba dive?" Ivan said.

"I can't think of another option right now," Aleks said.

During the next ten minutes, Ivan and Aleks pulled scuba gear out of the attic and carried it through the house to Ivan's large white SUV.

* * *

Ivan checked his phone for the time; it was five in the morning. He asked Aleks to check the time line of the battle. "The Confederates approached the fort about 8:00 a.m.," Aleks said.

This gave them, at the most, a couple of hours to retrieve the silver near the old wagon bridge in the middle of the Chattahoochee River.

"Do you need our help?" Martha asked, referring to Catherine and herself.

"Yes, you ready to leave right now?" Ivan asked.

They threw shoes on and grabbed sweatshirts. Colleen asked everyone to be careful. She was staying home to prepare for the Fort Tyler fundraiser.

* * *

They loaded up into the SUV and headed out of the driveway, down the hill, across the railroad tracks, and toward the boat landing at the river.

"Hey, Dad, have you heard from Van lately?" Aleks asked.

The car grew uncomfortably silent. The family seldom spoke of Van's predicament in front of anyone new, and Aleks had brought him up in front of Martha. Ivan placed the blame for his conviction and incarceration on himself. If only he had chosen a different attorney or made him come in at his usual curfew on the night of the incident. He was convinced he was to blame and carried it with him.

"I haven't spoken to him for a week or so. He's been busy working for Mr. Crowder on the farm," Ivan said.

Martha's gaze shifted to Aleks.

"We should call and ask him to dive with us. He can share my equipment, and besides, we may need his help with these foreign nationals. Didn't you say he competed in the prison MMA?" Aleks asked.

"Yes," Ivan said, "but it's too early to call him."

Meanwhile, Catherine had already called. "Hey, it's Cat. What are you doing? … Okay, well, here's Aleks. He wants to speak to you."

She handed off the phone to Aleks, and he started with the invitation.

"Hey! What are you up to?" Aleks asked.

"Sleepin', man. What are you doing up so early?" Van asked.

Aleks asked him to meet them for the dive. "I'd love to! This is the craziest thing. Are you all doing something illegal?" Van asked.

"If we get caught, it will be difficult to explain, but no, it's technically not illegal," Aleks said.

"Do you think I'll remember how to dive?" Van asked.

"Tell him it's like riding a bike," Ivan hollered.

"That's my dad; he heard you." Aleks laughed.

"Tell him to meet us at the river, downtown West Point, past West Point Tire by the boat ramp, and to come now and pack some dry clothes too."

Ivan and Aleks looked at an old photograph of the wagon bridge and located the place in the river where a piece of its footing remained.

Van rolled up next to Catherine in his old Honda. The headliner was hanging down over his passenger seat. He pushed it up and waved at Catherine and Martha, who were sitting in the truck.

Aleks and Ivan were pulling the canoe off the top of the truck.

"Hey, Van! You ready for a treasure hunt?" Aleks asked.

"Why not?" Van said.

Van helped Aleks load the scuba gear while Ivan held the canoe in knee-deep water. Then Aleks sat down in the back and Ivan in the front, and Van stepped in the middle. They picked up their paddles and headed toward the train trestle.

They arrived at the point where the support from the old wagon bridge peeked out from the water. "It should be right under us," Aleks said.

"True, unless the current carried it further down the river. It'll depend on the weight of the chest," Ivan said.

Aleks told Van to wait in the canoe and they would take turns or buddy-breathe.

Ivan and Aleks jumped into the murky water and put on the buoyancy compensators (BC) and fins. Van handed them their dive lights.

Aleks knew there were artifacts from the war in the river but never thought he'd see them firsthand. There he was looking at a Confederate cannon that had been under water for 150 years. He took out his phone in its waterproof case and snapped a few pictures of it. *That was too good to pass up,* he thought.

His father tapped him on the shoulder and motioned for him to come in his direction. Ivan pointed to his eyes with his index and middle fingers, giving Aleks the dive sign to look at something. It was another artifact; this time, it was a wagon and again completely intact.

Underneath the wagon, settled into the bottom of the river, was a chest. Ivan picked up a rock and hit at the lock. Aleks took a try at it, and it finally broke loose.

They opened the chest to find Mrs. Griggs's silver. Ivan pointed to the chest and then gave the thumbs-up dive sign to surface. Aleks worked to pull the wagon off the chest, but it wasn't budging. He and his father worked together to pull it loose so they could lift it from the floor of the river. It was no use; they needed help.

Aleks surfaced and managed to scare the bajeebers out of Catherine. She and Martha were sitting on the front bumper of the SUV, and Catherine let out a scream so loud it sounded like a monster had attacked her.

"What's wrong with you, Cat?" Aleks asked as he floated on his back, adding air to his BC. "Is she okay, Martha?" he asked.

"Yes," she said.

"Martha, this is our cousin, Van," Aleks said.

"We've already met," Van said.

"Well, I'm not fine, Aleks. You shouldn't scare people like that!"

"Cat, I was coming up to show you this." In his hand, he held a cake server. "On the back, it has a G for Griggs. There's an entire chest down there. We'll bring it up with your help, Van," he said.

* * *

Aleks wiped his mask and swam with Van toward the bottom. They had an extra mask for Van, but he and Aleks had to buddy-breathe from Aleks's regulator since they only had two air tanks. They swam twelve feet in each direction and then surfaced again. "The visibility is terrible down there; it's less than two feet," Aleks said.

"Has Dad surfaced?"

"No, we haven't seen him," Catherine said.

"We thought you were with him," Martha said.

"You can't find him?" Catherine asked, sounding panicked.

"Don't get all upset. I'm sure he's fine," Van said.

Aleks and Van went down to search for Ivan. Van pointed to the air tank; they had ten minutes left, barely enough time to find Ivan and bring up the chest, Aleks thought. They felt along the bottom in a six-foot radius of the chest. Van dropped the regulator; bubbles shot up from the valve, and air rushed out. Aleks grabbed for the hose and reined it in on his third try. He gave himself air and then put it in Van's mouth. Van's hands were busy poking a stick around in a hole. Something caught it, and Van struggled to pull it out but lost it in the hole. Aleks shined the flashlight in the hole but saw nothing. Then he spotted a stream of blood toward the surface. The boys followed it up and found Ivan. His right arm was bleeding, and in his left hand he held on to the largest freshwater fish any of them had ever seen.

"Look at this monster! Have you ever seen a catfish this big?" Ivan asked with a laugh. "He tried to spin me around by my arm. He grabbed hold of my hand and practically swallowed it."

"Daddy, are you okay?" Catherine hollered from the bank.

"Yes, I'm fine, just some little sandpaper cuts from this catfish." He threw it in the boat. "We'll have Mama freeze this monster and fry it up next week. My granddaddy used to make the best catfish, nothin' better," he said.

"Dad, was he in that hole?" Aleks asked.

"Yes and I made the mistake of sticking my hand in. He grabbed hold of it, and I wasn't sure what had me. People catfish noodle for these big ones, but I've never done it," he said.

"They call it hand-fishin', and he looks to be a wicked seventy-pound flathead," Van said.

"Dad, do you need a bandage?" Aleks asked.

"Nah, I'm fine, just a scratch," Ivan said.

Ivan and the boys headed down for the real treasure. Ivan and Aleks pushed up on the barrel of the cannon, lifting it enough for Van to pull out the piece of the leather chest pinned down to the river floor. Van took a breath and slowly emerged, blowing out bubbles on his way to the surface. Ivan and Aleks ascended with the chest. The rusted lock fell off as they lifted it into the canoe.

It was almost six thirty and sunrise occurred a few minutes earlier. Aleks looked up at the bank to Martha and Catherine waiting for them. He noticed the sunlight reflecting on Martha's hair. Aleks was in the front and lifted himself up out of the boat, handing Martha his fins. He leaned in toward her and planted an unexpected kiss on her cheek.

"What was that for?" she asked.

"Thanks for your help with everything," he said.

"Aleks, let's load up. We only have so much time," Ivan said.

"Wow, my little cousin is all grown up!" Van said with a laugh.

"Well, and you are so welcome for my help too, Aleks," Cat said.

"Thank you, Cat," he said. "You want a kiss?" he teased.

"No, thank you. Eww!"

"Hurry up, guys! Get the truck loaded. We should leave for Adam immediately," Ivan said.

"Wait a minute! Leave for where? You found Adam?" Van asked.

CHAPTER EIGHTEEN

Preparing for the Battle

THE DIVING GROUP found Colleen in the dining room, assembling a floral arrangement of roses and hydrangeas for the centerpiece.

"Hey, Aunt Colleen, you have something that will fit me?" Van asked.

"Oh, of course, we would love to have you come for the fundraiser dinner."

"No, Mama, we are taking him with us to find Adam," Aleks said.

"They've gotten you involved in this crazy business of theirs?" she asked.

"Yes, we have," Aleks said.

"We need him dressed right away," Ivan said. "I'm sorry about the party tonight. I know you needed us to help set up," Ivan said.

"I'll manage with Catherine's and Martha's help. Unless Martha is going with you?" Colleen asked.

"I want to go," Catherine said.

"Catherine, you and I will stay here and help your mum," Martha said.

While Colleen pulled clothes for Van to wear, Aleks and Ivan gave him the abridged version of Adam's disappearance.

"Time travel, are you kidding me?" Van hollered. "You joking me? Are we doing a reenactment? Come on. You guys don't have to lie to me; I'll help ya out if you need another guy. I have to tell you though, I'd rather be dressed as a Yankee," he said with a chuckle. "My New York family would have a conniption if they knew I was dressin' up as a rebel. So if we could keep this among us?" he asked sarcastically.

Aleks could tell that Van didn't believe them.

"This is serious," Ivan said. "Your cousin needs you. I don't know if you've heard, but Aleks may be indicted on charges related to Adam's disappearance."

"What?" Van asked. "No, I haven't heard anything lately. I'll do whatever you need me to do."

Van's playful demeanor turned stoic as they packed a high-powered rifle with a scope and night vision, a handgun, and a short sword.

"Mama, did you pack the antibiotics?" Ivan asked.

"Where are they?" she asked.

"I put the injectables in the refrigerator," he said.

"What else are you taking?" she asked.

"Some protein bars and water. You know how crabby Aleks gets when he's hungry," he said.

She pulled Ivan aside in the kitchen. "I'm worried. How will you protect yourself? What if you don't come back?" Her head fell against his chest, knocking up against something hard. "What are you wearing?" she asked, tapping on his chest.

"It's a bulletproof vest. Remember my echo tech whose brother was a police officer? He gave me these vests. We are all three wearing them. I know you are worried, but you shouldn't be. I promise to bring Aleks and Van back safely; with our superior weapons and knowledge, we'll be fine."

"Aleks, you ready? Van, you ready?" Ivan hollered down the hallway.

Their haversacks were packed, and Aleks had his slung across one shoulder. Ivan found him on his knees in his room saying a prayer. Van walked in behind Ivan, and the three finished the prayer together.

"And lead us not into temptation, but deliver us from evil: For thine is the kingdom, and the power, and the glory, for ever. Amen."

"You ready?" Ivan asked.

"Yes, sir!" Aleks said.

"Let's go jump the rails you've told us about!" Ivan said.

They went to the backyard, before going behind the tree house, turned, and waved at the three women looking out from the kitchen window. Then they disappeared behind the shed.

* * *

Colleen, Catherine, and Martha watched from the kitchen window as the men walked off to battle. Colleen stayed calm for her daughter and Aleks's friend.

"We aren't the first women to watch men leave for this battle, and our battle will be over tomorrow. That's not so bad, right?"

"That's right, Mama. This time, the war won't last four years."

"Aren't you two the least bit worried? They took out of here with heavy weapons and antibiotics. That's not normal where I come from," Martha said nervously.

"Would anyone like some tea?" Colleen asked.

"Yes, let's have some tea," Martha said.

CHAPTER NINETEEN

Time Piece Turns, Tick-Tock, Tick-Tock

EACH OF THEM had a piece of silver and eight tachyon rocks from the yard. "When the compass spins and the railroad watch starts, be ready to go," Aleks said.

"Go where exactly?" Van asked.

"We'll arrive in 1865 on a train close to West Point," Aleks said. "Listen, in order to return you must be with me and you must have at least five of these rocks on you. Do not lose your rocks."

Aleks noticed Van looked nervous and asked his dad to put his arm around Van.

"Point the compass on the rock; timepiece turns, tick-tock, tick-tock." Aleks recited the words as he and Adam had done many times before.

A thunderous roar came from the back of the shed.

"This is it! Hold on, and don't let go!" Aleks hollered.

They were sucked into its vortex for what seemed like longer but only lasted seconds, and then they dropped smack dab into the engine car of an 1860s locomotive.

The engineer's eyes widened; he looked panicked as he grabbed for the gun next to the door. Ivan held the engineer from behind, holding his arms down while Van pried the gun from his hands.

"It's okay, sir. We are Confederates heading to the fort to meet General Tyler," Aleks said. "We were told by General Tyler to check out the engine. You can't be too careful around here right now. There're rumors that the Union have sent spies in to take the railroad before its cavalry shows up."

The engineer calmed down, and Ivan released him. "I'm the engineer of this train. My name is Stephen. Sorry about that. I didn't mean to pull my gun on ya. The general told us to be expectin' Yankees. You all gettin' off here in West Point?" he asked.

Van leaned over the side and threw up. Time travel had triggered his motion sickness.

"You okay?" Aleks asked.

"I'm all right," Van said.

Stephen told them that the railroad bridge was jammed with traffic for at least a quarter of a mile outside of West Point. Ivan and Aleks agreed that they could arrive in West Point much quicker on foot and decided to exit the train.

"Thanks, Stephen," Aleks said, and they waved good-bye.

"Take care of yourselves, and tell General Tyler hello for me," Stephen said.

"This is déjà vu all over again," Aleks said.

"The first time Yogi Berra is quoted in the 1800s," Ivan said with a chuckle.

Van was in a state of disbelief and hadn't spoken a word since they disembarked the train.

The atmosphere of the town had changed significantly in the 24-hours since he and Martha had been there. The Confederates were fortifying the area to defend the bridges, warehouses, and depot. This railroad going from West Point to Montgomery and then to the Gulf Coast was one of the Confederate supply routes. It had been this area's lifeblood—supplying food, ammunition, and weapons and the transport of soldiers throughout the southeastern war theater.

People were buzzing with activity. Refugees who had come in from Montgomery after it surrendered to Federal forces four days earlier were warning townspeople of the Union's approach. It looked similar to a modern-day panic before a snowstorm or a hurricane; however, this was devastation of another kind.

The time travelers kept a steady pace from the depot to the Griggs house. Van asked to look around town, but Ivan said it was too risky with the heavy Confederate presence. "If someone recognizes Aleks, we'll be detained." Ivan insisted they keep to their plan.

Van looked to Aleks for an explanation.

"I have a bounty on my head," Aleks said.

"No way, you have a bounty on your head in 1865?" Van shrieked. "I've gotta hear this one."

"It's this sword right here," Aleks said, pulling the short sword from the inside of his jacket. "I took it at Gettysburg, and I'll leave it here before we go back. Maybe they'll take the bounty off of my head if I return the sword. It belongs to a famous Alabama general."

* * *

"There it is; do you see it?" Ivan asked.

The house was a bright spot on the hill. The plantation looked quiet. The front staircase outside reached from the front yard to the second-level balcony; otherwise, the stone house looked almost exactly like home to the time travelers.

They arrived at the second-floor balcony entrance, and Aleks tapped the doorknocker and found the door ajar. He pushed open the large mahogany door.

"Hello? Anyone home? Mrs. Griggs?" Aleks called.

CHAPTER TWENTY

The Griggs Plantation 1865

"MAY ISA HELP you?" Mammy asked peeking out the door. "Why, if it ain't Masser Aleks! It sure is you, and you's come back fur Adam, hasn't ya, boy?"

Mrs. Griggs ducked her head into the hallway from her bedroom. "Is that Aleks at the door, Mammy?"

"Yes, ma'am, Mrs. Griggs. I hope we are not imposing. This is my father, Dr. Ness, and my cousin, Van, and we are here to defend your town at the fort. General LaGrange is headed in this direction and expected anytime now."

Aleks introduced his father and Van to Mrs. Griggs. She offered her hand, first to Ivan and then to Van. Then, she held her arms out toward Aleks and hugged his neck.

"Aleks, you and your family are always welcome at the Griggs home. We were terribly worried about you and your plantation when we heard news that the Yankees had burned Atlanta. We kept asking our Atlanta friends if there was word of the Ness Plantation but heard nothing," she said.

Aleks looked at his father and then back at Mrs. Griggs. "We were one of the few to be spared. There is nothing left, Sherman's men looted everything but we'll be able to rebuild after the War," Aleks said.

"I am so sorry. What about Mrs. Ness and the rest of your family?" she asked.

"Mrs. Ness and our daughter are with her parents. They are all safe," Ivan said.

"We are about to have Easter breakfast. Would you please join us in the dining room? It may be our final meal at the Griggs house," she said, wiping a tear from her eye.

"We would love to join you for breakfast," Van said.

"Isn't your home made of limestone, Mrs. Griggs?" Ivan asked.

"Yes," she said.

"I think you'll find it withstands cannon fire," Ivan said.

"Excuse me, Mrs. Griggs, may I go see Adam?" Aleks asked.

Mrs. Griggs shook her head, unable to speak from an overflow of emotions.

Mammy answered for her. "He's downstairs in de kitchen. Masser Aleks, he's been a missin' ya sometin' fierce."

"I've been looking for him everywhere," Aleks said.

"Why, of curse you has," she said with a smile that lit up the entire hall.

Aleks thanked them both, and then into the dark downstairs, he ran. There was a loud crackling and popping sound coming from the stove, and it was just loud enough to cover up Aleks's entrance into the kitchen. He walked up and quietly stood behind Adam. He said, "Point the compass on the rock."

Adam turned around fast and nearly hit his head on the low ceiling when he jumped with surprise. "You found my message on the table!" he shouted.

The boys hugged, and neither could contain their emotions. They both sobbed openly.

Dorothy walked out of the cellar and scolded Aleks as soon as she laid eyes on him. "Well, Masser Aleks, we's ben lookin' fur ya fur a mighty long time now. Where's ya been? Adam thinks ya done lef' him fur good. Masser Griggs, he's a good masser, but Adam wants to goes home. This catchin' ups gonna half ta wait till afta breakfast. We's got ta feed dis family now and add one more to da table."

"Mrs. Dorothy, would you mind adding three more? There are three of us in all; my dad and cousin are also with me," Aleks said.

"Good glory, Aleks, don't you be callin' me Mrs. tha'll gets you a whoopin' round here," Dorothy said quietly so just Aleks and Adam could hear.

"She's right Master Aleks, if it don't get you a whoopin' it might get Dorothy in trouble with the new black overseer. He whipped me good for calling her Mrs. He said Mrs. is not for slaves," Adam said.

Aleks laid his hand on Adam's arm. "A black man did this? You have marks?" Aleks asked.

Adam nodded yes.

"Does Mrs. Griggs know?" Aleks asked.

Adam shrugged his shoulders.

"Most everyone has marks from whippin's since dis overseer," Dorothy whispered. "The masser hire him cuz plantin' season is here and de masser is off to War. Shhh, someone's a comin'. We bes be quiet," she added.

Ivan and Van entered the kitchen where they found the boys talking with Dorothy.

"Now, where'd you all comes from?" Dorothy exclaimed. "All dis company and commotion, dear Jesus, what's gonna happen next?"

Aleks introduced them to Dorothy, and Van told her it was pleasure to meet her and her breakfast sure did smell good.

"The first-floor floors are dirt, like you always told us," Van said. "And look, Uncle Ivan, your office is a kitchen and your den is a slaves' quarters! Jeez, how do ya like that?"

Aleks stayed near the stove, talking to Adam. "Listen, Adam, it's time for us to go."

"I just need to stay until the end of the battle," Adam said.

Aleks interrupted him. "No, everything has changed. We need to leave as soon as we can get you out of here."

"What do you mean?" Adam asked.

"For starters, you are classified as a missing person, and I am the main suspect in your case," Aleks said.

"I don't understand how anyone could think that," Adam said.

"It makes perfect sense; the authorities found your haversack in my bedroom, and now they are certain I did something to you. They are accusing me of withholding evidence."

"Do you know why I didn't travel back last time?" Adam asked.

"Yes, it was the rocks. You only had one rock left in your haversack. I've done some work at the MIT lab with a friend. I'll explain more later."

"I knew it! I knew it had to be the rocks," Adam said and then started to tell him the story of what he'd been through during the last two years. He explained that when the time window opened, the force of Aleks's reentry pushed him against the train door; he hit his head and lost consciousness. When he woke up, there was French gentleman speaking to him.

Ivan and Van walked over and interrupted the boys' reunion.

Ivan gave Adam a hug. "Let's have this conversation outside," he said.

They walked out of the first-floor servants' entrance out from under the balcony over to the large oak tree in the front yard. Aleks asked Adam to finish telling them what had happened to him.

"When I woke up from hitting my head from the force of the time window pushing me back, a Frenchman asked me if I was okay and where my master was. I told him that my master was riding on top of the train. It was the first thing that popped into my head," Adam said.

"You're going to love this. The Frenchman was Mr. Verne, and he told me that my master was not riding on top of the train and that he had indeed seen him disappear like a flash of light right before his eyes."

"Who was the man?" Ivan asked.

"It was Jules Verne."

"*The* Jules Verne! Are you certain? I didn't think he came to America until after the war," Ivan said.

"He said no one knew of his travels. His family was protective of him, and they wouldn't allow him to travel to America so he told them he had gone to visit friends in the South of France. He told me that, 'God made America in six days and on the seventh he rested.' He loved everything about our country, even the war. He wanted to see it for himself. For several months, I traveled with him through Virginia, Tennessee, and Georgia. He said I was his servant. He took care of me and promised to get me back to Georgia; in exchange, I told him things about the future and time travel. He promised not to use it to manipulate world events, that he would use it only in his writings and treat it like the impossible made possible through science fiction."

Ivan thought about Verne's writings. "It all makes sense now; you told him about the moon shot?" Ivan asked.

"Yes, sir, and I also told him about submarines. Mr. Verne and I parted ways in West Point. He took the train south from there. I debarked the train and headed to the Griggs house. I'd made it back to safety, but while walking up the road here, I was captured by a bounty hunter. He was the nastiest son of a gun I've ever met. His trench coat was lined with guns and knives, and he carried a sword on his belt. He told me there was a bounty on my head, and he reckoned he might as well be the one to collect it. He tied my hands and put me in the back of a wagon; there were eight of us blacks, all covered with a tarp and transported through Alabama and Mississippi. I didn't think I would survive because this man clearly didn't like me. He said I spoke like an uppity Nigger and called me Passé Blanc."

"What's that?" Ivan asked.

"It means that I was so light that I could pass for white. He took us to Pass Christian, to work on a plantation. He said they needed Negroes like me to work in the house. I was on that farm for no more than part of a night when I escaped. I snuck off to the harbor, the same area where we'd met your cousin during the Battle of Ship Island, and then I took a ferry to New Orleans. Once there, I made my way to the Treme, the oldest settlement of free Africans in the United States. I sought shelter at St. Augustine Church and told my story to the parishioner—all but the time travel—and he made arrangements for my transportation back to Georgia."

"How did you know to go to New Orleans for help?" Ivan asked.

"My grandmother had told me about the free community," Adam said.

"We are thankful you are alive and well. We need to get you out of here," Ivan said.

"Yes, sir, I can't wait to go home. I'm sorry for the trouble I've caused you," Adam said.

"Why are you sorry? You're the one who was left. It'll all be fine when you get home," Aleks said.

"My parents must be worried. I've missed them so much," Adam said.

"They have been devastated," Aleks said. "There's something we have to tell you." He explained how they'd found a letter written by Mrs. Griggs. They told him that she'd called him a hero.

"It says 'Adam Griggs IV is a hero'?" he asked with a smile.

"Yes, but there is something else too," Ivan said. "She says that you—"

Before Ivan was able to finish, Dorothy interrupted. "You best gets your boys into the house, Masser Ivan, or Ms. Griggs will gets afder me fur makin' yous cook yur own breakfas. Gets upstairs to de dining room. Breakfas is ready.

"Adam, gets those biscuits off da fire and on the dumbwaiter, rights now. You don't wants to burn no biscuits," Dorothy shouted with delight at the thought of all the company fussing over her cooking. "Isa 'fraid we gonna hafda make another batch of everything," she said with a smile.

* * *

Mrs. Griggs was waiting for the Ness men so they could say the blessing. It looked and felt like most Easters inside the Griggs House. This remote area of the South had gone mostly untouched by the war until this point. There had been no Yankee occupation like in New Orleans or other areas of the South. Its homes and churches were still standing, and its railroads were operational; however, on this Easter morning, unlike all the others, its church pews would be empty of worshipers and the town would be filled with armed men.

This town and its people had been expecting the war and had started preparations on the fort about three years earlier. The fort had three cannons that covered the bridges, the town, and the railroad. The fort was directly behind the stone house.

The house seemed strangely normal, considering the rumors of the coming conflict. Mammy was in the center of the hallway retrieving breakfast food from the dumbwaiter, which was situated in the main hall. It was on a pulley system, and Adam was sending food up.

"I hopes Ms. Griggs don't have a spell from all dis company comin' in on her all at a once. Dat and de war is comin' too. Oh Lord!" Mammy said to herself.

The Ness family walked through the second-floor balcony entrance into the main hall and turned to the right into the dining room. Mrs. Griggs asked Dr. Ness to take the place at the head of the table in Dr. Griggs's chair and then requested that he bless the food and pray for the protection of Dr. Griggs, General Tyler, and all the brave men in the war. Ivan ended the prayer by saying, "Thank you, Lord, for already answering our prayers. Amen."

Aleks gave him a nudge under the table.

"Thank you, Mrs. Griggs, for taking good care of Adam. It has been a long couple of years wondering if he was dead or alive or if he'd suffered at the hand of a cruel master. Knowing that he was with you is a relief," said Aleks.

CHAPTER TWENTY-ONE

General Is Shot

MEANWHILE, AT THE Griggs House, 150 years in the future, Colleen sat anxiously looking at the clock on the stove every few minutes. She wondered what was taking the time travelers so long. It had been over an hour since the guys had left for 1865. Couldn't they just get Adam and jump back?

Catherine found her in the kitchen. "Why is General barking?" she asked.

"I'm not sure. Would you check on him?" Colleen asked.

She called his name, but he didn't come to her. His bark sounded like it was coming from the crawlspace. Cat pushed ajar the small Alice in Wonderland–looking crawlspace door, but there was no sign of the golden doodle.

"I've tried treats and everything; I can't get him to come. He's growling at something, but it's so dark under there that I can't see him," Catherine said.

Martha entered the kitchen and asked about the dog.

Colleen stepped outside and called for him, but he still didn't come. She got a flashlight and headed toward the crawlspace but stopped abruptly at the sound of a loud explosion followed by a puff of smoke from the crawlspace. General's barking turned to a yelp.

"Catherine, call nine-one-one!" Colleen shouted.

Colleen pushed the kitchen door shut and locked it behind her. "Follow me," Colleen instructed Catherine and Martha.

She took the girls to the attic where they waited for the police to arrive.

"Mama, what are you doing?" Catherine asked.

She'd retrieved Ivan's handgun from the top shelf of the closet.

"I heard a gunshot coming from the crawlspace," Colleen said.

Martha interrupted. "Do you think the Germans followed us here?"

"I'm scared, Mama!" Cat cried.

"I heard the police car pull up," Colleen said. "Everything is going to be fine. You girls stay here."

* * *

She stepped across the driveway to the squad car. Everything was quiet outside, including the dog. She could see the officer had her dog in the backseat of the squad car.

It was nearly nine in the morning, and her mind was filled with worry about her husband and boys and now their family dog. "Was he shot? He looks like he's bleeding," she said to herself.

The officer carried the fifty-pound canine to the kitchen for her. Catherine and Martha met them at the door. "Is he okay, Mama?"

"He's been shot in the hind leg. He needs to be taken to the vet. The police officers have asked me to stay here to fill out a report. I need for you and Martha to take General to the vet."

"I don't want to leave you," Catherine said.

"I am fine. I need you to take care of the dog."

"We're not going to leave your mama, darling. She'll be fine while you're gone," Officer Bock said.

"What if the person with the gun is still under our house?" Catherine asked.

"We've searched under the house and all around your property, and now we are checkin' every square inch of the inside," Officer Bock added.

"Please go with Martha and show her where the vet's office is located. I promise, I'll be fine," Colleen said.

* * *

The doorbell rang. Colleen looked up to see Chief Laurent at the kitchen door.

"Come on in, Chief. Did you find anything else?"

"There's no one on your property, but it does look as if someone was underneath your house earlier this morning. We found fresh marks and some bullets under there. The bullets are musket shells that, if I'm not mistaken, date back to the Civil War. They look too old to have been shot from a modern-day weapon, and one had blood on it. For now, we'll assume the blood is from your dog," he said.

Colleen's mind raced with thoughts about Ivan. *The chief and his officer will think I'm crazy if tell him it was a Confederate soldier who shot my dog. He'll think it was a reenactor or that I'm certifiable.* "Yep, absolutely nuts!" she said out loud.

"I'm sorry, Mrs. Ness, what was that you were saying?" the chief asked.

"Oh nothing," she said.

"Mrs. Ness, the odd thing is that it looks like the perpetrator only has one foot. There is one boot print for the right foot. Anyway, are there any other doors underneath the house? Any rooms under the house?" Chief Laurent asked.

"Not that I'm aware of," she said.

"I know your house was built before the Civil War. We thought surely there were secret doors or hiding places that were used during the war," the chief said.

"No, not that I am aware of—and honestly, I think my parents would have told us about them when Ivan and I took over the house." Colleen opened the closet door in the dining room. She pulled out a large cardboard tube and opened it. Inside of it was a large roll of paper. She set it on the table and unrolled a set of blueprints.

She spent the next thirty minutes examining the blueprints with the chief while she answered the officer's questions. "All we have, Mrs. Ness, are the musket shells, footprint, and an injured dog. I'm afraid it just doesn't add up," the officer said.

"I don't see anything here on the blueprints that we haven't already searched," the chief said. "I'm going to place an officer over here to keep an eye on things for the next twenty-four hours."

Officer Bock spoke up and informed her that they would call her with the forensic report on the dog. "If there is something traceable, then we'll have a case. I'm sorry we don't have a more substantial lead," he said.

"Here is my direct number," the chief said, handing her his card. "Call if you hear or see anything else. And one more thing, was Dr. Ness at home when you heard the shots?"

"No, sir, he is out of town."

"We'll need to speak with him when he returns. When do you expect him?" the chief asked.

"He is supposed to arrive home late today."

"Please ask him to give us a call at the department."

"I certainly will. Thank you so much," she said.

CHAPTER TWENTY-TWO

Morning of the Battle of West Point 1865

ALEKS SAT AT the table thinking how time changed everything. It was the same day, the same house, on the same street in front of the same fort; yet everything was different when separated by 150 years.

Mrs. Griggs announced that General Tyler had sent a messenger by the house and ordered them to vacate. "They fear the Union will take over our house and that it will be destroyed." In her calmest voice, she politely requested that after breakfast the men help her family load their wagon and travel across the river.

Persia interrupted. "Mother, where will we stay in West Point?"

"We will be at the Reed's home."

"I'm not going to Major Reed's. I'm going to the fort!" J. W. announced.

"I'll keep a good watch on him," Ivan said.

"Mother, my friend Isham Stanley will be at the fight. He told his uncle that '… anyone that will not fight when the enemy comes right into his own home would be a mighty sorry somebody.'"

"Where is General Tyler now?" Persia asked.

"He is at the fort preparing for the Yankees," Mrs. Griggs said. "He raised the flag that the ladies of West Point made for him. Your father presented it to him, and he has promised to defend it with his life."

Mrs. Griggs stood and dismissed everyone from the breakfast table. "Please put some biscuits in your pockets for later. You may get hungry at the fort," she said. "Children, we will leave right away. Make haste, Persia, and fetch your jewelry box. J. W., get the family Bible from the parlor." Mrs. Griggs excused herself and hurried out of the dining room, calling for Mammy.

"What is that?" Aleks asked.

The clanking sound seemed to be coming from Mrs. Griggs, for it happened with each of her steps.

Persia leaned in to Aleks and whispered, "That's some family silver clanging together. I must have sewn it too close together." She giggled as the clanging kept time with each of her mother's footsteps.

"Persia?" Mrs. Griggs called from the hallway.

While the house servants cleaned up from breakfast, Ivan and the boys carried baskets packed with food, blankets, and valuables to the horse-drawn carriage that waited under the front staircase.

"Ms. Griggs, I cants get them vases buried. Dat red clay won't budge," Jim said.

"I thought I told you to do that last night, Jim."

Ivan interrupted. "Let me find a good spot for Jim to bury the vases. I know all about this Georgia clay and have dug in it many times."

"Why thank you, Dr. Ness," she said. "You can't imagine how much better I feel having you all here with Dr. Griggs away."

"This war won't last much longer, Mrs. Griggs, and you'll be fine," he said with confidence that she did not understand but found comforting.

Ivan and Jim walked out the back door with the familiar vases. Ivan passed by these vases every day; they sat on the mantel in his present-day living room.

"Listen, Jim, I need to speak with Adam before we bury the vases. Do you know where he is?" Ivan asked.

"He already at da Fort. He's a-helpin' General Tyler with the munitions and such. General Tyler axed fur a strong boy ta help wid munitions so I sent him. Adam said you wouldn't mind since you would be meetin' him up der," he said.

"That's fine. Van and I will head there after I help you bury these vases," Ivan said, taking the shovel and digging in the back corner of the yard.

When he was finished, Ivan asked a servant to call for Van and Aleks to join them in the backyard. They were helping pack Mrs. Griggs's carriage.

The servant returned with Van because Mrs. Griggs requested that Aleks escort them to the wagon bridge at the river and then walk back up the hill with J. W.

Ivan was irate. "It's his teenage brain. He's not thinking about consequences." Ivan fussed all the way to the fort with Van following behind him.

* * *

Jim assisted the ladies as they stepped up into the carriage; Mrs. Griggs, Persia, and Dorothy sat on one side while Mammy's large constitution filled up more than half the other side, leaving just enough space for J. W. to squeeze in next to her. Aleks stepped in and saw that short of sitting on someone's lap there was no more space. "I'll help Jim up front," he said, shutting the door and climbing up top. "You've got the best views up here, don't you?" Aleks looked at Jim and smiled. *It was difficult not to be excited,* he thought.

Mrs. Griggs told Jim they were ready to leave. She turned back to look at her home and patted away tears with her handkerchief.

"It's gonna be okay, Mama," Persia said. "General Tyler promised he'd keep us safe from the Yankees."

She held her daughter's hand and said, "I know, darling, and I feel better that J. W. will be with Aleks and his father at the fort. Seems we've always known them."

"Mama, I think Aleks and J. W. favor, don't you?" she asked.

* * *

The story of the battle was playing out before them. Aleks knew it like he'd lived it once before. Today he'd be written into the story of that infamous battle. "I feel like we are riding out of the mural," he said.

"What's dat?" Jim asked.

"There's a painting on the wall in my house, and it looks a lot like the Griggs home."

"Yesa, Masser Aleks, on some days dis town looks pretty like a painting, but today the Yankees is gonna mess it up."

Aleks nodded his head but had nothing else to say. Of course Jim didn't understand that Aleks was speaking of the mural in his home. It depicted the morning of the Battle of West Point. J. W., Persia, Mrs. Griggs, and General Tyler—they were all in the painting. If there was a connection between his time travel and the mural, he had yet to discover it.

His hometown would have been unrecognizable if it hadn't been for his house. The yard looked nothing like it did in the present day. It was a working plantation with fields and fences. The absence of the one-hundred-year-old trees that lined the property allowed a clear view from the house to the fort and down to the river.

As they crossed through the downtown area toward the wagon bridge, the streets were in a state of panic. Men, old and young, some barely able to lift a musket because of war injuries and others too young to go to war until then, all headed uphill for the fight.

Aleks thought back to what his mom had said about the recruits at the fort. They were outnumbered about sixty Union for every Confederate, and the Union weapons were sixteen times better than the Confederate weapons.

Jim brought the carriage to a stop, and J. W. gave Aleks their marching orders from his mother. The boys were to gather their weapons and haversacks and leave the carriage before they crossed the river. The bridge over the Chattahoochee was filled, bumper-to-bumper, with every kind of vehicle. They were carrying military supplies and people's personal property.

They'd barely reached the top of the riverbank when Aleks heard Mrs. Griggs's voice.

"Is that your mama hollering for us?"

"Sounds like her. She's always telling me to do something," J. W. said. "Okay, Mama!" he hollered back.

Aleks pulled out his binocular scope and spotted Mrs. Griggs's carriage near the middle of the wagon bridge, rocking back and forth. Jim was holding tight to the horse's reins. "Something's wrong, J. W. Why didn't I think of it earlier!" Aleks said, referring to the silver chest that was on the carriage. "We've gotta go back!"

Aleks and J. W. heard Persia's shrill screams coming from the carriage. A wretched-looking man, not bigger than a buck-twenty, had pulled Persia from the carriage and held her with his left arm wrapped around her neck and his right hand holding a knife to her throat. Aleks could see other people who were near the bridge exiting their carriages, trying to help Persia, but the attacker was threatening to kill her and jump from the bridge with her if they didn't meet his demands. Mrs.

Griggs pleaded with him to take what he wanted and leave her daughter unharmed.

Aleks and J. W. had entered the wagon bridge and ducked down out of sight, closing in on the attacker. They walked along the right edge, out of his view.

Aleks heard Mrs. Griggs tell Jim to lift the box of silver from the back.

"Mrs. Griggs, if I leave go of dis horse, we's gonna be in the river. They's all upset by da screamin'."

"Do what I say, Jim," she said.

About that time, Aleks and J. W. came around the other side of the carriage, and Aleks motioned for J. W. to take the reins.

The attacker was distracted when Jim walked toward him with the box, and then Aleks ambushed the attacker from behind and caught his leg in a hold that took him right off his feet. The thief dropped the box on the bridge next to the horses.

What happened next would have seemed impossible had Aleks not seen it with his own eyes. The horse looked like he purposely nudged the silver box into the river; the same silver box Aleks, Van, and his dad had recovered earlier that morning.

"And there it goes," Aleks said.

"Goes what?" asked the attacker.

"The box of silver," he said, as he grabbed the man by his neck and shoulder.

"You's best be gettin' that box, boy."

"No, sir, I'll get it later," he said.

"What are you doing to me, son?"

"I've got you in a half nelson. The more important question is can you swim?"

"I reckon so. My daddy threw me in before I could walk."

"When you come out of the river and walk out on the bank," Aleks said, pointing to the side opposite downtown West Point, "I want you to walk toward Atlanta and I want you to thank God with every step that you were given another chance," he said.

"You should shoots him on de spot," said a servant who was driving another carriage across the bridge.

"If I catch him bothering anyone again, I'll shoot him," Aleks said and then flipped the man over and dropped him into the swiftly moving water.

Jim took control of the horses and was ordered by Mrs. Griggs not to stop for anyone until they reached the Reed home.

Poor Persia was hysterical with fright and took deep breaths into her mama's handkerchief. "Don't fret, honey. Mama will shoot the next person who tries to rob us. I have Dr. Griggs's pistol by my side."

* * *

At last, J. W. and Aleks headed to the fort. Union soldiers were getting closer. Aleks showed J. W. the black smoke in the sky off to the southwest.

Union Colonel LaGrange was approaching West Point with orders to secure the bridges. The Union would need them as an alternate river crossing if their attempt at crossing in Columbus was unsuccessful.

"Can you believe we'll be shootin' guns and drawin' swords instead of going to church on Easter? The good Lord knows I've been dreamin' of this. Never thought I'd get a chance to shoot at a Yankee. I'm excited, and to be honest, I'm sorta scared too," J. W. said.

"Don't be scared. You won't die," Aleks said.

"How come you know that? Are you an angel or somethin'? Our preacher says sometimes there are angels who walk among us and that we should be nice to everyone in case we meet a stranger who's an angel. I don't think I believe that because it all sounds silly to me."

"I've heard that too," Aleks said and added, "I'm no angel, but there are some things I know for sure; stick close to me and my daddy and you'll be fine."

* * *

To Aleks, the fort looked much like the descriptions he'd read. Colonel LaGrange of the First Wisconsin Cavalry said it looked like "a remarkably strong earthwork, thirty-five square yards, surrounded by a ditch twelve feet wide and ten deep …" It was set high on a vantage point to the west of town that allowed views of every approach into the town of West Point. It was built to defend the Atlanta and West Point Railroad; the route went from Atlanta to the Gulf Coast.

Aleks and J. W. entered the fort with the other defenders as the hour of engagement grew near. Inside the fort, there was an air of excitement and rage. The war had finally arrived, and it was their time to fight the

Yankees in their own backyard. Just as Aleks had read from accounts of the battle, some were teenage boys who had served as home guards and had not seen the war while others were veterans, unfit to fight, who convalesced at the local hospital.

Additional Confederate forces included those who had entered West Point after facing defeat in Selma on April 2. This group consisted of fourteen artillerymen from the Pointe Coupee Battery of Louisiana and a few from a South Carolina battery and a Georgia battery. Also in the mix of the who's who of fort defenders were the owner of the local West Point hotel, his young son, and a publisher of a Tennessee newspaper.

Aleks spotted his dad and Van walking away from one of the cannons and toward the center of the fort.

"Dad! Dad!" Aleks hollered and jumped up and down, waving his hands, but Ivan couldn't hear him above the crowd of soldiers.

"They are headed to the magazine," J. W. said. "Wait till you see all the ammunition!"

The magazine was a large semisubterranean structure made of timber and dirt and looked like a large mound. Aleks and J. W. walked around from behind it. Ivan and Van were walking up to its front side. They all met up at the door of the magazine where they found Adam with Big Adam, handing out ammunition to soldiers.

"Hey!" Aleks said. "Are you ready?"

"I'm ready," J. W. said. "Ready to fight!"

Aleks was referring to them leaving for 2015 before the fight started. "Hey, J. W., are any of your friends up here in the fort?" Aleks asked. He was thinking J. W.'s friends would distract him so he didn't follow them out of the fort when they were leaving for 2015.

"There's Isham Stanley," J. W. said.

"General Tyler wants you and Isham to stay toward the back of the fort," Aleks said. "I'll come back there and join you after I speak with my dad."

* * *

Ivan patted Adam's shoulder. They stepped to the side of the magazine and the three of them—Ivan, Van, and Aleks—huddled around Adam.

"It's time for us to leave," Aleks said with a huge smile on his face.

“Yes, sir, Masser Ness, I can’t waits ta get home,” he said, glancing around to see if anyone was listening in on their conversation.

“We’ve gotta get you out of the fort! Your life is in danger,” Ivan said.

“I don’t mean to be disrespectful, but everybody here is in danger,” Adam said.

“If you die here today, we can’t travel back to the same point. The time window we’ve traveled through closes when it passes the 150-year mark. Aleks discovered that he could move forward on the time line but never backward; that’s why he couldn’t go back to the time when you were both in Gettysburg,” Ivan said.

“No, I can’t leave yet, not before we save Big Adam. We need to get him out of the fort and to safety. If he stays here, he’ll die,” Adam said.

“Didn’t you hear my dad?” Aleks said. “We are out of time! We have to leave now before the fighting starts.”

A cannon fired from the front of the fort.

“It’s too late!” Aleks said. “It’s already started!”

CHAPTER TWENTY-THREE

General Tyler Captured by Men in Blue

BACK IN THE twenty-first century, the Griggs House was preparing for a hundred guests. Ivan and Colleen were the hosts of the Fort Tyler Dinner in less than eight hours. Their guests had purchased tickets in advance, and the event was sold out. It was an annual event that served to raise funds for continued upkeep and restoration of the historic site known as Fort Tyler.

There was no chance she could cancel the event. She sat at the large secretary desk in the main hall, using her nervous energy to return phone calls. From the kitchen, she heard the sounds of clanking pots and dishes as the cooks prepared the best pork loin, angel biscuits and banana pudding—this side of Montgomery.

She had Martha and Catherine outside in the courtyard, preparing centerpieces of lanterns and magnolia leaves for each round dinner table on the brick patio.

Colleen's phone was ringing. She answered it in hopes it was news about her dog's shooter.

"Mrs. Ness?"

"Yes, this is she," she answered.

"This is Chief Laurent. We've brought in someone who fits the profile of your shooter. We'd like you to come down to the police department and see if you can identify him. He doesn't have any form of ID, and I have a feeling he's one of the fort reenactors gone bad, real bad. When we arrested him this morning, he was dressed in a Confederate uniform and said the date was April 16, 1865."

"Yes, Chief, I'm on my way," Colleen said and then ended the phone call and opened the sunroom door. She leaned out to speak to Catherine and Martha in the courtyard. "Hey, ladies, I'm headed to the police department. They have a shooting suspect in custody. I have a feeling this has something to do with your brother."

"We are going with you," Catherine said and jumped into the Land Rover with her mother, and Martha followed.

"Wow, usually my life is so boring. Not much happens in this little town! We don't even have a Starbucks," Catherine said.

* * *

The officer assisting with the investigation greeted them at the West Point Police Department. "Mrs. Ness, we'll need you and the girls to come through security."

"Beep, beep!" The metal detector sounded. Martha was taken to the side and searched.

"I don't have any weapons," Martha said.

"No problem, ma'am. This is only a routine safety measure. Do you have anything metal on you—jewelry, a belt, or change in your pocket?" he asked.

"Let's see here … Oh, I have this rock," she said with a smile.

The officer put the sensor near the rock, and it beeped repeatedly. "Well, that's it. It's the rock in your pocket. Here, you can have it back. I doubt you'll be hurtin' anyone with it. Unless you are into stoning," he said with a laugh. "But then you'd be a stoner and that's illegal too," he said and bent over laughing.

"Officer Bock! Please get ahold of yourself! These are ladies," the chief scolded.

"Pardon me, ladies. I didn't mean to offend you," Bock said.

"It's all right," Colleen said. "I'm use to Dr. Ness's jokes."

"Is that one of the rocks from the yard?" Catherine asked curiously.

"Yes, Aleks gave it to me a while back. I haven't worn this sweatshirt in a while. Didn't realize it was still in there," Martha said.

"Come this way, ladies," Officer Bock said. "You will be given a photo lineup. There will be six photos with the suspect placed randomly in the six pack," he explained. "Let me know when you are finished, and I will escort you to the chief's office."

"The girls may look at them too, but we are most interested in whether you recognize one," he said.

Colleen sat at the long rectangular table with the girls, and they passed the photos down the line. Colleen recognized the photo of General Tyler. It matched the one in her sunroom from 1865.

She handed General Tyler to Catherine, and Catherine gave her a look of surprise. She stood up from her chair. "Catherine, sit down, please," Colleen said, kicking her under the table.

"Is there someone you recognize?" Bock asked Catherine.

Looking at her mom and seeing a look of dissatisfaction, she said, "No, sir, I was wondering if I could use your bathroom."

"Yes, it's outside this door and to the left," he said.

Martha showed no reaction to any of the photos.

"Okay, I am ready to see the chief now," Colleen said. "This photo is familiar," she said, holding up General Tyler's photo. "I believe he is a reenactor. I don't recognize any of the others."

"I think your daughter is still in the restroom. Would you mind checking on her before we go into the chief's office?" he asked.

Colleen pushed through the bathroom door, and Martha followed.

Colleen placed her hand on her chest and gasped.

"Mrs. Ness, what's wrong? You look like you've seen a ghost," Martha said.

"That's General Tyler," Colleen said.

"Who?" Martha asked.

"The man in the photo is the spitting image of General Robert Tyler," Colleen said.

"The man the fort is named after?" Martha asked.

"Yes, I recognized him too—from the picture of him in our sunroom," Catherine said. "What are we going to do, Mama?"

"I can tell you what we are not going to do; we are not going to identify him as General Tyler. We have to go back out there now. Let me do all the talking," Colleen insisted.

They walked out, and she felt like the cat that'd swallowed the canary.

"Please come this way. Chief Laurent will speak with you now," Bock said.

"Mrs. Ness."

"Hi, Chief, you know my daughter, Catherine. This is our family friend, Martha. Martha is visiting from Boston where she is a graduate student at MIT."

"It's nice to meet you. I'm sorry you all had such a scare this morning. We found the man you identified on the empty lot next to your home. He was walking with the help of a crutch toward the back of the lot and appeared to be heading to the fort. He had a weapon, and it had been recently discharged. We are quite certain he is the one responsible for shooting your dog. Since it was an unusual set of circumstances, I had one of my men pick up the bullet and take it to the lab in Montgomery. We have not received the report yet but expect it by later this evening. I need to ask you a few questions for the record." The chief asked her if she recognized the man in the photo.

"Yes, I believe he is part of the reenactment group that comes from Columbus every year for the Fort Tyler anniversary," Colleen said.

"Do you have any idea what he was doing under your house?"

"No, sir, I do not, but it's normal for us to have reenactors walking through our yard or requesting tours of our home prior to the Fort Tyler Dinner. If he's the reenactor who always plays the general, I've never felt threatened by him or any of the reenactors for that matter," she said. "How old is he?" she asked.

"He says he's thirty-five and his name is General Robert Tyler of Tennessee. He says he is in good health with the exception of his war injury."

"What is that?" she asked.

"He lost his left leg in an 1863 Civil War battle in Chattanooga, and he gives the account in such detail that if it wasn't for my desk calendar, he'd have me convinced. Did you see him this morning before the shooting?"

"No, sir," she said with a nervous laugh.

"Listen to this; he says he saw you this morning and asked you to vacate your property so your family would not be harmed by the Yankees. He also said that he didn't mean to hurt no one this morning and that his intentions are to protect this town and the family of Dr. Griggs. Honestly, he sounds like he needs to be admitted to the frickin' crazy wing at the hospital. Please pardon my language, Mrs. Ness. We see stupid criminals every day, but this is the first time I've seen this kind of crazy.

"I have one more question for you, Mrs. Ness. If the ballistics show that your dog's gunshot wound was caused by the general's gun, are you planning to press charges?"

"No, sir, we do not plan on pressing charges," Colleen said. "Chief, have you considered taking him to the fort to have the other reenactors identify him?"

"Yes, we plan to take him there on our way to the hospital."

"Which hospital, Chief?" she asked.

"Randolph County, it's known to have the best crazy wing in the country," he said with a wink.

Colleen and the girls watched from the Land Rover as General Tyler, a tall, thin dark-haired man with a long mustache, was taken to the police car and put in the backseat. The absence of his left leg confirmed his identity for Colleen.

"Where are we headed now?" Catherine asked.

"We are following him to the fort. I want to keep track of him until your father and the boys return," she said.

"Mama, doesn't he die in the fort at noon?"

"He's not going to die today because there's no way he'll be in the 1865 fort at noon. What time is it?"

"It's already eleven o'clock," Martha said.

* * *

It was a short five-mile drive from the police department to the historical site. At the front of the fort was a small paved parking lot with a Civil War monument. A fence surrounded the area below the fort with a gate at its entrance. Next to the fort, there was an open field where several campsites were set up. The soldiers stationed there demonstrated the life of a Confederate soldier. Some men gathered around a pot of stew cooking over an open flame while others performed drills. Women in day dresses sat under a white tent and reenacted a tea, and in the distance, a lady at a spinning wheel demonstrated how it turned cotton into thread.

Colleen and the girls stayed in their car, parked across the parking lot from Chief Laurent, and watched General Tyler have an outburst in the backseat of the police car. "I don't know what is upsetting him more—being in a car or watching the Union reenactor talking to the Confederates," Colleen said.

Next, the chief opened his door and left the squad car, leaving Officer Bock with the general. The chief walked through the fort gate, up the paved pathway, and toward the top of the fort. They lost sight of him in the heavily wooded area along the winding path. About ten minutes passed before the chief returned to the car with some Confederate reenactors.

While the chief was in the fort, Colleen moved her car next to his vehicle.

"Mama, we look nosy," Catherine said.

"It's okay. We're not doing anything unlawful," Colleen said and rolled down her window to listen.

"Would you men please identify this gentleman for me?" the chief asked.

"Yes, sir, Chief," said David Wayne, the event organizer and a reenactor.

"Yep, he's our General Tyler," Wayne said and the others nodded in agreement. "Look, Chief, I don't know what this fella did to warrant the backseat of your car, but surely it's not bad enough to keep him from the hundred-and-fiftieth reenactment. The ladies put all this work into the candlelight tour, and we need this guy to make our event a success," Wayne said. "I guess you could say he's sorta like our star player. After all, Chief, where would Auburn be without its Cam Newton or Bo Jackson?"

David leaned his head into the squad car. "We were wondering when you planned on showin' up. What'd you do to end up in this mess?"

Colleen leaned her head out the window but still couldn't hear anything the general was saying so she decided to get out of her SUV.

"Mama, are you crazy?" Catherine asked.

Colleen shushed her and stood as a quiet bystander directly behind David Wayne and the Chief.

The general explained what had happened to him. "I do not understand this carriage or how it runs without horses. I can tell you that this morning while I surveyed the area for Yankees, I spoke with Mrs. Griggs and told her of our concern for her family and asked she and her family to vacate their house below the fort. I rode my horse around the house and was riding back up to the fort when a strong gust of wind pushed me from my horse. I hit my head on a rock, and when I woke up, I was under the white house. I was disoriented; I did not recognize my surroundings. I surveyed the area, looking for the enemy, and then a large dog the size of a small horse appeared out of nowhere. He startled me so that I dropped my gun, and it accidentally misfired. After my gun fired, I heard Mrs. Griggs call out a name over and over again. It was shortly thereafter, while leaving the area near the house, that these Yankees dressed in their new uniforms shackled my hands and took me to their prison."

"Look at him, Chief. He's the best Tyler reenactor we've ever had. He's the spitting image of Tyler and doesn't get out of character. If I didn't know better, I'd think he was Tyler. He is not a threat to anyone, and you know better than to think any of us are a threat. My wife says we are just a bunch of boys playin' Johnnies and Yanks with blanks," David said with a chuckle.

"All right, David, we've been friends since childhood, I'm going to grant you this request. I will post Officer Bock at the front of the fort. General Robert Tyler is not to go anywhere except with you until we get the ballistics back from Montgomery and gather more information on him," Chief Laurent said.

Colleen stood next to David. "Mrs. Ness, are you okay with this agreement?"

"Yes, Chief," she said.

General Tyler stepped out of the car with the help of David and Colleen. David gave Colleen a funny look when he saw the general appeared not to have his left leg. "I don't remember you missing a leg," David said under his breath but in earshot of Colleen.

The police car headed out of the fort parking lot, and General Tyler looked around and then made his way into the fort. David followed him.

"Girls, you stay in the car. I'm going to speak with General Tyler," Colleen said.

"Mrs. Ness, this could be dangerous," Martha said.

"No, all accounts of the general report that he is a complete gentleman. I'll be fine," she said.

"Excuse me! Excuse me, General Tyler?"

He stopped on the cement pathway and turned slowly toward Colleen.

"Yes, ma'am?"

"General Tyler, I am Mrs. Ness. I live in the house below the fort, and I was wondering if you would come have a cup of tea or coffee with me. I know it has been a long day already and you are confused and tired. I would like to speak with you in private. I have news about the war."

"Pardon me, ma'am, but this has been a strange morning indeed. I am under orders to defend this city from Wilson's troops. I am proceeding up this hill and plan to take a look with my field glass. If my troops are successful in defending your home, I would be delighted to have tea in your company. I fear, however, that your home will be somewhat uninhabitable after the cannons bear down upon it. Earlier today, the United States Army took over the property and they are operating their weapons from it. I am sorry, ma'am, but we have no choice but to fire back."

"General, does the fort look different to you?" Colleen asked.

"Yes, ma'am! It seems my mind is playing terrible tricks on me." He drew his sword and said, "I cannot allow you to follow me into battle."

"But, General Tyler, would you please take a minute and look around. You can't tell me it looks the same as this morning. Look at the trees and the walkway; notice the back of my house and the flag in the fort. General Tyler, the flag in the fort is the American flag, and if you look carefully, you'll see it has more stars than before the war. I beg you, take a look at it. General Tyler, please come with me to my home so I can help you."

A group of Confederate reenactors greeted him and said, "General Tyler, we are ready to shoot the thirty-two-pounder. The Yankees are approaching from the west, and there are snipers targeting our men from the house below the fort. Can we have your orders to direct our cannon on the stone house?"

It was then General Tyler took out his field glass, raised it to his eye for a better view, and stepped into what was supposed to be his final moments. A small plane flew over startling the general. He lost his balance and fell to the ground. Colleen was not far behind him and offered him her hand.

"It's not safe in the fort for you," he said.

"General Tyler, what did you see in your field glass? Did you see any Yankees at my house, or did you see more horseless carriages and a yard that looked unfamiliar? Please come with me, and let's have some tea or coffee."

The general walked to the reenactor nearest him and said he needed to borrow his horse. The young man told him he was welcome to ride it as long as he had it back to him in a couple of hours. He had the horse there as part of the day's festivities.

Tyler tied his crutches on the horse and mounted. "Wow! You are in great shape compared to these other reenactors," David said. "Where are you headed?"

"I am taking the lady to safety," General Tyler said.

"I can't allow you to leave the fort; it's the chief's orders," David said.

"It's fine, David," Colleen assured him. "I'll let Officer Bock know on our way out. He can follow us to my house. I've invited the general to my house for coffee, and I'll return him to you in time for the candlelight tour."

Colleen offered her hand to the general, and he lifted her up onto the horse.

"My name is Colleen Ness," she told him.

He rode down the hill and past Officer Bock, who was guarding the gate but didn't notice the general and Colleen leaving because he was busy watching the young ladies practice the Virginia reel. As they rode past the Land Rover, Colleen motioned for Martha and Catherine to follow them.

Robert Merrill's Sketch of the Battle of West Point

Union soldier Robert Merrill, of the First Wisconsin Cavalry that took the Fort, sketched a drawing of what he witnessed at the Battle of West Point. After the war, he carried the drawing back to his home in Wisconsin where it stayed with his family for generations.

In 2011, the Merrill sketch returned to West Point and was donated to Rea Clark and the Fort Tyler Association by the Artist's great granddaughter, Merrilyn Shaw. Robert Merrill became an accomplished artist later in life.

CHAPTER TWENTY-FOUR

Operation Fort Tyler

THERE WAS AN air of confusion in the fort. General Tyler's absence had left the men without direction. Captain Celestino Gonzales, second in command, took over in Tyler's absence but received a shot to the abdomen from a sharpshooter early in the fight.

Ivan took the captain to the center of the fort behind the bombproof where Dr. Alexander Reese had set up a hospital.

Aleks and Van stayed near Adam and helped with the ammunitions.

With Tyler MIA and Gonzales seriously wounded, Colonel James H. Fannin was the next in command. Aleks recognized him from a photograph as well. He approached the time travelers and asked, "You boys seen General Tyler?"

"No, sir," said Aleks. "He went down early this morning to check on Mrs. Griggs. Now, that house is infested with Yanks and ain't nobody gettin' in or outta there without a fight, sir."

* * *

Union sharpshooters had positioned themselves on the rooftops in the nearby stables and in the Griggs's house and backyard.

The 1,200 cavalry of the First Wisconsin were riding in from the south and heading up the hill on all sides.

Colonel Fannin ordered the cannonade and firing of the muskets.

"Do you hear them singin' that terrible song?" J. W. shouted to Aleks. He had checked back in with Aleks near the ammunition. "My daddy said they'd sing that song."

"Glory, glory, hallelujah! Glory, glory, hallelujah!" The Yankee army hit the chorus as they rode and marched onto the plantation and up the hill.

"That's the 'Battle Hymn of the Republic,'" Aleks said excitedly.

"Can we help with ammunition?" J. W. asked.

"Sure. Who's your friend?" Aleks asked.

"This is Isham Stanley," J. W. said.

"Happy birthday!" Aleks announced.

"Thank you. How did you know it was my birthday?" Isham asked.

"J. W. mentioned it," Aleks said. He knew J. W. had not mentioned it; instead, it was something he'd read in one of the history books about the battle.

"Today is my seventeenth birthday, and I'm sure going to enjoy shooting at those Yankees, though I am not a bit mad at them," Isham said.

"I'm Aleks, and this is my cousin Van," Aleks said.

"Nice to meet ya. Is someone making ham and eggs over there?" Isham asked.

"I don't believe so," Van said.

"Well, they are making me hungry. I keep hearing them say, 'Ham and eggs! Ham and eggs!' I'd like some ham and eggs," said Isham.

"They ain't makin' no ham and eggs, boy!" shouted another Reb.

"Well, what are they makin'?" he asked.

"Boy, they is makin' hand grenades," the Reb said.

"Oh, I'm not ripe on technical terms for some munitions of war," Isham replied.

Aleks explained to Isham that the soldiers were making hand grenades. The fuse on the grenade had to be cut the right length so when it was lit and thrown over the parapet, it would explode by the time it struck the ground. It required good judgment in cutting the fuses, for if cut too long, the Yankees could throw them back into the fort where they would explode among the Confederates.

* * *

"Aleks, I'm going to check on Big Adam," Adam said. "He's been injured. See, he's over there by the fort doctor."

Aleks and Van stayed close behind Adam as he went to his ancestor's side.

Big Adam told the boys how he'd been toward the back, helping carry water when he saw a sharpshooter aiming for one of the men in the fort. Big Adam said he rushed to push the soldier out of the way. He saved the soldier's life but landed on a railroad spike that was sticking straight up from the ground. The spike went through his heel.

Blood was spurting from his leg like a broken water main. Dr. Reese said he'd take his leg off right after the fighting ended.

Dr. Reese told him to pray. He pulled out the spike and wrapped Big Adam's leg and foot with a dirty shirt from a dead Yankee, gave him a jigger of whiskey, and left Big Adam's side to tend to the next injury.

Adam saw an expression of hopelessness on his ancestor's face and sat down next to him. He leaned toward Big Adam and said, "It'll be all right. I know a doctor who can fix your leg."

"Ain't no use. You hears de doctor; he's gots to take it," Big Adam said.

"Here comes the other doctor," Adam said as he pointed to Aleks and Van bringing Ivan over from the opposite side of the bombproof.

He explained to Ivan that Big Adam had a puncture wound from a railroad spike and the fort doctor planned to amputate it.

"First things first," Ivan said as he took an injectable from his bag and gave Big Adam what felt like a bee sting in his arm, and then another shot followed.

"What kinds of a doc is you?" he asked.

"I'm the good kind that's gonna keep you alive without taking off your leg," Ivan said with a laugh. He worked quickly, washing the wound out with antiseptic, and then suturing the incision. "Listen, don't you let anyone take your leg," he said and added, "because it's gonna heal and be just like new."

"But, Doc, he ain't gonna listen ta me. He'll cuts my leg clean off if you don't talks ta him 'bout it," he pleaded.

"I'll take care of it. Don't you worry!" Ivan insisted.

Adam pointed out the doctor who was now caring for other wounded. Ivan reminded Adam that it was time for him to take cover near the powder magazine. It was nearing the end of the battle, and their main concern now was to keep Adam uninjured. "Go over by the magazine and stay put," Ivan instructed. "We'll get you on our way out of the fort."

* * *

Ivan went to speak with the fort doctor. "Hope you don't mind, Doc, but while you've been tending to these men, I took care of Big Adam, Mrs. Griggs's field hand. He's fine and won't need anything else," Ivan said.

"Did you amputate his leg?" he asked.

"No, but I cleaned the wound with whisky and bandaged it up. I would leave it alone and let it heal. Honestly, you don't have time to care for the slaves when you have captains and soldiers to tend to; let me do that."

"What's your name?" he asked.

"I'm Dr. Ness."

"Nice to meet you, Doc. I'm Dr. Reese."

Ivan cared for many wounded that day, even a few of the artillerymen from the Pointe Coupe Battery of Louisiana. As the Civil War doc administered last rites, Ivan came along behind him with antibiotics and ointments for their wounds. The two doctors worked into the evening.

"I've never seen or heard of anything like this before; I have no deaths to report," Dr. Reese said. "Captain Gonzales seems in stable condition. We'll want to move him to the Griggs house, along with the other wounded as soon as the fighting ceases."

Sometime around six in the evening, the Yankees breached the fort by climbing in on ladders and the Confederates on the hill surrendered.

"Hey, Dad." Aleks tapped his father on the shoulder.

Ivan was administering care to another injured soldier.

"It's time. We have to leave *now*."

"Let's go!" Ivan said.

Aleks grabbed Adam and headed out of the fort behind Van.

"Where are you going?" J. W. asked.

No one stopped to respond, and they didn't stop until they came to the rocks near the back of the Griggs home, on the edge of the fort. J. W. ran after them and stopped only for a moment to pick up some shiny rocks.

"Your mother will be thrilled. We have Adam, and we'll be home in time for the Fort Tyler dinner," Ivan said.

"Speaking of Tyler, did anyone see him?" Van asked.

They stepped into the area by the outcropping of rocks where the present-day tree house stood and held on to each other. Aleks had the railroad watch and compass in his hands. No one in the fort had noticed the time travelers' exit because the soldiers' attention was on capturing the flag.

Aleks pointed the compass to the rock and Adam recited, "Jumpin' the rails down the track; all wheels turn, click-clack, click-clack." They heard the roar of the train, and they were gone.

CHAPTER TWENTY-FIVE

Jumpin' the Rails to 2015

IT WAS AS Adam remembered it: the blinding light, the blaring sound, and then a free fall where he lost his stomach. The landing was always a mystery until it happened, and this time, it was slap dab in a carload of cotton.

"What are the chances of this?" Adam yelled. He pushed his way through several bales and came up with it stuck in his hair.

"Well, at least you didn't have to pick this cotton by hand," Aleks said sarcastically.

"Thank God things have improved in the last 150 years," Adam said.

Ivan jumped into a tae kwon do stance.

"What's wrong with Uncle Ivan?" Van asked.

"We're not alone," Ivan said.

"Aliens?" Van asked, laughing.

"Ancient aliens?" Aleks added with a laugh.

"Guys, he's serious," Adam said, pointing to a bale of cotton moving at the top of the stack.

"Hey! It's me," J. W. said, spitting cotton from his mouth. "Where are we?"

"Are you kidding me?" Aleks said.

"What do you mean by that?" J. W. asked.

"We'll tell you later," Aleks said.

Adam and Aleks pulled open the door and determined they were about a mile from downtown West Point. "When the train slows down to change tracks, we'll have about two minutes to jump," Aleks advised.

"Why should we jump when the train stops in West Point?" J. W. asked.

"It no longer stops in West Point. We have to jump," Ivan insisted.

The train's whistle blew as it neared the trestle and began to slow down. They watched from the door as it passed over the Chattahoochee River. Aleks told them to jump as soon as it cleared the bridge. Aleks jumped off and rolled a couple of times down the embankment. Next Van jumped and then Adam came after him, but Ivan waited until J. W. was out before he jumped from the train.

"Where are y'all going? I can't jump in my hoopskirt! Mama will have Mammy switch me worse than a runaway if I go show my pantalets to a bunch of menfolk," she said. It was Persia; she'd entered the time window too. "I declare you men are absolutely too rough."

"What's she doing here, Dad?" Aleks asked.

"Did you say the rocks have something special about them? Allowing time travel?" Van asked.

"Yes," Aleks said.

"I gave her some rocks when we were at breakfast. She thought they were pretty, and I had extra."

"She must have gotten close enough to us when we jumped that she came through," Aleks said.

"Hold on, Persia! I'm coming," Aleks hollered as he ran after the train, caught the handle on the side of the door, and pulled himself back on. He held on to the outside door and rode into downtown West Point, all the while having no luck persuading Persia to jump off with him.

They looked like a planned reenactment event for the group that had gathered for a historical tour outside the restored West Point Train Depot.

"Looks like chivalry in action," one man said. "Just look at her period day dress."

"Why, isn't she beautiful? A real Southern belle being saved by her soldier," said another.

"What is she yelling? She's almost made me believe she's in distress," the tour guide said. "I don't believe this was on my itinerary for the tour. Let's see here: train depot tour, fort reenactment, Fort Tyler dinner, and candlelight tour. I don't see a train demonstration. A nice treat, nonetheless."

Aleks and Persia passed by city hall and the police station.

Aleks saw the police chief, Aaron Laurent, waving at the train engineer. Someone must have radioed the train engineer because the train slowed to a stop.

Aleks sent a text message to his parents letting them know to come ASAP.

"Aleks Ness, what in the world is going on here? I'm sure you have a good explanation for us. Is this part of the reenactment events for today's Fort Tyler Celebration? I sure wish y'all would tell me this stuff ahead of time," the chief scolded.

The police chief paused long enough to take a sip of his coffee and shake his head.

"Yes, sir, it was a silly idea. I thought it was cleared by the railroad company and the train had scheduled a stop in West Point, just like it used to back during the war. I'm so sorry for causing all this trouble."

The train engineer hollered and waved his hands in disgust from the platform.

"What's he sayin'?" asked the chief. "He sounds like a damn Yankee. Please excuse my language, miss. I can't understand a word those Northerners say. Hard to believe we are speakin' the same language sometimes, ain't it?" he said with a chuckle and motioned for one of the deputies to take the report from the train engineer.

The ambulance blared and flashed its lights, making a full-fledged emergency entrance into the depot parking lot.

"What's the matter, darlin'?" the chief asked.

Persia looked like a frightened animal in the middle of a busy street. She ran the opposite direction of the EMS, and Aleks caught her before she ran into the street. Persia placed her hands over her ears, closed her eyes, and sobbed, "I want my mother."

Aleks had his arm around her. "This is my cousin, Persia Griggs. She and her brother are in town for the reenactment. Persia is shaken up from our train ride. It's my fault. I'm so sorry that it frightened you, Persia."

The medics attended to Persia in the back of the ambulance. She screamed when they tried to take her from Aleks.

"I'm not leaving you," he said and sat with his arm around her while they checked her vitals. She thought the blood pressure cuff was trying to harm her when the EMTs pumped it full of air and it squeezed her arm. They needed Aleks to hold her while they removed it.

"She's okay," Aleks told the men. "Listen, my parents are on their way and my dad can check her vitals later," Aleks said. "Here comes my father now," Aleks said, pointing to his parents SUV.

Colleen and Ivan drove into the depot parking lot. Aleks walked Persia around to the back door of the Land Rover. She refused to get in the car.

"I've never seen anything that could go without horses," Persia said to Aleks. "This doesn't look safe."

Ivan left the SUV to speak with the chief of police. "Chief Laurent, I'm terribly sorry. We thought we had clearance for this railroad reenactment. You know, my wife here gets me into these things, and most of the time, I don't know about it till she's telling me what to wear and where to stand."

"We can't apologize enough, Chief," Colleen said from the car. "This is obviously a misunderstanding. I hope you plan to attend the 150th Anniversary dinner tonight," she said with a smile that caused the chief to forget the incident.

"I would love to attend, but you know that I can't afford no fancy Fort Tyler dinner on what the City of West Point pays me."

"I know the city can't afford to pay you what you're worth. Colleen and I want you to come as our guest. We'll see you at 7:30 p.m. Oh, and bring that pretty new girlfriend of yours," Ivan said with all the charm he could muster and then motioned for Aleks and Persia to get in the car.

"I'll be there. Thank you for your generous invitation," the chief said.

"About this incident, Ivan, he's a good kid," the chief said, slapping his hand down on the frame of the car window. "I ain't never had no trouble out of him, but he better never—and I mean *never*—let anything like this happen again. Trains ain't nothin' to mess 'round with. Hopefully we got all this quieted down before our local newspaper catches wind of it. With his friend's disappearance, this would put Aleks in a bad light."

"Thanks, Chief!" Ivan and Aleks both hollered.

"This young lady is Persia Griggs?" Colleen asked.

"Yes, Mama, she came back with us and so did her brother, J. W.," Aleks said.

"Yes, Persia, I've met your brother. He is at our house. The boys are sitting out on the front patio waiting for you all to arrive."

They pulled down West Point's main street, took a left by Point University and the bank, and drove up Eighteenth Street.

"Where is my brother?" Persia asked.

"He is at our house with Adam and Van," Ivan said. "We will be there in a minute."

Persia had a calmer disposition with the thought of seeing her brother. Her crying turned to a sniffle.

"Are you my aunt?" Persia asked.

"Yes, I am your aunt Colleen," she said.

"Then, Dr. Ness, you are my uncle?" she asked.

"That's right; this is your uncle Ivan," Aleks said. "I told Persia that we are cousins."

"Why don't you have on your dress and hoop?" Persia asked. "You are wearing pants like men wear."

"I'll be wearing one tonight for the dinner," Colleen said.

"How does your carriage run without horses?" Persia asked.

"The horses are under the hood of the car," Ivan said.

"Dad, she doesn't understand," Aleks said, seeing the confused look on her face.

"Persia why aren't you at the Reed's home in West Point with your mother?" Aleks asked.

She told them how she'd ridden back to the house with Jim, who'd been sent to help carry wounded from the fort to the house.

"I'm surprised you came back to the house so quickly after the cease-fire," he said.

"Mama doesn't know I went with him. I wanted to go home, and my mama told me I had to wait so I snuck in the carriage before Jim left for the fort."

Ivan whispered to Colleen, "Apparently, teenage girls are an age-old problem."

"Oh hush," she said.

"Jim found me when we arrived at the house, and he threatened to tell my mama to give me a good switchin' if I didn't stay put in the carriage." She went on to tell them that she waited as long as she could and suffered such a terrible fright from all the Yankees that she decided it would be safer to find Dr. Ness and the others. That was when she walked up to the fort and saw them near the bottom of the fort by the big rocks. "I wondered what you were doing and was about to ask when the wind kicked up so, and then I don't remember a thing until I woke up in the cotton bales on the train … This looks similar to my home, but where are the fields and who put this black fence around my house?" she asked.

Aleks opened the door when they drove into the driveway. "We'll get out here and walk up with the rest," Aleks said.

Van, Adam, and J. W. met the car in the driveway by the front gate. Aleks hopped out and coaxed Persia out of the car. It took some doing to maneuver the hoopskirt through the backseat and out the door, but it finally popped out behind her.

"J. W.!" Persia sobbed. "Are you okay?" she asked.

"I'm fine. We traveled into the future. Van and Adam explained it to me," J. W. said.

As the gate opened, J. W. spotted the plaque on the column. "Look it here, Persia; it says that it is our house. It even has our names on it." J. W. read it out loud. "The Griggs Home 1858, placed on the Register of Alabama Historical Places in 1976, Home of Dr. and Mrs. Ivan Ness."

CHAPTER TWENTY-SIX

The Griggs Home 2015

THEY STEPPED ONTO the front patio and opened the downstairs door.

"Come this way." Aleks motioned to them.

"No, sir, this is the servants' entrance," J. W. said. "I am not going in the servants' quarters. Where is the front staircase?" he asked and then turned and went back outside.

Van opened the old heart-pine doors, giving Persia her first glimpse of the crystal chandelier, mahogany paneling, and marble floors.

Martha ran downstairs and greeted them. She and Catherine were dressed for dinner in silk ball gowns and hoopskirts. The familiar attire calmed Persia.

"You made it, and I can't wait to hear all about it," Martha said and grinned at Aleks.

"Martha, these are my cousins, Persia and J. W."

"The ones in the mural?" she asked, unable to catch herself before the words slipped out. "She looks traumatized." She spoke to Persia. "Here, have a seat here." She took Persia by the hand and guided her to the settee in the foyer.

"Where's my brother?" Persia asked.

Aleks spun around and went outside to grab him but didn't see him. "J. W.? J. W.?"

He ran first to the side of the house by the neighbors' and then to other side by the empty lot. He was nowhere. He ran to the backyard and looked behind the tree house and into the garage. "J. W.? J. W.?" he called.

Aleks left the garage and went through the sunroom door at the back of the house. "J. W.? J. W.?"

Adam came up the stairs from the first floor and entered the main hallway.

"Have you seen J. W.?" Aleks asked.

"No, he didn't come in the downstairs with us," Adam said. "Aleks, is my mother here?" he asked.

"Have you checked the kitchen?"

The boys headed toward the kitchen and ran into Catherine in the dining room. "You stink, Aleks," she announced as she gave him a big hug.

"I've had this wool jacket on in 80 degrees and I need a shower. I wouldn't be hugging me," he said with a laugh.

"Oh my gosh, Adam, its you!" she said giving him a big hug.

He nodded his head emphatically.

"Do your parents know?" she asked.

"We are looking for Mrs. Mary," Aleks said. "Is she in there?" he said, pointing to the swinging door between the kitchen and the dining room.

The door swung open, and out of the kitchen and into the dining room stepped the housekeeper and cook, a young Thai lady wearing a grease-spattered apron. She untied the apron with one pull and laid it on the chair next to the door.

"Is it true, Catherine? Is this the boy you were saying was lost for two years?" she asked.

Adam stood with a confused look on his face, and Aleks was speechless as well.

"Um, Cat, where's Aunt Mary, and who is this lady?"

"What do you mean? You know Miss Kamie," Catherine said.

""I'm sure Mr. Aleks remembers me," she said with a sweet smile and slight bow of her head.

"No, Cat, I don't know her; I've never seen her before."

"Stop it, Aleks. This is supposed to be a good day, and this is no time for your teasing. Grrr," Catherine growled.

"Welcome home, buddy! We missed you! Whew, you and Aleks both smell funky. You better get home and take a shower too," Catherine said.

Aleks watched Miss Kamie as she introduced herself to Adam as if they had never met. That seemed likely to him since Adam had been gone for two years, whereas he had only been gone for a day. "You tired and confused, Mr. Aleks. You sit down at the table. I get you glass of water. I heard you brought home a guest with you from college. Her name is Martha?"

How could she possibly know Martha? he wondered.

Miss Kamie was speaking, but Aleks was no longer listening; his mind was contemplating the theories about time travel. *I have to talk to my Dad,* he thought. *I wonder if he's noticing the changes too. He has to be, and what about Van? And no one else notices that anything has changed? What about Catherine? What does she remember, and when did it change?* It was too complex a problem to solve right now. The fundraiser was about to start, and he was filthy. He looked at Miss Kamie, fussing over him and speaking to him as if she'd known him for years.

"Okay, thank you, Miss Kamie, for the water. I'm feeling much better now."

"Your memory better now, and you remember me?" she asked with a bow.

"Yes, ma'am, I was only teasing Catherine."

"I know you like to do that, Mr. Aleks."

"Oh, yes, ma'am."

Aleks headed to his room to clean up before the party. He'd told Adam he could use his bathroom to clean up as well.

* * *

Adam was also in shock because the lady in the kitchen was not his mother. What had he done? By saving Big Adam, had he done something terrible to his mother?

"Catherine, where can I find my parents?" Adam asked.

"Your mama is at the bank, and your father is in Montgomery."

"You are talking about my mother, Mary Griggs. She's at the bank?"

"Yes, she's always worked there," Catherine said.

"Thanks, Cat!" Adam left the kitchen and went down the hall behind Aleks, but instead of following Aleks to his room, he took the stairs and went out the downstairs doors.

* * *

The doors slammed shut, and Aleks turned to see that Adam was no longer following him down the hall. "He didn't leave the house, did he?" Aleks said out loud.

"Adam?" Catherine asked.

"Yes, Adam," Aleks said.

"Yes, I think he's going to the bank to see his mom."

Aleks opened the large door at the front of the house and stepped out onto the balcony. He saw the back of Adam. He was walking down the sidewalk in the direction of the bank. "Adam, what are you doing?" Aleks asked.

Adam turned around and told him he was going to see his mom.

"Come back, and we'll call her to come here," Aleks said.

"It's only a block away. I'll be back," he said.

* * *

He entered the bank lobby, and one of the tellers screamed his name. A lady from one of the offices with a window came over, hugged his neck, and told him how happy she was that he was back. Then a customer walked by him and said, "I can't believe this isn't all over the papers—your return and all. Maybe the police will finally have enough evidence to put that Ness boy away."

He heard his mother's voice from down the hallway. *Is she a janitor?* he wondered, as he glanced up and saw her coming out of the ladies' restroom. He was frozen.

She ran toward him and threw her arms around him. "My baby! My baby!" she cried. She held his face in her hands.

Adam was so shocked by the changes he was lacking emotion; his face showed nothing, although he was so thankful to be home.

"Is this any way to greet your mama?" she asked. "Come up to my office so we can talk in private and call your father. Does he know you are home?"

He followed behind her, up the grand staircase and through the double doors at the end of the hall. She pushed them open. The name on the desk read "Mary Griggs."

"First things first, Adam, we need to let the police know and have our attorney submit your testimony into evidence. Was Aleks responsible for your disappearance?"

"Absolutely not, Mama! He had nothing to do with it. Mama, he had a good reason for not saying anything. If he hadn't done that, I may have never made it home."

"This doesn't make any sense to me, but I trust that you have a good explanation for your disappearance."

Her phone on the desk rang in on her private line.

"Let me take this," she said. "Yes? … Oh hello, Colleen. Adam is sitting here with me now. Thank you for checking on him," she said.

After she hung up, she said, "You can't leave without telling someone where you are going. Mrs. Ness was worried something had happened to you. She said she was getting ready to call me to come to their house, and when she looked for you, you were gone and Catherine told her that you had come down to the bank."

"I'm not going anywhere, Mom," Adam said.

"Did anyone hurt you?" Mary asked. "Did you get kidnapped and forced to work the fields?"

"Why do you ask that?" he asked.

"Have you looked at yourself? You are dressed like a field hand and have cotton in your hair."

He turned and caught a glimpse of himself in the large mirror on the wall opposite his mother's desk. She was right.

"Let's call your father, and after you have time to clean up, we'll take care of the other details."

Adam's father was on his way home from Montgomery, and she reached him in the car. She told him of the wonderful news and decided they'd meet at home.

He couldn't stop staring at his mother as they walked out of the bank together. Her hair was smooth and neat, she was dressed like the boss, and her car was different from the vehicle she had driven two years earlier. "From a Toyota to a BMW, wow, Mama, I like your car," he said.

"Come on now, Adam. I've not had a Toyota since that Corolla I had when you were five," she said with a laugh. "This car is almost two years old."

Adam just smiled and thought to himself that this day would make a good episode for *The Twilight Zone*. "We have plans to attend the Fort Tyler dinner tonight, but we'll cancel. I know that Colleen will understand."

What is she doing? he thought. *Why are we driving up next door to the Ness home?*

"Get out of the car, honey. We are home."

The name on the mailbox said Griggs and the license plate on his mother's BMW said "MaryG." The house and yard were immaculate.

Adam stopped outside the front door to read the historic plaque. It was the Adam Griggs House c. 1876. "What's this?" Adam asked.

"You mean to tell me that after living here your entire life, you've finally noticed the historic plaque?" his mother scolded.

"I guess I've been gone so long that everything looks new to me," he said. "Tell me about Adam Griggs, the one on this plaque."

Adam learned later that his family history had changed for the better because Big Adam was saved from his fate at the Battle of Fort Tyler. Big Adam's loyalty and hard work had served him well. His family stayed with Dr. and Mrs. Griggs after the war. They chose to stay and work the land as sharecroppers. It kept them from enduring added hardships of other newly freed slaves. Some former slaves moved to areas outside of town and built shantytowns where poverty and disease thrived.

Dr. Griggs wrote a contract allowing Big Adam and his descendants to earn two acres of the Griggs plantation by farming it for ten years. Big Adam was a proud man the day the contract was completed and the two acres had his name on the deed; a celebration ensued, ground was broken, and the first bricks were laid soon after for the Adam Griggs Home.

* * *

The decor inside the house looks as nice as that in Aleks's home, he thought.

"Hey, Mama, do you mind if I take a shower while we wait for Daddy?" he asked.

"Of course you can. You don't need to ask. Do you remember where your room is?" she asked with a laugh. "Up the stairs, first room on your left, and you'll find that nothing has changed."

His shower and room looked like they belonged in a fancy hotel. There were framed photos on the dresser of Adam with his parents and one with him and his father. "Why does my dad have on a robe?" he said out loud to himself.

Next to that photo, there was a letter and a note from his father. The note read, "Dearest Adam, my dreams do not have to be your dreams, but I hope you will become a Harvard man if that is truly your heart's desire. All my love, Dad."

It was written on Alabama Supreme Court letterhead, and his father's name was listed under the title of "Chief Justice." The letter was addressed to him, and the return address was Harvard Admissions Office. He held it in his hand and flipped it back and forth several times, looking at the address.

"Welcome home, Son!"

Adam recognized his father's voice. Adam and his dad embraced, and his father cried. This was rare; his father seldom showed this kind of emotion.

Adam stood there looking at his father, who was dressed like a businessman and spoke like an educated gentleman. He couldn't take his eyes off of him.

"What is it, Adam? You look like you are seeing me for the first time. I haven't aged that much, have I?" he asked with a laugh. "Although this term of court we have a capital case."

"No, Dad, it's just that I'm so happy to see you," Adam said.

"We'll get caught up after you clean up. I'll be downstairs."

* * *

Adam could hear his parents talking as he came down the staircase. They were sitting in the next room. He could see the lights on from the entryway. He stood there a moment and listened.

"We have to contact the police immediately. I know you would like to put this off, but it has to be done," Judge Griggs said.

"Can't we just enjoy the evening with our family together for the first time in two years?" Mary asked.

"Has he said anything to you about where he was or why he didn't contact us?" Judge Griggs asked.

"No, nothing except that Aleks was not at fault," she said.

"I think we need Aleks to come over here so we can speak with the boys together before the police question them," Judge Griggs said.

Adam walked into the formal living room and stood in front of his parents, who were sitting in the wingback chairs in front of a marble fireplace.

"We would like for Aleks to come over so we can speak with you both," Judge Griggs said.

"They have a dinner tonight," Adam said.

"Honestly, Adam, I don't care about the dinner. I care about my son and how I have no idea where he's been for two years and the last person who saw him just found him. We need some answers, and we need them now. You could both be facing charges," he said.

"He'll be happy to talk to you too, but promise me that you won't call the police chief until we've had a chance to tell you our story. I'll run over and get him," Adam said and ran out the front door.

"Adam, wait! Adam!" his mother yelled.

* * *

She watched him walk next door and enter the Nesses' sunroom. She'd stay at her window and watch until she saw him come back home.

Judge Griggs stood up from his chair and paced back and forth.

"I'm going over there," he said. "We are going to get to the end of this right now, party or no party! I'm sorry, Mary; it has to be tonight!"

The door slammed behind him, and she watched her husband march down the steps that joined their lots and through the brick patio where the tables were set up for the party. People from the community who'd arrived and taken their seats were thrilled to see the chief justice and stopped him for a handshake and a hello on his way to the door.

CHAPTER TWENTY-SEVEN

Modern-day Changes

ALEKS ENTERED HIS bedroom and pulled clean clothes from his dresser to wear for the fundraiser. He was exhausted from the day but planned to stay at the dinner for a couple of hours. He lied down across his bed, closed his eyes, and fell asleep.

* * *

Meanwhile, Catherine, Persia, and Martha were in Catherine's bedroom having tea and cookies. Martha suggested it to settle Persia down, but she refused to have any. Catherine and Martha were the ones eating; Persia was still too upset.

"Mama is going to think the Yankees have kidnapped us," Persia said and continued sobbing into her handkerchief.

"I know you are frightened and confused. Here, let me show you a picture in the hallway that will make you feel better."

Catherine took Persia's hand and led her down the hallway toward the mural, and Martha followed behind them.

Persia recognized herself and J. W. in the painting. "Catherine, that's how my house looked this morning," she said with curious eyes and a broad smile. "That's it! How do I get there?" she asked.

"My brother will take you back once we find J. W."

Persia lingered at the mural. She ran her hands across the painting of her home from 1865, her mother, and J. W. "Oh my, and there's General Tyler," she said.

Persia was feeling somewhat better; Catherine and Martha walked her back to the bedroom to prepare for the event. The girls fixed their hair and then helped Persia with hers. Catherine used the curling iron for Persia's sausage curls.

"Ouch! That's hot! Did you have that pole in the fireplace?" Persia asked.

"No, silly, it's plugged into an outlet."

Persia examined her curls and the curling iron. None of it made any sense, but it sure was nice and much quicker than making curls with rags tied in her hair and having to sleep in them all night.

"Do you think I can bring one of your hot poles home with me?" she asked.

Catherine laughed and said, "I'll gladly give you mine, but you'll have to heat it in the fireplace and the handle will melt."

"You'd need electricity too, and that doesn't get invented for another twenty years," Martha explained.

"Well, I guess you can take it with you, and when you get these outlets in your house, then you'll have my curling iron to plug into them," Catherine said.

Persia sat in Catherine's upholstered rocking chair. She ran her hands over the yellow silk gown that puffed up around her, and admired the silk white lace trim on the edge of the bodice and the sleeves. It had an off-the-shoulder neckline, giving it a more mature look than what younger girls wore. The hoopskirt and boots she wore were hers. She'd put them on that morning.

"The dress you are wearing is from a costume stop," Catherine said.

"What is a costume stop?" Persia asked.

"Oh, never mind, it's not important right now," she said.

"My mother had my dress made for tonight's dinner. The corset is a bit uncomfortable, but the dress is so beautiful that I don't mind." Catherine's dress was the pale lavender dress she'd worn last year. It was also a silk with lace, but the neckline was more modest.

Martha sat on the edge of Catherine's bed. She was wearing a green-and-white ball gown. It was borrowed from Mrs. Nancy, a local historian and reenactor, and was patterned after the one Scarlett wore in *Gone with the Wind*.

"This is confusing for me. Your house looks similar to mine, but in my house, your room is where the dining room is located, and Aleks's room is the parlor," Persia said.

"I know this is all strange to you," Martha said. "Aleks will return you to your mother as soon as he is able to."

"When will that be?" Persia asked.

"Before the night is over," Martha said.

"You will feel right at home here tonight," Catherine said. "We have Civil War reenactors and period dancing, and it is all to remember the time when you were alive."

"Whatever do you mean, the time when I was alive?" Persia sobbed.

"Oh, I didn't mean to say that you are dead," Catherine said, holding her hand up over her mouth.

"I think you've said quite enough, Catherine," Martha said.

"What I meant to say is that you will feel right at home. I know my dad and brother will fix everything for you," Catherine said.

* * *

Aleks was startled when he woke up. He wondered what time it was and if he'd missed the dinner, if J. W. had been found, and where Adam was. He checked the time and saw the party was about to begin. He'd take a quick shower and find Van and his father.

The door to his bathroom was shut. Aleks turned the doorknob.

"Hmm," he said to himself. "Why is my door locked?" He grabbed the screwdriver from his desk and popped the doorknob open.

He opened the door, and inside he found a man asleep in his dressing area—a man who looked enough like General Tyler that he could be mistaken for his twin. Aleks quietly closed and locked the door back and ran into the hallway. Catherine's door was ajar. He pushed it open and asked where he could find their mother.

"She's upstairs getting ready," Catherine said.

"Hey, Aleks, can I talk to you for a second?" It was Adam. He'd come down the hallway and was dressed in normal clothing. He had obviously cleaned up. "Why aren't you cleaned up yet?" he asked.

"I laid down for a minute on my bed and accidently fell asleep," he said. "I need to ask my parents something. I'll be right back. You can go in my room, but do me a favor and don't go in my bathroom. I'll explain in a minute."

Aleks took the steps three at a time and knocked frantically on his parents' bedroom door.

"Come in," Colleen said.

"What's the matter with you?" she asked. "Looks like you've seen a ghost. Oh, you found General Tyler. I'm sorry, honey. I meant to tell you but forgot."

"Mama, how do you forget to tell me that you locked General Tyler in my bathroom?" Aleks asked. "Dad, did you know?" he asked.

Colleen nodded her head yes that she'd already told Ivan. "While you were in the kitchen talking to Miss Kamie, your father helped me move the general down the hall to your room. He said he was feeling tired from the day's events. I gave him a blanket and told him to rest there."

"He's apparently a heavy sleeper because he didn't hear me when I came in the bathroom. Dad, could you move him to the chair by my bookshelf so I can take a shower?" Aleks asked.

"Can you take a shower in our bathroom? It would be easier at this point to let him sleep," Ivan said. "He's feeling ornery, and I'm afraid he'll draw too much attention if we roust him."

"Yes, of course," Aleks said.

"But take a quick one," Ivan hollered after Aleks. "You don't have time for one of those thirty-minute showers."

"I know, Dad!"

"We'll see you downstairs, Aleks," Colleen said.

Colleen and Ivan spoke quietly about the general as they walked down the staircase.

* * *

Guests for the fundraiser entered through the downstairs doors where Fort Tyler board members Raymond and William were greeting guests, giving out name tags, and directing them to the main hallway and out the sunroom door to the patio.

Ivan looked up to see the steady stream of visitors passing through the hall. He and Colleen turned in the opposite direction of the guests toward the children's bedrooms.

Colleen managed to slip into Catherine's room unnoticed by the guests. Ivan, on the other hand, was noticed.

"Hey, Ivan!" The familiar voice belonged to his friend Ben from Columbus.

"Hey there, so glad you could make it tonight," Ivan said.

"Susan and I wouldn't have missed it," Ben said.

"Where's Colleen?" Susan asked.

"She'll be out in a minute. She's checking on the children."

Catherine's bedroom opened and out stepped Colleen with the three young ladies. Persia was seemingly recovered from her travels, and the three of them were giggling at Aleks. He'd run down the staircase in front of them with nothing but a towel on. Catherine yelled his name out, trying to warn him to stop, but he was too fast down the steps, and instead of warning him, she'd accidently drawn everyone's attention to him. The crowd of guests in the hallway heard her, turned to look, and saw Aleks run from the staircase to his room.

Aleks ran right in front of his mother. Colleen shook her head, smiled, and said, "Good evening, everyone. As you can see, my family is not entirely ready for the dinner, but I have good news, our dinner is ready for us. Please follow me," she said. Her elegance and charm turned the guests' attention back to the dinner. She gracefully walked by them in her white silk ball gown that shimmered in the light of the hallway chandeliers.

"Here she is now," Ivan said. "Colleen, would you please show Ben and Susan to their table. You have them sitting with us, right?"

"Yes, of course," Colleen said.

"I'll see you shortly. I need to check on Aleks," he said with a wink.

* * *

Colleen passed into the sunroom and paused by the curio filled with artifacts. Friends of hers were looking at the Civil War surgical set—Jodi and Ed from Auburn and Cindi and Chris from Atlanta.

"Good evening!" she said. "I'm glad you all were able to join us."

Colleen glanced out the window to check on the dinner and saw the caterer setting out the salad plates at each place setting. "It looks like dinner is about to be served." Colleen motioned for them to follow her to the patio. "I'm sure Ivan will give you a demonstration with the surgical set later," she said, laughing.

"That's right," Jodi said. "Didn't he use the knife to lance a spider bite on your leg?" she asked.

"And I have the scar to prove it," Colleen said. "The surgical set is made of surgical steel, and Ivan assured me it was sterile and never dulls. He was right."

"Being married to a doctor has some advantages," Cindi said with a laugh.

Colleen opened the sunroom door and found Judge Griggs standing directly in front of her. She was startled at first. She didn't know he had walked up the back steps to the door. "Oh, Judge, I'm so happy you decided to join us," Colleen said. "You all remember our neighbor and good friend, Judge Adam Griggs," she said. "Where's Mary?"

Colleen stepped back to allow her guests access to the door. "I'll meet you out there," she said to them.

"It's nice to see you all," Judge Griggs said and moved to the side of the door with Colleen. "I'm not here for the dinner, Colleen. I'm here to speak to our sons," he said softly. "I know this isn't the best time, but it can't wait."

"Ivan is in Aleks's room, but I thought Adam was at home," she said.

"Adam came over to see Aleks about thirty minutes ago," he said.

"Okay then, he is probably in Aleks's room too. I think you'll understand everything much better once you've heard their explanation," Colleen said.

She knew it was risky for anyone else to know about the time travel, but this wasn't anyone; it was Adam's father. He needed proof, and with General Tyler, maybe convincing him would not take as long. Colleen did not have time to analyze it further; she had a patio full of guests, the musicians were playing, and the first course was served.

CHAPTER TWENTY-EIGHT

The Judge and the General

JUDGE GRIGGS KNOCKED on Aleks's door. "Ivan, it's Adam," he said. He waited a moment, and finally the door unlocked. Aleks opened it, shut it behind him, and locked it.

"Hey, Dad," Adam Jr. said. His son was sitting in the drafting chair in front of the desk.

"Hi, Son," Judge Griggs said. "Ivan, can the four of us talk?" he asked.

"Of course," Ivan said.

"Have either of you contacted the police?" Judge Griggs asked.

"No, we haven't; we wanted to explain things to you and allow you time to reunite with Adam before the police and the media descended upon you," Ivan said.

"Mary and I appreciate your thoughtfulness, and I don't mean to sound crass, but we've been reunited and now one of us needs to contact the authorities," he said. "The last thing we want is for the authorities to think we've withheld information about the case."

"Dad, there's some business we need to take care of before we talk to the police," Adam said.

"Please explain," Judge Griggs said.

For the next hour or so, Judge Griggs listened as they told him about the time travel. At first, he shook his head in disbelief, but the more they talked and with Ivan's experiences, he started believing their story.

"So, you're telling me that General Tyler is locked in here and that Persia and J. W. came through the time window too?" Judge Griggs asked.

"Yes, Dad," Adam said. "After Aleks returns these people to 1865, then we can talk to the police."

"We don't know exactly when the time window closes, but it is close to the 150th anniversary," Aleks said.

Then they explained that General Tyler was on loan from the police department after the incident earlier that morning. "We can't risk Tyler being arrested," Aleks said.

A knock on Aleks's door stopped their conversation. "Who is it?" he asked.

"Aleks, it's Martha. Your mother asked me to check on you. The dinner is over, and the caterer is asking if she wants plates set aside."

"Yes, thanks, Martha. Have you met Adam's father, Judge Griggs?" Aleks asked.

"No, but it's a pleasure to meet you, sir," she said.

Aleks explained Martha's connection to the time travel research and their trip together. She also vouched for the man in the next room. He was the spitting image of the photo in the sunroom, and his story matched up too.

"Did you show him the photo of us in front of the house?" she asked.

"No, I forgot," Aleks said and pulled out his phone. He showed Judge Griggs the time-travel photos from that trip and the ones he snapped at Gettysburg.

"Okay, okay, okay, I believe you. How do we find this J. W.?" he asked.

The four of them left Aleks's room and walked through the empty house, downstairs, and out the front door. Their search for J. W. would begin with the Ness property and the fort.

* * *

After the dinner, while the period dancers were demonstrating dances and getting audience participation, David Wayne came down from the fort to use the bathroom in the Ness home. He went to Aleks's room and knocked on the bathroom door. No one answered. David knocked again. With no answer, he assumed there was no one in there and turned the knob, but it was locked. David knocked again. There was a commotion on the other side of the door, and the doorknob popped.

The door opened, and David stepped back to allow the other person out of the bathroom. "Hey, sorry about that," David said, leaning in enough to see General Tyler sitting in a chair. "Did I wake you up?" David asked.

The general's hair was all pushed up in the back from sleeping on it.

"You old rascal, you. You're catchin' a few winks while the rest of us are workin' our butts off up at the fort," David said with a chuckle. "We were wondering where you were. Good news is the candlelight tour hasn't begun. I can get you positioned before the first group comes through," he added.

Tyler was silent. He seemed disoriented but cooperative. He grabbed his crutch and hat and followed David down the main hall to the sunroom.

"I haven't heard any more from the police chief. I guess everything is fine and you can go home after the tour," David said. "Chief Laurent has been at the dinner. He and his girlfriend are sitting next to Colleen at the front table, closest to the dancers."

On the way through the sunroom, David stopped to speak with a fellow reenactor who had also come in to use the restroom. While David was speaking to the other soldier, General Tyler was surveying the sunroom shelf with the grapeshot. He slipped an iron ball into his jacket pocket.

"Have you met our General Tyler?" David asked the other reenactor.

"No, sir," Marty said.

David introduced Marty to General Tyler, and the general commenced with his questions about the battle.

"Were you men defending the fort this morning?" General Tyler asked, straightening his uniform.

"Yes, sir, General," David said.

"What's the status of the fort and our men?"

"Your men fought hard all day. It was a valiant fight of 120 Confederates against 1,200 Union. It lasted until evening when General Fannin commanded the men to surrender."

"Surrender?" the general shouted. "What do you mean we surrendered?"

"Gosh darn, he's good!" David said. "What'd I tell you?" he asked Marty.

"Yes, sir, the Union Army, under the command of General LaGrange, breached the fort by climbing across the parapet on ladders," Marty said.

"Where are my men currently?" Tyler asked.

"Some were taken as prisoners and marched off toward Macon," David said.

"How many losses did we suffer?" Tyler asked.

"No losses," David said.

"Tell me your name and where you are from," Tyler said.

"I'm Marty Prestin from Pine Mountain."

"You know, David and Marty, I'm in a quandary here. I started my day defending a town in need of defending, but now it seems a peaceful place, showing no marks of war, except for those in this sunroom wall," Tyler said, pointing to the cannon marks on the white limestone wall. "How those marks got on the inside of this room is a puzzle I am unable to solve."

"I think this presentation of yours will do just fine for the tour. Let's get up to the fort," David said.

"He's going to win himself a Oscar with a performance like this one. Where'd you find him, David? He's the real thing!" Marty said.

"Believe it or not, he just showed up," David said.

They took Tyler outside and up to the fort, through Judge Griggs's fort entrance in his backyard. Meanwhile Officer Bock was still stationed at the main gate, awaiting orders from Chief Laurent concerning Tyler. Bock and the chief were under the assumption that General Tyler was at the fort where they had left him earlier that afternoon.

No one noticed anything unusual about the general. He appeared to be a reenactor headed to the fort with David. Anyone who would have stopped the general from leaving the house had missed his departure. Colleen and everyone at her table, including the chief and his date, as well as Van, Martha, Persia, and Catherine were all dancing.

CHAPTER TWENTY-NINE

Fighting Breaks Out at the Fort

THE ENCHANTED APRIL evening came with a glorious sunset that swept across the sky to the east. There was only light humidity, and a quiet breeze danced on the lawn and in the treetops. Hoopskirts twirled, and candlelight flickered; the guests were captured in the romance.

"I'm going to sit out the next dance and have dessert before it's all gone!" Catherine told Martha and Persia.

They congregated at the dessert buffet, situated in front of the courtyard fence, which was adorned with an antique climbing rose.

"Red velvet cake is my favorite. I love America. Everything is wonderful!" Martha exclaimed.

"The English have the best fish and chips. It's all I ate when we were in England last summer," Catherine said.

"Catherine, that German keeps putting his name on my dance card," Persia said.

"You don't have to dance with him because his name is on your card. My mama has the dance cards for fun; they aren't real. Just like the hand fans; it's another fun way to remember the past."

"Oh, okay," she said. "He has asked me where I live and then asked to borrow my cell phone. When I asked him what a cell phone was, he looked at me and said that he knew I wasn't from here and that he'd find out where I was from."

"Oh my goodness! We need to get you to a safe place," Martha said. "Where is Aleks?"

"The last I heard was that a group of them were searching for J. W."

"Let's go find them," Catherine said.

The three young ladies scooped up their hoops and began milling around the fort.

"Excuse me, Mr. David, have you seen my brother?" Catherine asked.

"I saw him earlier," David said.

"My brother is missing," Persia said. "Have you seen my brother?" she asked.

"How old is your brother?" David asked.

"He is twelve years old," she said.

"We will certainly send them home if we see them," he said.

* * *

Ivan had his night-vision binoculars out, and the search party was in full swing, searching every tree and lot within a two-mile radius. The problem was that J. W. would fit in with the reenactors on this night.

They split up, with Adam and Judge Griggs searching their yard and then the empty lot next door and Ivan and Aleks searching the wooded area around the fort. It had been a good hour, and there was still no sign of J. W.

Ivan had changed into his Union officer's uniform after he returned from 1865. His Confederate garb was dirty, and there was no time to wash it before the dinner. He thought nothing of it until General Tyler spotted him.

* * *

"Boom! Boom! Boom!"

"Aaaah!"

"It's okay, Persia; those aren't real bullets," Catherine said. "The reenactors are demonstrating their weapons."

"She's not going to understand," Martha said. "We should take her back to the house."

Persia screamed and ducked behind the parapet.

During the disturbance, General Tyler sneaked over to one of the cannons and loaded it with the grapeshot from the house.

Ivan realized at that moment he was watching the real General Tyler from 1865 load the cannon and rushed the general to stop him, but it was too late; he'd already lit the fuse.

The general spotted Ivan coming toward him. He lifted his rifle given to him as a prop and fired it at Ivan. He had loaded it with live musket shells from his pocket.

Ivan hollered at him not to shoot, but it was too late. The general was convinced he was defending the fort and Ivan was a Yankee.

Ivan, hit in the left arm, made it to the general before he could reload. He knocked the general's crutch from under him and hit him in his left forearm; the rifle flew up in the air, and David Wayne caught it as he rushed in to see why Ivan was tackling General Tyler.

"The cannon!" Ivan hollered.

Boom!

The cannon, which was pointed down at the house, shot the 150-year-old grapeshot right into the Nesses' attic.

"Who loaded live ammunition in that cannon?" David asked.

"It was an accident," Ivan said.

"Why are you sitting on top of the general?" David asked.

"He shot me with his rifle," Ivan said.

"I'm so sorry," David said. "The chief left him in my care. I thought he was harmless."

"He is harmless," Ivan said. "I'm certain he didn't know the ammunition was live."

The general was facedown in the grass with Ivan sitting on top of him and restraining his hands behind his back.

"I am defending this town for the ladies of West Point. To my death!" Tyler said.

Ivan placed his hand over the general's mouth.

* * *

Officer Bock saw smoke coming from the Ness home and heard the screams after the cannon fired. He radioed for the fire department and some backup.

The few dinner guests who had forgone the candlelight tour were shaken up and ran scared out to the front yard and then to their cars. Guests who were doing the candlelight tour didn't know anything out of the ordinary had occurred; cannons and muskets being fired were normal parts of the reenactment. Colleen's friends from Auburn and Atlanta had no idea that anything had happened. They were at the medical tent station for the candlelight tour, learning about Civil War injuries.

For the most part, General Tyler's offense was concealed by the darkness. It was past sunset, and visibility was low. The only lighting at the fort was by candles.

* * *

Aleks was not far behind his father when the shooting occurred. He checked on his dad. His father told him he had everything under control with the general and that he needed him to keep looking for J. W.

Aleks headed back down by the line of trees surrounding the fort. He heard a tree rustle above him. He looked up and saw J. W. looking down at him.

"Why's he in a huff?" J. W. asked.

"J. W., come down, right now. We've been looking for you all night," Aleks said. "Persia is all upset."

"No, she's not," J. W. said. "I've been watchin' her. She's had dinner, and she's been dancin' with some Muggins."

"Listen, J. W., how would you like to have some dinner? You hungry?" Aleks asked.

Aleks took J. W. to his tree house and messaged Adam, Van, and Ivan that J. W. had been found.

"You know what I think?" J. W. asked as they climbed the stairs to the tree house. "The man dancing with Persia was too old for her, and he looked like he was following her around. I even saw him walking behind her at the fort."

The guys stopped at the top of the tree house steps.

"What did he look like?" Aleks asked.

"He was tall and had blond hair," he said. "He was at the fort before your dad was shot."

Adam met them at the tree house with a few plates of food from the kitchen per Aleks's request. Aleks unlocked the door, turned on the lights, and found a movie to play for J. W.

"Listen, I need you two to keep him here until I get back. I'm going to find Persia."

* * *

Back in the fort, Ivan explained to David that the general was delusional.

"Listen, David, this guy didn't mean any harm. He may need psychiatric care and meds. I know you have a lot going on with the candlelight tour. I'm good here and will keep an eye on this guy," Ivan said.

"Are you sure?" David asked.

"Yes, and Van is on his way to help out," Ivan said. "Have you seen him lately?" he asked.

"Van?" David asked.

"Yes, he's huge. He's been working out, and he deadlifts four hundred pounds," Ivan said.

"Uncle Ivan, are you exaggerating?" Van said with a laugh.

Ivan had messaged Van to grab the duct tape out of the garage and come up to the fort to sit with General Tyler.

"Good to see you Van," David said. "Holler if you need my help with this guy. All right, I'm going to check on the tour stations; make sure they're goin' smoothly," he said. "Check in with me later, and let me know the status of General Tyler here," he said and waved good-bye.

Ivan lifted his hand from the general's mouth long enough to administer the duct tape, and then he taped his hands behind his back. "I'm sorry, General, but you give me no choice. I can't have you shooting people. We are not going to hurt you. We are taking you home tonight," Ivan said.

Ivan situated Van and General Tyler down by the rocks behind the tree house. "I'll be back with the Griggs children and Aleks," Ivan promised.

CHAPTER THIRTY

After the Cannon Fire

IVAN ENTERED THE house and met up with Keith, their neighbor from across the street, a retired police officer. He'd come in from the front door. Colleen was in the living room, and she saw them enter at the same time.

"Ivan, I've been calling you and messaging you. Why didn't you answer?" she asked.

He turned around, and she saw his left arm. His shirtsleeve was soaked with blood.

Colleen screamed, "Ivan, your arm! Were you shot?" she asked.

"Do you need my help?" Keith asked. "I told my wife it sounds like you're still fighting the war over here. Is the smoke real? And what about the blood on your shirt?" he asked.

"There are no serious injuries. I was nicked in the arm by a musket shell. Nothing I can't clean up on my own," Ivan said.

"Who shot you?" Keith asked.

"It was an accident. One of the reenactors had a live musket shell," he said.

"Was it the general?" Colleen asked.

"I'll fill you in later. Keith, would you stay here with Colleen? I need to take care of a few things, and I don't want her alone," he said.

"Ivan, what about the cannon that shot through the back of the house? Have you spoken to the police? Officer Bock is outside taping off the crime scene," Colleen said.

"The police have it under control. Have you heard from Catherine and the girls?" he asked.

"Yes, we've been messaging. She's on her way in from the fort," she said.

* * *

Following the explosion, Catherine and Martha ran toward Judge Griggs's gate entrance. Reaching the bottom of the steps between their house and the neighbors', Catherine and Martha noticed that Persia was no longer with them.

"Where did she go?" Martha asked.

"I don't know. I thought she was walking with us," Catherine said. The girls retraced their footsteps, calling out Persia's name.

A reenactor along the candlelit path said he saw the girl going toward the house with a tall blond gentleman. "If I'm not mistaken, he sounded German."

"Come on, Cat! We have to get the police!" Martha tripped on her hoopskirt, ripping the bottom of the gown with her shoe and landing on her face and elbows. Several reenactors came to her rescue and helped her back up. She brushed herself off and thanked them for rushing to her side.

"I'm fine, nothing some tea won't fix," she said with a smile.

Martha and Catherine headed back for the gate. They ran into Judge Griggs in his backyard. He was sitting out on his patio.

"You ladies okay?" he asked.

"Hello, Judge," Martha said.

"We've found the boy," Judge Griggs said, referring to J. W.

"Where are Aleks and Adam?" Catherine asked.

"They are all in Aleks's tree house," he said. "I'm here keeping an eye on things."

"Have you seen a girl in a yellow dress come through here?" Martha asked.

"There was one earlier who came through with a gentleman from the party," he said.

"Did you see where they went?" Martha asked.

"They walked toward the front yard," he said.

"Thank you, Judge," Martha said.

* * *

Martha and Catherine stopped at the top of the steps and noticed the tree house lights.

However, they heard Aleks's voice coming from the courtyard over to their right and on the same level as the patio. The courtyard was surrounded by shrubbery with a canopy of two large crape myrtles, which limited their view of the courtyard from up on the hill.

They heard two voices; one was Aleks's, and the other sounded like it belonged to a man with a German accent. They sounded argumentative, but the girls couldn't hear what was being said.

Aleks opened the courtyard gate, and the large blond man followed close behind him. The girls lost sight of them as they entered the sunroom and went into the main hall.

"Where do you think they are going?" Catherine asked.

"I don't know, but we are going in there to find out," Martha said.

"I'm going to let my daddy know what's going on; he'll know what to do," Catherine said.

* * *

Colleen fussed over Ivan's arm for as long as he'd allow.

"That's enough, Colleen; I'm fine," he said.

Aleks passed by the living room but didn't look up to see his parents standing there with Keith. "Looks like our boy genius has found a kindred spirit," she said to Ivan.

"Seems strange to me that Aleks isn't curious about the hole in the house or the blood all over my shirt. This guy must be fascinating. Who is he?" he asked.

"Um, said he is a visiting professor at Auburn in the physics department," Colleen said.

"How did he hear about the dinner?" Ivan asked.

"I'm not sure, but I told him that you speak fluent German because he is from Germany," she said.

Without explanation, Ivan left the living room and walked down the hallway, stopping at Aleks's bedroom door; it was not pushed all the way closed. Ivan stood off to the side and listened.

"Look," Aleks said, "I think you've enjoyed a little too much wine this evening. Please allow me to call you a cab."

"Listen, Aleksandr, we have your friend, and she told us everything with the exception of the formula. My friends found you at MIT, but you slipped away from them. Don't kid yourself; we know you are time-traveling. Now, you either share it with us willingly or we kill the girl."

"Who is the girl?" Aleks asked.

"We have Miss Persia Griggs. She is like a frightened little mouse," he said and then let out a sadistic laugh.

"You get pleasure from scaring a young girl?" Aleks asked, sounding disgusted. "What are you planning to do with the gun you have in my back? My parents' home is practically in the middle of town. The police department is minutes from here, and the police chief is at this fundraiser. Don't you think he's armed?"

"Listen, Aleks Ness, all I have to do is send a message to the person who's holding your cousin in the laundry room, and she will be shot immediately. He has a gun to her head, and when he pulls the trigger, no one will hear it because he has a silencer. I am giving you exactly five minutes to tell me how you time-travel. After that, we kill her and then the rest of your family become targets."

"She has nothing to do with this," Aleks said.

Aleks retrieved his notebook with formulas and talked to the German. "I have been working on a formula, but we haven't been successful," he said. "Why do you think that I am capable of time travel? I'll go through my formula with you. Please give me more time. Please don't harm her."

* * *

Ivan left the door and took the staircase downstairs. He ran through the den past Ben and Susan and into the safe room.

"Hey, Ivan, you never showed up for dinner. Everything okay? I heard some cannon fire. I thought it was part of the reenactment, but look at you. What happened?" Ben asked.

Ben worked for the US Immigration and Customs Enforcement (ICE). He and his wife, Susan, were sitting in the den with some other guests watching *Gone with the Wind*.

He followed Ivan into the safe room.

"We have a hostage situation in our house. There are two Germans; one is holding a young woman at gunpoint while the other is making demands on Aleks. If Aleks doesn't give him what he is asking for, they are threatening to kill the young woman," Ivan said.

"What do you have in there that I can use?" Ben asked, pointing to the safe. "Is your arm okay?"

"Yeah, I'm fine, just a little nick from a musket shell. I'll pour some peroxide and alcohol on it and wrap it up later," Ivan said.

"You are one tough dude," Ben said.

Ivan had a short sword, some camouflage, and several guns in the safe.

"Here, Ben," Ivan threw some camouflage at him. "Put this on; you can't crawl under the house in your suit. Go through the small outside door near the kitchen; it is for the crawlspace, which goes under the house and leads to the laundry room. The German said she is in the laundry room with an armed man. I'll come around from the outside and distract them as you come through the crawlspace."

"Sounds like a plan, but let me grab my weapon from the car. I'm not crawling under the house with this sword you just handed me," he said with a laugh.

"Oh, here, I meant to hand you this," he said as he handed him a semiautomatic shotgun.

"Now, you're talkin'. How do we explain this to the folks in your den?" Ben asked.

"I'll handle it," Ivan said.

He and Ben walked out of the safe room. Ben was heavily armed and wearing Kryptek camouflage.

The room was empty. Susan and the other couple had gone up for the candlelight tour.

"I'm going to send Colleen a message and tell her to gather our daughter and her friend and go to the safe room," Ivan said.

CHAPTER THIRTY-ONE

Hostages

AFTER THE CANNON raised the roof on the house, guests grabbed their hearts and then their belongings and headed for the exit.

"I believe I've experienced quite enough of the past for one evening," one guest said on her way through the house and out the front door.

Another guest said, "You hear about people like this—those who live in the past and are still fighting the war. Well, this is a perfect example of why the South gets a bad name. I'm sure the media will get ahold of this and make us all look like backwoods hicks."

A kinder guest said, "It's beautiful and all, but who could live here? I bet they have ghosts too."

* * *

Catherine and Martha walked into the house and found Colleen in the living room.

"Mama!"

She held up her hand for Catherine to wait a minute; she was finishing up a phone call with the police chief.

Police Chief Laurent told her that the musket shell from the dog's leg matched General Tyler's firearm. "We'll need you down at the station tomorrow morning to finish your statement. And another thing, the DA is expected to press charges since this little episode with the general has cost the City of West Point several thousand dollars," Chief Laurent said.

"I want you to know that Officer Bock has begun the investigation into that cannon fired into your home tonight. We think the General Tyler reenactor is connected to that incident as well. Have you seen him tonight?" he asked.

"No, sir," she said.

"Let me know if you need anything," he said.

"Thank you, Chief. I'll let Dr. Ness know and have him bring me down in the morning," she said. Colleen ended the call and looked up to see Catherine and Martha standing in front of the couch.

"Hey, honey, what's going on?" Colleen asked Catherine.

"We can't find Persia," she said.

"Have you seen her?" Martha asked.

"No," Colleen said, looking down at her phone. "Your father just sent me a message telling us to head for the safe room immediately. He said he is getting Persia."

The girls followed Colleen down the hall and downstairs to the safe room. She put in the code for the ten-by-ten-foot room and closed the door. It locked behind them.

They sat on chairs. A desk, a gun locker, and some jewelry safes were inside.

"Do you know where Aleks or the other guys are?" Martha asked.

"Aleks was in the house, talking to a guest from the party," Colleen said.

"I'm scared, Mama," Catherine said, crying.

"Everything is going to be okay." Colleen wrapped her arms around Catherine and rubbed her back.

* * *

Ben accessed the crawlspace from the small outside door near the driveway, the same door that General Tyler had come through twelve hours earlier. The ceiling in the crawlspace was high enough in most places, which allowed him to walk bent over, but as he approached the exit on the other side, near the laundry room, the ceiling sloped, and his six-foot frame would only fit if he crawled on his hands and knees. When he reached the door, he waited for Ivan to give their cue word, "German."

* * *

Ivan felt above the doorframe in the usual spot for the outside laundry room key. It was gone. *How many times had he said to always put the key back?* He ducked down to the side of the door, which had a paned window in the top half. It was too risky to break the glass, and he was too large to fit through the small vent above the dryer.

The headlights of the vacating guests shined across the front of the house. He looked up at the door, and a headlight bounced off something shiny on the side of the frame. It was the key! He'd found it attached to a nail on the upper right side.

He grabbed it and wondered when Colleen had put it on a nail and why she thought it was a safe place to hide it—out where anyone could see it.

He entered the laundry room from the outside door. He sounded like he'd had one too many mint juleps. He didn't see the gunman but heard a clank sound that came from behind the wall near the washer. The birdcage was covered with a tablecloth to keep the birds from squawking. Ivan noticed it when he entered. It was in front of him a couple of yards, near the crawlspace door. Ivan figured the German must have done it to keep the birds from drawing attention. Otherwise, they were extremely loud when anyone entered the laundry room.

Ivan picked up some dirty linens from the floor and tripped around the corner by the washer.

"May I help you?" the German asked.

"I wish you could. Do you know how to get red wine out of antique linen? My wife had a fit for me to put stain remover on it immediately. It was her grandmother's. My wife, she's quite the slave driver, if you know what I mean," he said, slurring his words and stumbling as he walked. "Whew, you have to watch out for those mint juleps; they sneak up on you.

"Oh, I'm sorry," he said, seeing Persia sitting on a stool. "I didn't realize you had company. Persia, darling, what are you doing down here?" he asked. "Did Aunt Colleen put you to work?"

"No, sir," Persia said, looking frightened.

"We are getting acquainted. The war reenactment was so loud that we couldn't hear each other. I hope you don't mind that she suggested this quiet place," the German said.

"Not at all," Ivan said. "This was a smart place to come to get away from the noise," he added. "Would you mind if I start the washer and put these clothes in the dryer before I leave?" he asked, knowing it would cause the German and Persia to move into the space near the birdcage and closer to Ben.

The transition was made, and Ivan loudly asked the man if he was German. Ben leaped from the crawlspace door onto the German's back, and Ivan grabbed Persia and took her outside. The men knocked over the birdcage. The parrots escaped and flew around wildly. When the dust and feathers cleared, the German was handcuffed and laid out on the floor.

During the altercation, Ivan took Persia to the safe room to join Colleen and the girls. "You'll be fine in here," he told them as he stepped outside the safe.

"Wait, Ivan! Where are Aleks and the boys? What's going on?"

"I don't have time to explain now. Trust me and stay here until I call you on the safe phone," he said.

There was an emergency phone on the wall that had never been used. It was a satellite phone that Ivan had insisted on installing when they built the room. Colleen had thought it was ridiculous at the time, but after the events of the last week, ridiculous things were the norm.

Persia sat down in the corner of the room. She looked like a frightened animal again.

"Come here, Persia," Colleen said. "Everything will be fine. Uncle Ivan will take care of everything. He always does."

Martha covered Persia with a blanket and sat next to her with her arm around her.

"Would someone please explain what's going on?" Catherine asked.

"There are some German men after your brother's research," Colleen said.

* * *

Ivan made his way back to the laundry room. He instructed Ben to have the German call his friend, the one holding Aleks against his will and say the girl told him everything.

"You are crazy," the German said and spit in Ivan's face. "He'll never believe me."

Ivan responded, "I'll give you until three, and then my friend here will shoot your left hand and on five he will shoot your right hand. Do you get the picture?"

Ben held the gun on the German while Ivan dialed the number and held the phone up to his mouth. "Steiner, bring the boy to the laundry room. I have the missing part of the equation," he said.

Ivan ended the call.

"Steiner knows something is wrong," the German said.

Ivan took a washcloth, forced it in the German's mouth, and covered it with duct tape. "I've grown tired of his German accent," he said to Ben with a smile.

"They've come out of Aleks's bedroom and are in the main hallway," Ben said, pointing to the security monitor. "I'll be here watching and will step in when you need me," he said.

"I've got the monitors on my phone. I'll watch and take him down in my office." Ivan walked the fifteen feet from the laundry room across to the front of his office near the door. He hid out of sight from Steiner and Aleks, who came down the stairs and into the office.

Ivan took a martial arts stance as he readied himself to defend his son against the madman. Aleks entered the office first and then Steiner. Ivan knocked Steiner off his feet with a roundhouse kick to the side. Steiner's gun fired in the fall. The bullet nearly hit Ivan's prize artifact, an *Allosaurus* fossil, but nicked a fossilized nest of dinosaur eggs instead.

"Watch out for my fossils!" Ivan hollered.

The bronzed eagle perched on top of a pedestal broke Steiner's fall; its talons sank deep into his back. Ivan manipulated Steiner's wrist and removed the gun from his hand.

"Great job, Doc!" Ben said, watching from the laundry room's entrance. "I'll take it from here."

"Where's Aleks?" Ivan hollered.

"I'm right here, Dad," he said, sticking his hand up from behind the desk.

"You take on the Union and Confederate armies but are afraid of a couple Germans?" Ivan said with a chuckle.

"The Germans' weapons are slightly more accurate than the Civil War kind, and besides, you looked like you had it under control. You always tell me about your mixed martial arts fighting, and now I've seen it for myself. Wow, you weren't exaggerating."

"It's all muscle memory, Aleks. Muscle memory," Ivan said.

"Is he bleeding to death?" Aleks asked, referring to Steiner, who was moaning from the pain.

"He'll be fine," he said and plucked out the eagle's talons with a quick jerk. Steiner hollered. "Aleks, I need a clean towel, cotton gauze, peroxide, rubbing alcohol, and medical tape. It's in my upstairs bathroom over the sink.

"Listen, Ben, I know you're required by law to follow protocol, but I need you to hold off for twenty-four hours."

"Why's that, buddy?"

"Aleks has to return three missing persons."

"Does this have anything to do with his friend Adam?" Ben asked.

"Yes, can you hold off booking them until I let you know it's all clear? Should have it done by the time you get to Columbus," Ivan said.

"You've till 8:00 a.m. We never had this conversation. Now, can you help me put these two in the back of my car? I'll take them to a holding cell in Columbus."

"You need someone with you? These guys are too dangerous to transport alone," Ivan said.

"No worries, I have my wife with me," Ben said.

"I forget that she's an agent too," Ivan said.

"Don't let her delicate constitution and sweet demeanor fool you!" Ben said. "I've notified the officer on duty to expect us in an hour. I'll message you when we arrive. We won't process anything until Monday morning anyway. Our administrative assistant doesn't come in on the weekends."

"I can't thank you enough," Ivan said.

"Always glad to help you out!" Ben said.

* * *

While the German plot was being foiled, Adam and J. W. were still in the tree house, watching the movie *Back to the Future*. They were so engrossed that it took Aleks more than one try to get their attention.

Adam unlocked the door.

"Did you find Persia?" J. W. asked.

"Yes, Persia is safe. I was held at gunpoint by a German, and then my dad performed a roundhouse kick that would make Jackie Chan proud," he said.

"Oh great!" Adam said.

"Did you hear what I said?" he asked.

"No, what'd you say? Speak up; the movie is a little loud," Adam said.

Aleks pulled the plug on the TV. "Why'd you do that?" J. W. asked.

"Give us five more minutes; it's the funny part where he meets his mom and doesn't know it's his mom," Adam said.

"Come on!" Aleks hollered.

"Come on, J. W. He's right," Adam said. "I'll tell you what happens at the end."

* * *

The boys arrived at the safe room shortly after Ivan. "Let us in, Supermodel," Ivan said.

"What was that?" Aleks asked.

"That's our secret code so your mother knows it's me," he said. "No one else knows I call her supermodel," Ivan said.

"We all know now, and I'm not sure we wanted to," Aleks said with a laugh.

Aleks helped pull open the door as his mom pressed the release button from the inside. The boys explained that the Germans had been arrested and taken off the property. Everyone was safe, and it was time for J. W., Persia, and the general to leave.

"Persia, do you have everything that you brought with you?" Aleks asked.

"Yes, but I need to change into my day dress. I borrowed this dress from Catherine. I have everything else though."

"J. W., do you have everything with you?"

"Yes," he said.

Ivan suggested that Aleks take Van with him on the mission.

"Adam, you stay home this time!" Ivan said.

"I'm not going to argue with you," Adam said.

"Persia and J. W., I can never thank you enough for the kindness you showed me while I was at your house," Adam said and reached out to shake Persia's hand, but she leaned in and gave him a hug.

"We will miss you, Adam. We will miss all of you. Thank you, Dr. Ness, for saving me from that terrible man," she said. "I'm so frightened, Aunt Colleen," she said. "What if we can't get back home? You have all been so good to us, but I miss my father and mother."

"Don't cry, Persia. Aleks will get you back home," Colleen said.
"Come on; let's get out of here," Aleks said.

* * *

Martha grabbed Persia's day dress from Catherine's room. It was a navy cotton material with a lace collar. "Here is your dress, Persia," Martha said.

"Thank you, Martha," Persia said. "Where can I change my dress?" she asked.

They were outside the back of the house and walking toward the tree house.

"Don't worry about it," Catherine said.

"That's right; you may keep it," Colleen assured her.

The rest of the group stopped at the foot of the hill and said their good-byes.

Ivan walked the group up behind the tree house. There he found Keith sitting with Van and the general.

"Here's the key for the general's handcuffs." He handed them to Aleks. "Unlock him right before you make a run for it," Keith said with a laugh.

Keith had been standing watch with Van over the general. Van had asked for his help so he assisted Van after Colleen and the girls went to the safe room. At Van's request, he'd brought a pair of handcuffs for the general. They had replaced the duct tape with the handcuffs.

CHAPTER THIRTY-TWO

Missing Persons

COLLEEN INSISTED ON taking Ivan to the emergency room to have his gunshot wound from the general taken care of while Van and Aleks took the time travelers back to 1865. They arrived on a train en route from Macon to West Point. The boys kept the general in handcuffs until they arrived in West Point. Aleks knew it was no use trying to convince him that he and Van were the good guys.

"Listen, General, I like you. My parents even have a photograph of you in our house. Please don't take offense by this gun pointed at you. We really are on your side. When we arrive at the fort, we will surrender you to the First Wisconsin Regiment. I will tell the Union officer that by orders of Colonel LaGrange, you are to be given a horse and a day's rations and allowed to check on your wounded men at the Griggs home."

Aleks donned a Union officer's jacket and carried his Confederate coat in his haversack in case they encountered the other side of the conflict. Van wore an Auburn T-shirt under his jacket.

"How awesome would it be if someone saw my T-shirt and yelled 'War Eagle'?" Van asked with a laugh.

"War Eagle!" Aleks hollered.

"War Eagle!" he yelled back. "That's it; the first 1860s War Eagle was by the Ness cousins," Van said proudly.

"War Eagle? What's a War Eagle?" asked J. W.

"It's the battle cry for Auburn," Van said.

The boys explained to the Griggs children that the university in Auburn would be renamed, and it would have a football team.

"War Eagle is what we yell when the team kicks off," Aleks explained.

"I still don't understand," J. W. admitted.

* * *

The group arrived at the edge of the Griggs home and explained to the Griggs children that it was time for them to part ways.

"We need your help; we have to take the general up behind your house without your mother seeing us. Can you keep her distracted while we do that?" Aleks asked.

They nodded their heads yes.

"There's one more thing," Aleks said. "You must not tell people you traveled through time. It needs to be your secret. You can tell your mother you were with us, but you cannot tell her about the future. Understand that your family and friends will think your minds are sick if you tell them," he said.

"We won't tell anyone. I promise," Persia said.

They all hugged, and Aleks took the short sword from his belt and gave it to J. W. "Give this to your mother. She'll know that it belongs to Colonel Oates from Alabama by the inscription here on the handle. Please ask her to have it delivered to him, saying it was found along the road on your way home."

"Will we see you again?" J. W. asked.

Aleks didn't respond, and he didn't ask again because his mother was outside calling for them.

"Where have you been?" she asked. "I was worried about you all night."

"We were with Aleks and Van," J. W. said.

"We thought you'd been captured and taken by the Yankees," she said.

The Griggs children turned and looked back in the direction they had come from, but the time travelers and General Tyler had gone.

* * *

Aleks donned the Union jacket, left Van at the rocks, and took Tyler to the Union soldiers lingering in the fort. The general was treated amicably.

Everything was finished. They could return home. He walked down the hill from the fort toward the rocks in the backyard. Van was coughing and wheezing.

"Are you all right?" Aleks asked.

"It's my asthma. The wagons and horses on the dirt roads are kicking up so much dust that it's hard for me to breathe," he said, walking a couple of feet before taking a seat on the hill.

Aleks rushed to his cousin's side. "Van? Van!"

His cousin's breathing sounded shallow, and his color looked pale.

"Come on, Buddy," Aleks said.

He lifted him over his shoulder and headed to the large boulders, their travel point. With the magnetic rocks back in their pockets and all the right pieces, they made it successfully home before sunrise.

Aleks entered the house carrying Van.

"Help! Dad? Mom? I need help! He's unconscious."

Ivan rushed into the living room and checked Van's vital signs. "He's okay; he just panicked."

Van started coughing and opened his eyes. "I guess I was wrong," he said.

"About what?" Ivan asked.

"My family does love me," he said. "Aleks had his chance to leave me in another time, and he brought me back anyway," he said with a cough and a laugh.

CHAPTER THIRTY-THREE

Time Travelers & the Investigation

THE CIA JOINED ICE in its investigation of the internationals since the Germans were rumored to have plotted against the U.S. president and even rumors were looked at with great scrutiny. Ben informed Ivan that Aleks and Martha would be interviewed by the investigators and it would be necessary to place them under protective custody for a couple of months or at least until the Germans were processed.

Martha was worried about this, and she spoke up. "Dr. Ness, I am homesick for my family and normally spend my summers with them in Grand Cayman."

"Let me speak with the CIA contact and see if we can set up a location on the island," Ben said and added, "I don't think anyone would think to look for you, Martha; your contact with the Germans was limited. Just one question though and I hate to be personal, but are you two dating?"

"Ah, no, sir, we are friends," Martha said with some hesitation and embarrassment from the look on her face.

"Dad, you've always said that guys are never just friends. That we always have an agenda?" Aleks said with a smile.

"I think what Aleks is saying, Ben, is that he and Martha have not been dating but he is hopeful."

"You and everyone else, I'm sure," Van said with a laugh.

"Okay, well you boys can fight over Martha later. Let Ben finish," Ivan said.

Ben instructed them to stay at the house until they were interviewed and briefed by law enforcement. "The appointments are set up for tomorrow morning. They will speak to you separately and then together. They may also decide to question the rest of you about the events during the night of April 16."

"We need to speak with you off the record, Ben," Aleks said.

"Okay, go ahead."

"Adam's two-year disappearance, the Germans, Persia, J. W., and General Tyler—they all have one thing in common: time travel. If it is shared with the wrong people or governments, it could threaten our national security."

"Okay, nice! The joke is on me!" Ben said with a laugh. "Ivan here," he said, patting him on the back, "promised he'd get me back for roasting him at his surprise party last year. Boy, you are good!" He laughed. "All right, now, Aleks, for the record, where are Persia, J. W., and General Tyler?"

"You're right; they were reenactors here from out of town. I think the general had too many jiggers of rum and took the role he was playing too seriously. He told me last night that he thought the cannon and musket shell were both blanks. Honestly, we turned our heads when the guy's wife came and picked them up last night."

"That's right, Ben; when you took the Germans to the holding cell, we let them leave for home," Ivan said. "Poor Persia said the German didn't hurt her, and you know, she had been traumatized enough."

"Well," Ben said, "you can choose to plead the Fifth during questioning. The CIA will be agitated, and after this, you will be watched and everyone you are close to will be scrutinized. In my experience, the CIA eventually gets answers," he warned.

"Is the Fifth Amendment similar to the English right to silence?" Martha asked.

"Yes, and I'm not sure how this works with Martha being a British citizen. Do you know, Ben?" Ivan asked.

"I'll check with our staff attorney," he said.

* * *

That evening, the Ness family sat in Colleen's rose garden. They had lighthearted conversation, a much-needed break from the events of the last week. The sky was saturated with hues of red, pink, and orange, and the moonlight illuminated the rose petals. Colleen glanced in the direction of the tree house and noticed fireflies, hundreds of them beneath the structure.

"Aleks, look over there," she said.

"I've never seen anything like this before!" Aleks shouted.

He walked toward them and circled around behind the tree house. The ground started shaking, and the water in the koi pond splashed over its edges. Catherine held on to Colleen, and Martha grabbed on to Catherine's arm. Aleks could see a bright light coming from beneath the shed.

"Be careful back there, Aleks," Colleen said.

"That felt like an earthquake," Ivan said.

"Did you see that light?" Van asked.

A flash of light shot across the yard like a shooting star traveling on a horizontal plane.

"I saw it," Ivan said.

"Aleks, you okay?" Colleen asked.

"I'm fine, but could you shine a light over here? It's pitch-black now."

Aleks walked out from the darkness. "Hey, Dad, is it possible that the earthquake was the time line closing down?" Aleks asked.

"I had the same thought. If you tried to return to the Civil War time line, it would be impossible to travel back," Ivan said.

"Please don't start that again," Colleen said.

"Start what?" Aleks asked.

"Time traveling! Haven't you had enough of that for a lifetime?" she asked.

"I don't care if I ever see another cotton field again as long as I live," Adam said.

"That's true, Adam; you had the worst of it," Aleks said.

"If the earthquake closed the time line, are the fireflies the souls from the past leaving once and for all?" Martha asked.

"That's creepy," Catherine said.

"I doubt it," Ivan said. "That sounds more like a sci-fi movie."

Colleen changed the subject by asking Adam if his parents would join them in the backyard for drinks. Adam said that his father had briefs to read over for court and that his mother had declined because she wasn't feeling well. With that, Adam excused himself and told everyone good night. Aleks followed him up the path toward the gate that connected their backyards.

"The truth is she was upset with my father last night for leaving her at home with no explanation. My father plans on talking to her this evening," Adam said.

"I was wondering what you thought about the changes that resulted from our saving Big Adam?" Aleks asked.

Adam explained that it was all too overwhelming to know exactly what his feelings were about it all. He was thrilled to see his family prospering, and he thought he'd grow accustomed to the larger home and better cars, but what about his old friends and his old school? That he wasn't sure about. Everything would be different, he said, except for him. "I grew up as the maid's son. I don't know if I'll fit into this new image," Adam said.

"Son," Ivan said, "you will be fine. You've what it takes to do well. I've always thought that about you."

Adam worried about his parents—what they knew and what would be kept secret from them. "They know about the time travel, but they can't know about the changes we made to the time line," Adam said.

Ivan agreed that it was too risky for the others—those who had not traveled with them to the Battle of West Point—to know that they had made changes, saved lives. This was the element of time travel that could be dangerous; it was also the reason the Germans wanted the formula.

"My mother and sister don't know about Big Adam. They don't remember any of the way things were before we left. We have to keep these things a secret. It's for everyone's good," Aleks assured him.

"Have you thought about the changes that must have taken place because of Gettysburg?" Adam asked.

Aleks looked at the ground, and he shook his head. Ivan asked repeatedly what changes they had made at Gettysburg, insisting they tell him what happened. Aleks explained the change in Pickett's Charge.

"Have you looked at the numbers?" Ivan asked.

"No, I haven't. I was too afraid to look, and honestly, when Adam was stranded, well, I didn't think of it any more after that," Aleks said.

Ivan said, "I think it's for the best that we keep it to ourselves. Hypothetically, if your actions caused people to die who otherwise would have survived you would be guilty of murder. This all sounds impossible but let's not take any chances. Aleks, if you have this written anywhere in your notebook entries, I want you to destroy them immediately."

The three of them called Van over to talk with them privately by the gate. They all agreed to keep the changes of the Battle of West Point to themselves.

"The changes that have occurred are all positive," Ivan said, "but if the Germans get ahold of it or if a terrorist gets this information, I'm afraid the changes would not be positive. I agree with you all taking the Fifth during your questioning tomorrow; this information must be protected and kept secret."

Adam brought up one last thing before heading home. "My father said he'd contact the police chief in the morning. He is going to remind him of a favor that he owes him—a political favor—hoping now that I'm home the investigation into my case will be closed and sealed. He said he knows of no other way to take care of it."

"I'm sorry, Adam," Aleks said. "For getting you mixed up in this and now your father is involved. I'm so sorry."

Adam hugged his lifelong friend. "It was a choice I made too," Adam said. Someone once said that 'with great power comes great responsibility.' "We've been given great power."

* * *

The CIA questioning was short, and the agency informed Aleks that he would be watched until they had their questions answered. Ben made arrangements for Aleks, Martha, and Adam to stay on Grand Cayman for the summer. Adam's parents were also convinced that it was best for Adam and the others to be protected until the Germans were taken into custody.

Martha and Aleks were allowed to finish up their semester studies online, and Adam's parents had made arrangements for him to begin his senior year course work during the summer. He had required reading to catch up on. One of his classes was Civil War history, merely a coincidence.

Once again, Catherine was too young and not part of the group. "I always miss out on the fun," Catherine exclaimed. "Why can't I go? I discovered what Aleks was up to way before anyone else knew. Well, it was probably the Germans and then me."

"So sorry, Cat, you'll have to stay here with your mother and me. Ben doesn't think we are in any danger," Ivan said.

"What about Van?" she asked. "He time-traveled. Shouldn't he be going to the island?"

Ivan explained that the Germans never made a connection with Van. As far as the authorities knew, Van was another guest at the fundraiser. "The other three were somehow connected to the Germans and are not safe until they are detained," he said.

* * *

Martha was quiet on the 30-minute drive to the Lagrange airport. Catherine chattered nonstop to anyone who would listen and Aleks tried not to be annoyed by his little sister.

"A private jet, are you kidding me?" Catherine blurted out, as they pulled up to the runway on the backside of the private airport. "Please don't tell me that they are taking that to Grande Cayman," she said.

"Makes me wonder if they know more than they are letting on," Ivan said quietly to himself.

"Who? The government?" Colleen asked. Ivan didn't say anything. He just shook his head.

Aleks had hopped out of the car and was retrieving their luggage from the back of the SUV when Adam walked up with his bag. His parents had driven him separately.

"Hey guys, I think you are going to enjoy your ride," Ben said. "My boss insisted on this instead of commercial. Apparently you all have the attention of some higher ups because I usually fly coach," he said with a laugh.

"You're right Mama," Catherine said.

"About what?" asked Colleen.

"Life's not fair," Catherine said.

"No, it's not Cat," Aleks said, giving his little sister a hug and then an unexpected kiss on her head. "I love you and I'll see you soon."

* * *

They said their good-byes and the three travelers boarded the plane and waved good-bye again from the window. As the jet taxied down the runway for takeoff, Colleen and Mary wiped tears from their eyes. Ivan put his arms around his wife and daughter.

"This will all be over soon and they'll be back by the fall," he assured them.

"That's right, Mary. We'll get this straightened out if Ivan and I have to take care of it ourselves," Judge Griggs said.

* * *

Steiner Voltberg and his accomplice were held as long as the German government would permit, but with no testimony from one of the victims and with Aleks pleading the Fifth, there was not enough evidence to keep them detained in the United States. They were extradited to Germany with pending charges of kidnapping and assault. The German government promised to hold them for questioning and bring them to trial on the charges if the U.S. Government submitted more evidence.

The Germans who'd threatened Aleks and Martha at MIT, Kyle Killar and Hans Spangenberg, were still at large. No one had seen them since that night in Boston, and the Department of Homeland Security had no record of them leaving the country.

The CIA was getting closer to discovering why the college students had taken the Fifth; they'd discovered the German's Civil War journal that mentioned Aleks Ness and Adam. This led them to evidence that pointed to Aleks's time-travel research. Their latest investigation included exhuming General Tyler's body for a DNA sample.

* * *

"Hey, Ivan, this is Keith here. The DNA matched; your General Tyler was indeed the same one in your mural, or should I say, the *original*."

"How do you know?" Ivan asked.

"Let's just say I've kept some of my connections with the CIA."

"I thought you were retired from the Jersey police department," Ivan said.

"I am, but some of those rumors about me being in the CIA—well, some of them were true," Keith said with a laugh. "Now the CIA is contacting Interpol to further its investigation in Europe."

"Time travel must be regulated," Ivan said. "It could be the most dangerous weapon in all of history."

PHOTOS

Author's son poses with Cover Artist and painting used for the cover art.

The author and her family in period dress pose outside
The Griggs Home before a community fundraiser.

Mural "Morning of the Battle" painted by "Jumpin' the Rails!" Cover Artist, Connie Wilkerson-Arp, adorns a hallway in The Griggs Home.

The author and her husband in period dress pose in front of the mural during a community fundraiser.

Guests arrive at a fundraising dinner at The Griggs Home.

Musicians, period dancers and reenactors arrive early to set up for the fundraising dinner.

Belles and Beaus Dancers.

Belles and Beaus Dancers entertain guests after dinner.

Belles and Beaus Dancers demonstrate The Broom Dance.

Guests at The Griggs Fundraiser watch the dancers before joining in for the Virginia Reel.

The Author's daughter playing with a friend during an 1860s period fundraiser at The Griggs Home.

Reenactors give a musket demonstration at the Fort.

The Author's children and a friend are dressed in period clothing and play in the Fort.

Reenactors set-up camp at Fort Tyler to commemorate the 150th anniversary of the Battle of West Point.

A Union reenactor at the Fort Tyler commemoration for the 150th Anniversary.

The Author with her children and a friend act as Civil War refugees during a Fort Tyler Association Candlelight Tour.

Confederate reenactors demonstrate their muskets from the balcony of The Griggs Home after inclement weather brought the Fort Tyler festivities inside.

ABOUT **JUMPIN' THE RAILS! II**

ALEKS ALWAYS KNEW his mother's ancestors were English immigrants, and there was an occasional reference to the Crown and a castle. What he didn't know was that they were direct descendants of the Broughton Castle Griggs in Branbury.

The family had three sons. The eldest son lived out his life in England, managed the family estate, and cared for their elderly parents. The middle son fled to Germany after the Crown rescinded its support of the family. He became a military strategist and waged war against England. The youngest son, Dr. Asa Griggs, immigrated to America, where he made his fortune as a doctor and a gentleman farmer of a cotton plantation. Aleks's mother was a direct descendant of Asa.

Dr. Griggs left for America to help support his family in England, but he was never able to return. He received word from his eldest brother only once, upon the death of their parents. His middle brother was never heard from again.

The middle brother changed his name to Schmidt, rose in the ranks of German command, and spoke the language fluently. Aleks crossed paths with Schmidt at Gettysburg. Schmidt was fascinated with the American Civil War and shadowed General Lee. Toward the end of the three-day battle, when Aleks and Adam were in the general's tent with Colonel Oates of Alabama, Schmidt briefly met and made note of the boys in his war journal. For a moment, Schmidt thought he recognized Aleks because he looked like a younger version of his brother, Asa, but he dismissed it as a mere coincidence. He also caught a glimpse of Aleks's phone. He wrote,

> What is this device? It looks like a magnifying glass, yet nothing is behind it. Or was it a photograph with light coming from within? Does it have a candle built into it? I saw a strange date, July 4, 2013. The year is not correct. When is this date? Is it a window to another place? I have my suspicions. My father had told me of his travel to other times. I thought him to be out

> of his mind because he was ailing in his later years, but now I question his sanity. When the boy's eyes met mine and he saw I knew of his powerful glass, he hid it before I could reach him. In less than a minute, the two were gone from my sight, and I never saw them again. For that matter, I never again saw such an interesting picture or window, nor had anyone else ever heard of it. I want to return home and speak to my father about his travel.

The secrets of time travel were rumored to be in the family castle in England and hidden in the secret compartment of a desk. Before coming to the United States, Kyle Killar and Hans Spangenberg went to England, ransacked the castle, and nearly killed the family living there. The time-travel formula was nowhere to be found, so they began their search for the Ness family, descendants of the Griggs, with a son named Aleks, the same one written about in their ancestor's Civil War journal.

* * *

Ivan pulled the letter from the box of family keepsakes. He opened the letter from Colleen's ancestor and read it.

> I'm terribly sorry to write you with frightful news. Our parents died in a fire. I'm uncertain what will become of us now; the fortune is lost, and the castle is in ruins. I wish you well, little brother, and hope that one day I will see you again. Enclosed in this package is a rock that belonged to our father. He said it had power beyond this world, so I want not for our middle brother to obtain it. He is consumed with power and aligns himself with evil men.
>
> Also, I've enclosed this letter from Father; in it, he explains how he used the rocks and traveled to other times. I have not found it to be true. I've tried to follow his instructions, hoping to travel back before the fire to save our parents and have not succeeded. I beg you to

travel to the time before the fire and save our parents. They were all I had left. Love, Jonathon.

Colleen entered his office. "You reread my family letter, didn't you?" she asked.

"Yes, and I think the only way to stop Killar is to travel to England," Ivan said.

"I agree," she said. "When are you telling Aleks?"

"Right away," he said.

Colleen's ancestor, the father of the three English boys who lived at Broughton Castle, had traveled the windows of time as well. About where he went and what he did, she had no additional information.

"Looks as if I'll need an extended leave of absence from my practice," Ivan said.

"I'm going with you," she said.

Catherine peeked around the corner. She'd been standing outside the door listening. "Me too," she said.

Author's son playing at the Fort during an 1860s period fundraiser.

AUTHOR'S NOTE

THE HISTORIC 1858 Griggs House sits on the Alabama–Georgia line. Its limestone Greek Revival structure stands directly below the highest point in Chambers County, Alabama. The stately home is known for its Civil War history.

Cannon marks left on the sunroom wall were made on Easter, April 16, 1865, when Confederate General Robert Tyler commanded 120 men against 1,200 Union troops from the fort behind the house. The Union used the house as cover during the fight. It was ransacked but not destroyed.

Many of the stories shared about the Battle of West Point are from firsthand accounts written by the Griggs family and others who witnessed the fight.

I became fascinated with its stories and from it came this historical science fiction adventure based on the Griggs House, its cannon marks, and Fort Tyler, the reconstructed Civil War fort behind the house.

The science fiction, medical, and historical information for the book came from the following sources: my husband, Lew, an engineer and cardiologist; Eleanor Scott's books on the Battle of West Point; Billy Clark's historical documents; a family letter on the Battle of Pass Christian; and Civil War literature and online resources.

My biggest challenge in writing this story was handling the topics of slavery and race fairly. These topics are tightly woven into the stories of the Civil War South, and to look closely at the time period is to look closely at these topics.

As a child, I knew little about race; however, in 1982, when my family moved from an all-white town in Wisconsin to a small town in Alabama, I encountered it for the first time and was shocked to witness a public Klan demonstration, hear rumors of a school race riot, and have my junior high principal explain what to do if someone pulled a knife on me.

In the early 1990s, as an Auburn University student, I met and became friends with a young black woman, Minnie Bryant. This friendship lends me a better understanding of racial division in communities and the sadness and shame created by skin color.

ACKNOWLEDGMENTS

THANK YOU TO Minnie Bryant for sitting on a bench outside Parker Hall with me as a 1990 Auburn University student and sharing her experiences of growing up black in a mostly white Southern community. The friendship between the characters Aleks and Adam is based on my twenty-five-year friendship with Minnie.

Support, insight, and inspiration for this story came from my family and friends. My husband Lew's brilliant scientific mind, my son's curiosity, and my daughter's encouragement brought this story to life. Thank you to my parents for serving as my first editors and to them and my brother and sister for their support from the first time I admitted I was writing a book. Thank you also to the many family members and friends who showed interest in my writing and waited patiently for this book's completion. Thank you!

A special thank-you goes to local historian Nanci Hendrix Rieder and the Fort Tyler Board and Association for sharing their enthusiasm for local history.

Thanks to the Griggs family, the descendants of the original owners of our home, for sharing their family's history. Dr. Griggs was an outstanding citizen and served in the Alabama legislature. Mrs. Griggs is remembered as being compassionate and caring toward all. I have used their names and the names of two of their children in this historical fiction.

Finally, a special thank-you to the Dr. Simmons family and the Gerald Andrews family, who also restored and preserved the Griggs House.

Printed in the United States
By Bookmasters